"I used to look at you,"
Holt said slowly. "A lot."

Wary, Suzanna lifted her head. "Really? I never noticed."

"You wouldn't have." His hand dropped away from her hair. "Princesses don't notice peasants."

Now Suzanna frowned, not only at the words, but also at the clipped tone. "What a ridiculous thing to say."

"It was easy to think of you that way—the princess in the castle."

"A castle that's been crumbling for years," she said dryly.

"You know, I've thought about kissing you for fifteen years." Holt watched the faint smile fade away from her face and the alarm shoot into her eyes. "That's a long time to think about anything."

He released her hand, but before she could let out a sigh of relief he cupped the back of her neck. His fingers were firm, and his grip was determined. "I'm just going to get it out of my system."

Dear Reader,

As usual, this month's Silhouette Intimate Moments lineup is a strong one, but there are two books that deserve special mention. First off, Nora Roberts completes her exciting "Calhoun Women" series with *Suzanna's Surrender*, the story of the fourth Calhoun sister and her successful search for love. You won't want to miss this book; Nora Roberts fans all around the world are eagerly collecting this new series from an author whose name is synonymous with the best reading in romance fiction today.

Another author of note is Judith Duncan. Her name may already be familiar to some of you, in which case you know that *A Risk Worth Taking*, her debut for Intimate Moments, promises reading pleasure well beyond the ordinary. For those of you who aren't familiar with her previous work, let me say only that the power of her writing and the depth of the emotions she captures on paper will astound you. This is a book that will haunt your memory long after you've turned the last page.

But I can't let these two special events keep me from drawing your attention to the other two books we're offering this month. Paula Detmer Riggs is an award-winner and a veteran of the bestseller lists, and *Silent Impact* is a perfect example of the deeply emotional style that is her hallmark. And let Marilyn Tracy introduce you to two characters who truly are *Too Good to Forget*. Memory—or the lack of it—can play strange tricks; in this case, those tricks lead to marriage!

In coming months, look for more of your favorite authors— Emilie Richards, Marilyn Pappano, Kathleen Eagle and Heather Graham Pozzessere, to name only a few—writing more of your favorite books.

Enjoy!

Leslie Wainger
Senior Editor and Editorial Coordinator

NORA ROBERTS

Suzanna's Surrender

SILHOUETTE·INTIMATE·MOMENTS®

Published by Silhouette Books New York

America's Publisher of Contemporary Romance

For my mother, with love.

SILHOUETTE BOOKS
300 East 42nd St., New York, N.Y. 10017

SUZANNA'S SURRENDER

ISBN: 0-373-07397-6

First Silhouette Books printing September 1991

Printed in the U.S.A.

Books by Nora Roberts

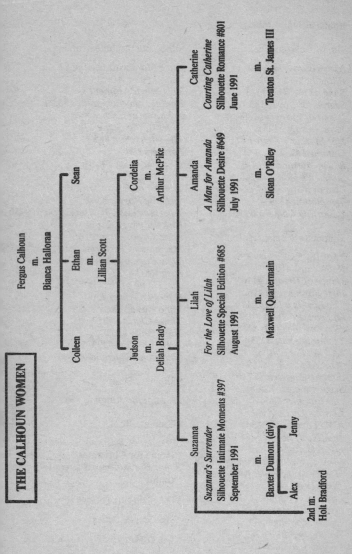

THE CALHOUN WOMEN

Fergus Calhoun
m.
Bianca Halloran

Colleen   Ethan   Sean
m.
Lillian Scott

Judson   Cordelia
m.   m.
Deliah Brady   Arthur McPike

Suzanna
Suzanna's Surrender
Silhouette Intimate Moments #397
September 1991

m.
Baxter Dumont (div)

Alex   Jenny

2nd m.
Holt Bradford

Lilah
For the Love of Lilah
Silhouette Special Edition #685
August 1991

m.
Maxwell Quartermain

Amanda
A Man for Amanda
Silhouette Desire #649
July 1991

m.
Sloan O'Riley

Catherine
Courting Catherine
Silhouette Romance #801
June 1991

m.
Trenton St. James III

Prologue

Bar Harbor, 1965

*T*he moment I saw her, my life was changed. More than fifty years have passed since that moment, and I'm an old man whose hair has turned white, whose body has grown frail. Yet my memories are full of color and strength.

Since my heart attack, I am to rest every day. So I have come back here to the island—her island—where it all began for me. It has changed, as I have. The great fire in '47 destroyed much. New buildings, new people have come. Cars crowd the streets without the charm of the jingling carriages. But I am lucky to be able to see it as it was, and as it is.

My son is a man now, a good one who chose to make his living from the sea. We have never understood each other, but have dealt together well enough. He has a quiet, lovely wife and a son of his own. The boy, young Holt, brings me a special kind of joy. Perhaps it is because I can see myself in him so clearly. The impatience, *the fire, the passions that were once mine. Perhaps he, too, will feel too much, want too much. Yet I can't be sorry for it. If I could tell him one thing, it would be to grab hold of life and take.*

My life has been full, and I'm grateful for the years I had with Margaret. I was no longer young when she became my wife. What we shared was not a blaze, but the quiet warmth of a banked fire. She brought me comfort, and I hope I gave her happiness. She's been gone for nearly ten years, and my memories of her are sweet.

Yet it is the memory of another woman that haunts me. This memory is so painfully clear, so complete. No amount of time could dull it. The years have not faded my image of her, nor have they altered by a single degree the desperate love I felt. Yes, feel still—will always feel though she is lost to me.

Perhaps now that I have brushed so close to death, I can open myself to it again, let myself remember what I have never been able to forget. Once it was too painful, and I lost the pain in a bottle. Finding no comfort there, I at last buried my misery in my work. Painting again, I traveled. But always, always, was pulled back here where I had once begun to live. Where I know I will one day die.

A man loves that way only once, and only if he is fortunate. For me, it was Bianca. It has always been Bianca.

It was June, the summer of 1912, before the Great War ripped the world apart. The summer of peace and beauty, of art and poetry, when the village of Bar Harbor opened itself to the wealthy and gave refuge to artists.

She came to the cliffs where I worked, her hand holding that of a child. I turned from my canvas, the brush still in my hand, the mood of the sea and the painting still on me. There she was, slender and lovely, the sunset hair swept up off her neck. The wind tugged at it, and at the skirts of the pale blue frock she wore. Her eyes were the color of the sea I was so frantically trying to recreate on canvas. They watched me, curious, wary. She had the pale and luminous skin of the Irish.

The moment I saw her, I knew I had to paint her. And I think I knew, as we stood in the wind, that I would have to love her.

She apologized for interrupting my work. The faint and musical lilt of Ireland was in the soft, polite voice. The child now in her arms was her son. She was Bianca Calhoun, another man's wife. Her summer home was on the ridge above. The Towers, the elaborate castle Fergus Calhoun had built. Even though I had only been on Mount Desert Island a short time, I had heard of Calhoun, and his home. Indeed I had admired the arrogant and fanciful lines of it, the turrets and peaks, the towers and parapets.

Such a place suited the woman who stood before me. She had a timeless beauty, a quiet steadiness, a graciousness that could never be taught, and banked passions simmering in her large green eyes. Yes, I was already in love, but then it was only with her beauty. As an artist, I wanted to interpret that beauty in my own way, with paint or pencils. Perhaps I frightened her by staring so intently. But the child, his name was Ethan, was fearless and friendly. She looked so young, so untouched, that it was difficult to believe the child was hers, and that she had two more besides.

She didn't stay long that day, but took her son and went home to her husband. I watched her walk through the wild roses, the sun in her hair.

I couldn't paint the sea anymore that day. Her face had already begun to haunt me.

Chapter 1

She wasn't looking forward to this. It had to be done, of course. Suzanna dragged a fifty-pound bag of mulch over to her pickup, then muscled it into the bed. That small physical task wasn't the problem. In fact, she was pleased to be able to make the delivery her second stop on her way home.

It was the first stop she wished she could avoid. But for Suzanna Calhoun Dumont, duty could never be avoided.

She'd promised her family that she would speak to Holt Bradford, and Suzanna kept her promises. Or tried to, she thought, and wiped a forearm over her sweaty brow.

But damn it, she was tired. She'd put in a full day in Southwest Harbor, landscaping a new house, and she had a full schedule the next day. That wasn't taking into account that her sister Amanda was getting married in little more than a week, or that The Towers was mass confusion in preparation for the wedding and with the remodeling of the west wing. It didn't even begin to deal with the fact that she had two energetic children at home who would want, and deserved, their mother's time and attention that evening. Or the paperwork that was piling up on her desk—or the fact that one of her part-time employees had quit just that morning.

Well, she'd wanted to start a business, Suzanna reminded herself. And she'd done it. She glanced back at her shop, locked for the night with the display of summer blooms in the window, at the greenhouse just behind the main building. It belonged to her—and the bank, she thought with a little smile—every pansy, petunia and peony. She'd proven she wasn't the incompetent failure her ex-husband had told her she was. Over and over again.

She had two beautiful children, a family who loved her and a landscaping-and-gardening business that was holding its own. She didn't even suppose Bax's claim that she was dull could apply now. Not when she was in the middle of an adventure that had started eighty years before.

There certainly wasn't anything mundane about searching for a priceless emerald necklace, or being dogged by international jewel thieves who would stop at nothing to get their hands on her great-grandmother Bianca's legacy.

Not that she'd been much more than a supporting player so far, Suzanna mused as she climbed into the truck. It had been her sister C.C. who had started it by falling in love with Trenton St. James III, of the St. James Hotels. It had been his idea to turn part of the financially plagued family home into a luxury retreat. In doing so, the old legend of the Calhoun emeralds had leaked to the ever-eager press and had set off a chain reaction that had run a course from the absurd to the dangerous.

It had been Amanda who had nearly been killed when the desperate and obsessed thief going by the name of William Livingston had stolen family papers he'd hoped would lead him to the lost emeralds. And it had been her sister Lilah who had had her life threatened during the latest attempt.

In the week that had passed since that night, the police hadn't turned up a trace of Livingston, or his latest known alias, Ellis Caufield.

It was odd, she thought as she joined the stream of traffic, how The Towers and the lost emeralds had affected the entire family. The Towers had brought C.C. and Trent together. Then Sloan O'Riley had come to design the retreat and had fallen in love with Amanda. The shy history professor, Max Quartermain, had lost his heart to Suzanna's free-spirited sister, Lilah, and both of them had nearly been killed. Again, because of the emeralds.

There were times Suzanna wished they could forget about the necklace that had belonged to her great-grandmother. But she knew, as they all knew, that the necklace Bianca had hidden away before her death was meant to be found.

So they continued, following up every lead, exploring every dusty path. Now it was her turn. During his research, Max had uncovered the name of the artist Bianca had loved.

It was a story that never failed to make Suzanna wistful, but it was just her bad luck that the connection with the artist led to his grandson.

Holt Bradford. She sighed a little as she drove through the traffic-jammed streets of the village. She couldn't claim to know him well—wasn't sure anyone could. But she remembered him as a teenager. Surly, bad tempered and aloof. Of course, girls had been attracted by his go-to-hell attitude. The attraction helped along, no doubt, by the dark, brooding looks and angry gray eyes.

Odd she should remember the color of his eyes, she mused. But then again, the one time she had seen them up close and personal he'd all but burned her alive with them.

He'd probably forgotten the altercation, she assured herself. She hoped so. Altercations made her shaky and sweaty, and she'd had enough of them in her marriage to last a lifetime. Certainly Holt wouldn't still hold a grudge—it had been more than ten years. After all, he hadn't been hurt very much when he'd taken a header off his motorcycle. And it had been his fault, she thought, setting her chin. She'd had the right of way.

In any case, she had promised Lilah she would talk to him. Any connection with Bianca's lost emeralds had to be followed up. As Christian Bradford's grandson, Holt might have heard stories.

Since he'd come back to Bar Harbor a few months before, he had taken up residence in the same cottage his grandfather had lived in during his romance with Bianca. Suzanna was Irish enough to believe in fate. There was a Bradford in the cottage and Calhouns in The Towers. Surely between them, they could find the answers to the mystery that had haunted both families for generations.

The cottage was on the water, sheltered by two lovely old willows. The simple wooden structure made her think of a doll's house, and she thought it a shame that no one had cared enough to plant flowers. The grass was freshly mowed, but her professional eye noted that there were patches that needed reseeding, and the whole business could use a good dose of fertilizer.

She started toward the door when the barking of a dog and the rumble of a man's voice had her skirting around to the side.

There was a rickety pier jutting out above the calm, dark water. Tied to it was a neat little cabin cruiser in gleaming white. He sat in the stern, patiently polishing the brass. He was shirtless, his tanned skin taut over bone and muscle, and gleaming with sweat. His black hair was curled past where his collar would be if he'd worn one. Apparently he didn't find it necessary to cover himself with anything more than a pair of ripped and faded cutoffs. She noticed his hands, limber, long fingered, and wondered if he had inherited them from his artist grandfather.

Water lapped quietly at the boat. Behind it, she saw a fish hawk soar then plummet. It gave a cry of triumph as it rose up again, a silver fish caught wriggling in its claws. The man in the boat continued to work, untouched by or oblivious to the drama of life and death around him.

Suzanna fixed what she hoped was a polite smile on her face and walked toward the pier. "Excuse me."

When his head shot up, she stopped dead. She had the quick but vivid impression that if he'd had a weapon, it would have been aimed at her. In an instant, he had gone from relaxed to full alert, with an edgy kind of violence in the set of his body that had her mouth going dry.

As she struggled to steady her heartbeat, she noted that he had changed. The surly boy was now a dangerous man. There was no other word that came to mind. His face had matured so that it was all planes and angles, sharply defined. The stubble of a two-day beard added to the rough-and-ready look.

But it was his eyes once again, that dried up her throat. A man with eyes that sharp, that potent, needed no weapon.

He squinted at her but didn't rise or speak. He had to give himself a moment to level. If he'd been wearing his weapon, it would have been out and in his hand. That was one of the reasons he was here, and a civilian again.

He might have forced himself to relax—he knew how—but he remembered her face. A man didn't forget that face. God knows, he hadn't. Timeless. In one of his youthful fantasies, he'd imagined her as a princess, lost and lovely in flowing silks. And himself as the knight who would have slain a hundred dragons to have her.

The memory made him scowl.

She'd hardly changed, he thought. Her skin was still pale Irish roses and cream, the shape of her face still classically oval. Her mouth had remained full and romantically soft, her eyes that deep, deep, dreamy blue, luxuriously lashed. They were watching him now with a kind of baffled alarm as he took his time looking her over.

She'd pulled her hair back in a smooth ponytail, but he remembered how it had flowed, long and loose and gleaming blond over her shoulders.

She was tall—all the Calhoun women were—but she was too thin. His scowl deepened at that. He'd heard she'd been married and divorced, and that both had been difficult experiences. She had two children, a boy and girl. It was difficult to believe that the slender wand of a woman in grubby jeans and a sweaty T-shirt had ever given birth.

It was harder to believe, harder to accept, that she could jangle his nerves just by standing ten feet away.

With his eyes still on hers, he went back to his polishing. "Do you want something?"

She let out the breath she hadn't been aware she was holding. "I'm sorry to just drop in this way. I'm Suzanna Dumont. Suzanna Calhoun."

"I know who you are."

"Oh, well…" She cleared her throat. "I realize you're busy, but I'd like to talk with you for a few minutes. If this isn't a good time—"

"What about?"

Since he was being so gracious, she thought, annoyed, she'd get right to the point. "About your grandfather. He was Christian Bradford, wasn't he? The artist?"

"That's right. So?"

"It's kind of a long story. Can I sit down?"

When he only shrugged, she walked to the pier. It groaned and swayed under her feet, and she lowered herself carefully.

"Actually, it started back in 1912 or '13, with my great-grandmother, Bianca."

"I've heard the fairy tale." He could smell her now, flowers and sweat, and it made his stomach tighten. "She was an unhappy wife with a rich and difficult husband. She compensated by taking a lover. Somewhere along the line, she supposedly hid her emerald necklace. Insurance if she got up the guts to leave. Instead of taking off into the sunset with her lover, she jumped out of the tower window, and the emeralds were never found."

"It wasn't precisely—"

"Now your family's decided to start a treasure hunt," he went on as if she hadn't spoken. "Got a lot of press out of it, and more trouble than I imagine you bargained for. I heard you had some excitement a couple weeks ago."

"If you can call my sister being held at knife point excitement, yes." The fire had come into her eyes. She wasn't always good at defending herself, but when it came to her family, she was a scrapper. "The man who was working with Livingston, or whatever the bastard's calling himself now, nearly killed Lilah and her fiancé."

"When you've got priceless emeralds with a legend attached, the rats gnaw through the woodwork." He knew about Livingston. Holt had been a cop for ten years, and though he'd spent most of that time in Vice, he'd read reports on the slick and often violent jewel thief.

"The legend and the emeralds are my family's business."

"So why come to me? I turned in my shield. I'm retired."

"I didn't come to you for professional help. It's personal." She took another breath, wanting to be clear and concise. "Lilah's fiancé used to be a history professor at Cornell. A couple of months ago, Livingston, going under the name of Ellis Caufield, hired him to go through the family's papers he'd stolen from us."

Holt continued to polish the brightwork. "Doesn't sound like Lilah developed any taste."

"Max didn't know the papers were stolen," Suzanna said between her teeth. "When he found out, Caufield nearly killed him. In any case, Max came to The Towers and continued his research for us. We've documented the emeralds' existence, and we've even interviewed a servant who worked at The Towers the year Bianca died."

Holt shifted and continued to work. "You've been busy."

"Yes. She corroborates the story that the necklace was hidden, and that Bianca was in love, and planning to leave her husband. The man she was in love with was an artist." She waited a beat. "His name was Christian Bradford."

Something flickered in his eyes then was gone. Very deliberately he set down his rag. He pulled a cigarette from a pack, flicked on a lighter then slowly blew out a haze of smoke.

"Do you really expect me to believe that little fantasy?"

She'd hoped for surprise, even amazement. She'd gotten boredom. "It's true. She used to meet him on the cliffs near The Towers."

He gave her a thin smile that was very close to a sneer. "Saw them, did you? Oh, I've heard about the ghost, too." He drew in more smoke, lazily released it. "The melancholy spirit of Bianca Calhoun, drifting through her summer home. You Calhouns are just full of— stories."

Her eyes darkened, but her voice remained very controlled. "Bianca Calhoun and Christian Bradford were in love. The summer she died, they met often on the cliffs just below The Towers."

That touched a chord, but he only shrugged. "So what?"

"So there's a connection. My family can't afford to overlook any connection, particularly one so vital as this one. It's very possible she told him where she put the emeralds."

"I don't see what a flirtation—an unsubstantiated flirtation—between two people some eighty years ago has to do with emeralds."

"If you could get past this prejudice you seem to have toward my family, we might be able to figure it out."

"Not interested in either part." He flipped open the top of a small cooler. "Want a beer?"

"No."

"Well, I'm fresh out of champagne." Watching her, he twisted off the top, tossed it toward a plastic bucket, then drank deeply. "You know, if you think about it, you'd see it's a little tough to swallow. The lady of the manor, well-bred, well-off, and the struggling artist. Doesn't play, babe. You'd be better off dropping the whole thing and concentrating on planting your flowers. Isn't that what you're doing these days?"

He could make her angry, she thought, but he wasn't going to shake her from her purpose. "My sisters' lives were threatened, my home has been broken into. Idiots are sneaking in my garden and digging up my rosebushes." She stood, tall and slim and furious. "I have no intention of dropping the whole thing."

"Your business." He flicked the cigarette away before jumping effortlessly onto the pier. It shook and swayed beneath them. He was taller than she remembered, and she had to angle her chin to keep her eyes level. "Just don't expect to suck me into it."

"All right then. I'll just stop wasting my time and yours."

He waited until she'd stepped off the pier. "Suzanna." He liked the way it sounded when he said it. Soft and feminine and old-fashioned. "You ever learn to drive?"

Eyes stormy, she took a step back toward him. "Is that what this is all about?" she demanded. "You're still steaming because you fell off that stupid motorcycle and bruised your inflated male ego?"

"That wasn't the only thing that got bruised—or scraped, or lacerated." He remembered the way she'd looked. God, she couldn't have been more than sixteen. Rushing out of her car, her hair windblown, her face pale, her eyes dark and drenched with concern and fear.

And he'd been sprawled on the side of the road, his twenty-year-old pride as raw as the skin the asphalt had abraded.

"I don't believe it," she was saying. "You're still mad, after what, twelve years, for something that was clearly your own fault."

"My fault?" He tipped the bottle toward her. "You're the one who ran into me."

"I never ran into you or anyone. You fell."

"If I hadn't ditched the bike, you would have run into me. You weren't looking where you were going."

"I had the right of way. And you were going entirely too fast."

"Bull." He was starting to enjoy himself. "You were checking that pretty face of yours in the rearview mirror."

"I certainly was not. I never took my eyes off the road."

"If you'd had your eyes on the road, you wouldn't have run into me."

"I didn't—" She broke off, swore under her breath. "I'm not going to stand here and argue with you about something that happened twelve years ago."

"You came here to try to drag me into something that happened eighty years ago."

"That was an obvious mistake." She would have left it at that, but a very big, very wet dog came bounding across the lawn. With two happy barks, the animal leaped, planting both muddy feet on Suzanna's shirt and sending her staggering back.

"Sadie, down!" As Holt issued the terse command, he caught Suzanna before she hit the ground. "Stupid bitch."

"I beg your pardon?"

"Not you, the dog." Sadie was already sitting, thumping her dripping tail. "Are you all right?" He still had his arms around her, bracing her against his chest.

"Yes, fine." He had muscles like rock. It was impossible not to notice. Just as it was impossible not to notice that his breath fluttered along her temple, that he smelled very male. It had been a very long time since she had been held by a man.

Slowly he turned her around. For a moment, a moment too long, she was face-to-face with him, caught in the circle of his arms. His gaze flicked down to her mouth, lingered. A gull wheeled overhead, banked, then soared out over the water. He felt her heart thud against his. Once, twice, three times.

"Sorry," he said as he released her. "Sadie still sees herself as a cute little puppy. She got your shirt dirty."

"Dirt's my business." Needing time to recover, she crouched down to rub the dog's head. "Hi, there, Sadie."

Holt pushed his hands into his pockets as Suzanna acquainted herself with his dog. The bottle lay where he'd tossed it, spilling its contents onto the lawn. He wished to God she didn't look so beautiful, that her laugh as the dog lapped at her face didn't play so perfectly on his nerves.

In that one moment he'd held her, she'd fit into his arms as he'd once imagined she would. His hands fisted inside his pockets because he wanted to touch her. No, that wasn't even close. He wanted to pull her inside the cottage, toss her onto the bed and do incredible things to her.

"Maybe a man who owns such a nice dog isn't all bad." She tossed a glance over her shoulder and the cautious smile died on her lips. The way he was looking at her, his eyes so dark and fierce, his bony face so set had the breath backing up in her lungs. There was violence trembling around him. She'd had a taste of violence from a man, and the memory of it made her limbs weak.

Slowly he relaxed his shoulders, his arms, his hands. "Maybe he isn't," he said easily. "But it's more a matter of her owning me at this point."

Suzanne found it more comfortable to look at the dog than the master. "We have a puppy. Well, he's growing by leaps and bounds so he'll be as big as Sadie soon. In fact, he looks a great deal like her. Did she have a litter a few months ago?"

"No."

"Hmm. He's got the same coloring, the same shaped face. My brother-in-law found him half-starved. Someone had dumped him, I suppose, and he'd managed to get up to the cliffs."

"Even I draw the line at abandoning helpless puppies."

"I didn't mean to imply—" She broke off because a new thought had jumped into her mind. It was no crazier than looking for missing emeralds. "Did your grandfather have a dog?"

"He always had a dog, used to take it with him wherever he went. Sadie's one of the descendants."

Carefully she got to her feet again. "Did he have a dog named Fred?"

Holt's brows drew together. "Why?"

"Did he?"

Holt was already sure he didn't like where this was leading. "The first dog he had was called Fred. That was before the First World War. He did a painting of him. And when Fred exercised the right *de seigneur* around the neighborhood, my grandfather took a couple of the puppies."

Suzanne rubbed suddenly damp hands on her jeans. It took all of her control to keep her voice low and steady. "The day before Bianca died, she brought a puppy home to her children. A little black puppy she called Fred." She saw his eyes change and knew she had his attention, and his interest. "She'd found him out on the cliffs—the cliffs where she went to meet Christian." She moistened her lips as Holt continued to stare at her and say nothing. "My great-grandfather wouldn't allow the dog to stay. They argued about it, quite seriously. We were able to locate a maid who'd worked there, and she'd heard the whole thing. No one was sure what happened to that dog. Until now."

"Even if that's true," Holt said slowly, "it doesn't change the bottom line. There's nothing I can do for you."

"You can think about it, you can try to remember if he ever said anything, if he left anything behind that could help."

"I've got enough to think about." He paced a few feet away. He didn't want to be involved with anything that would bring him into contact with her again and again.

Suzanna didn't argue. She could only stare at the long, jagged scar that ran from his shoulder to nearly his waist. He turned, met her horrified eyes and stiffened.

"Sorry, if I'd known you were coming to call, I'd have put on a shirt."

"What—" She had to swallow the block of emotion in her throat. "What happened to you?"

"I was a cop one night too long." His eyes stayed steady on hers. "I can't help you, Suzanna."

She shook away the pity he obviously would detest. "You won't."

"Whatever. If I'd wanted to dig around in other people's problems, I'd still be on the force."

"I'm only asking you to do a little thinking, to let us know if you remember anything that might help."

He was running out of patience. Holt figured he'd already given her more than her share for one day. "I was a kid when he died. Do you really think he'd have told me if he'd had an affair with a married woman?"

"You make it sound sordid."

"Some people don't figure adultery's romantic." Then he shrugged. It was nothing to him either way. "Then again, if one of the partners turns out to be a washout, I guess it's tough to come down on the other for looking someplace else."

She looked away at that, closing in on a private pain. "I'm not interested in your views on morality, Holt. Just your memory. And I've taken up enough of your time."

He didn't know what he'd said to put that sad, injured look in her eyes. But he couldn't let her leave with that haunting him. "Look, I think you're reaching at straws here, but if anything comes to mind, I'll let you know. For Sadie's ancestor's sake."

"I'd appreciate it."

"But don't expect anything."

With a half laugh she turned to walk to her truck. "Believe me, I won't." It surprised her when he crossed the lawn with her.

"I heard you started a business."

"That's right." She glanced around the yard. "You could use me."

The faint sneer came again. "I ain't the rosebush type."

"The cottage is." Unoffended, she fished her keys out of her pocket. "It wouldn't take much to make it charming."

"I'm not in the market for posies, babe. I'll leave the puttering around the rose garden to you."

She thought of the aching muscles she took home with her every night and climbed into the truck to slam the door. "Yes, puttering around the garden is something we women do best. By the way, Holt, your grass needs fertilizer. I'm sure you have plenty to spread around."

She gunned the engine, set the shift in reverse and pulled out.

Chapter 2

The children came rushing out of the house, followed by a big-footed black dog. The boy and the girl skimmed down the worn stone steps with the easy balance and grace of youth. The dog tripped over his own feet and somersaulted. Poor Fred, Suzanna thought as she climbed out of the truck. It didn't look as though he would ever outgrow his puppy clumsiness.

"Mom!" Each child attached to one of Suzanna's jean-clad legs. At six, Alex was already tall for his age and dark as a gypsy. His sturdy tanned legs were scabbed at the knees and his bony elbows were scraped. Not from clumsiness, Suzanna thought, but from derring-do. Jenny, a year younger and blond as a fairy princess, carried the same badges of honor. Suzanna forgot her irritation and fatigue the moment she bent to kiss them.

"What have you two been up to?"

"We're building a fort," Alex told her. "It's going to be impregnant."

"Impregnable," Suzanna corrected, tweaking his nose.

"Yeah, and Sloan said he could help us with it on Saturday."

"Can you?" Jenny asked.

"After work." She bent to pet Fred, who was trying to push his way through the children for his rightful share of affection. "Hello, boy. I think I met one of your relatives today."

"Does Fred have relatives?" Jenny wanted to know.

"It certainly looked that way." She walked over to sit with the children on the steps. It was a luxury to sit, to smell the sea and flowers, to have a child under each arm. "I think I met his cousin Sadie."

"Where? Can she come to visit? Is she nice?"

"In the village," Suzanna said, answering Alex's rapid-fire questions in turn. "I don't know, and yes, she's very nice. Big, like Fred's going to be when he grows into his feet. What else did you do today?"

"Loren and Lisa came over," Jenny told her. "We killed hundreds of marauders."

"Well, we can all sleep easy tonight."

"And Max told us a story about storming the beach at Normally."

Chuckling, Suzanna kissed the top of Jenny's head. "I think that was Normandy."

"Lisa and Jenny played dolls, too." Alex gave his sister a brotherly smirk.

"She wanted to. She got the brand-new Barbie and her car for her birthday."

"It was a Ferrari," Alex said importantly, but didn't want to admit that he and Loren had played with it when the girls were out of the room. He inched closer to toy with his mother's ponytail. "Loren and Lisa are going to Disney World next week."

Suzanna bit back a sigh. She knew her children dreamed of going to that enchanted kingdom in central Florida. "We'll go someday."

"Soon?" Alex prompted.

She wanted to promise, but couldn't. "Someday," she repeated. The weariness was back when she rose to take each child by the hand. "You guys run and tell Aunt Coco I'm home. I need to shower and change. Okay?"

"Can we go to work with you tomorrow?"

She gave Jenny's hand a quick squeeze. "Carolanne's watching the shop tomorrow. I have site work." She felt their disappointment as keenly as her own. "Next week. Go ahead now," she said as she opened the massive front door. "And I'll look at your fort after dinner."

Satisfied with that, they barreled down the hall with the dog at their heels.

They didn't ask for much, Suzanna thought as she climbed the curving stairs to the second floor. And there was so much more she wanted to give them. She knew they were happy and safe and secure. They had a huge family who loved them. With one of her sisters married, and two others engaged, her children had men in their lives. Maybe uncles didn't replace a father, but it was the best she could do.

They hadn't heard from Baxter Dumont for months. Alex hadn't even rated a card on his birthday. The child support check was late again—as it was every month. Bax was too sharp a lawyer to neglect the payment completely, but he made certain it arrived weeks after its due date. To test her, she knew. To see if she would beg for it. Thank God she hadn't needed to yet.

The divorce had been final for a year and a half, but he continued to take out his feelings for her on the children—the only truly worthwhile thing they had made together.

Perhaps that was why she had yet to get over the nagging disillusionment, the sense of betrayal and loss and inadequacy. She no longer loved him. That love had died before Jenny had been born. But the hurt ... Suzanna shook her head. She was working on it.

She stepped into her room. Like most of the rooms in The Towers, Suzanne's bedroom was huge. The house had been built in the early 1900s by her great-grandfather. It had been a showpiece, a testament to his vanity, his taste for the opulent and his need for status. It was five stories of somber granite with fanciful peaks and parapets, two spiraling towers and layering terraces. The interior was lofty ceilings, fancy woodwork, mazelike hallways. Part castle, part manor house, it had served first as summer home, then as permanent residence.

Through the years and financial reversals, the house had fallen on hard times. Suzanna's room, like the others, showed cracks in the plaster. The floor was scarred, the roof leaked and the plumbing had a mind of its own. As one, the Calhouns loved their family home. Now that the west wing was under renovation, they hoped it would be able to pay its own way.

She went to the closet for a robe, thinking that she'd been one of the lucky ones. She'd been able to bring her children here, into a real home, when their own had crumbled. She hadn't had to interview strangers to care for them while she made a living. Her father's sister, who had raised Suzanna and her sisters after their parents had died, was now caring for Suzanna's children. Though Suzanna was aware that Alex and Jenny were a handful, she knew there was no one better suited for the task than Aunt Coco.

And one day soon they would find Bianca's emeralds, and everything would settle back to what passed for normal in the Calhoun household.

"Suze." Lilah gave the door a quick knock then poked her head in. "Did you see him?"

"Yes, I saw him."

"Terrific." Lilah, her red hair curling to her waist, strolled in. She stretched out diagonally on the bed, plumping a pillow against the tiered headboard. Easily she settled into her favorite position. Horizontal. "So tell me."

"He hasn't changed much."

"Oh-oh."

"He was abrupt and rude." Suzanna pulled the T-shirt over her head. "I think he considered shooting me for trespassing. When I tried to explain what was going on, he sneered." Remembering that look, she tugged down the zipper of her jeans. "Basically, he was obnoxious, arrogant and insulting."

"Mmm. Sounds like a prince."

"He thinks we made the whole thing up to get publicity for The Towers when we open the retreat next year."

"What a crock." That stirred Lilah enough to have her sitting up. "Max was nearly killed. Does he think we're crazy?"

"Exactly." With a nod, Suzanna dragged on her robe. "I couldn't begin to guess why, but he seems to have a grudge against the Calhouns in general."

Lilah gave a sleepy smile. "Still stewing because you knocked him off his motorcycle."

"I did not—" On an oath, Suzanna gave up. "Never mind, the point is I don't think we're going to get any help from him." After pulling the band out of her hair, she ran her hands through it. "Though after the business with the dog, he did say he'd think about it."

"What dog?"

"Fred's cousin," she said over her shoulder as she walked into the bath to turn on the shower.

Lilah came to the doorway just as Suzanna was pulling the curtain closed. "Fred has a cousin?"

Over the drum of the water, Suzanna told her about Sadie, and her ancestors.

"But that's fabulous. It's just one more link in the chain. I'll have to tell Max."

With her eyes closed, Suzanna stuck her head under the shower. "Tell him he's on his own. Christian's grandson isn't interested."

He didn't want to be. Holt sat on the back porch, the dog at his feet, and watched the water turn to indigo in twilight.

There was music here, the symphony of insects in the grass, the rustle of wind, the countermelody of water against wood. Across the bay, Bar Island began to fade and merge into dusk. Nearby someone was playing a radio, a lonely alto sax solo that suited Holt's mood.

This was what he wanted. Quiet, solitude, no responsibilities. He'd earned it, hadn't he? he thought as he tipped the beer to his lips. He'd given ten years of his life to other people's problems, their tragedies, their miseries.

He was burned out, bone-dry and tired as hell.

He wasn't even sure he'd been a good cop. Oh, he had citations and medals that claimed he had been. But he also had a twelve-inch scar on his back that reminded him he'd nearly been a dead one.

Now he just wanted to enjoy his retirement, repair a few motors, scrape some barnacles, maybe do a little boating. He'd always been good with his hands and knew he could make a decent living repairing boats. Running his own business, at his own pace, in his own way. No reports to type, no leads to follow up, no dark alleys to search.

No knife-wielding junkies springing out of the shadows to rip you open and leave you bleeding on the littered concrete.

Holt closed his eyes and took another pull of beer. He'd made up his mind during the long, painful hospital stay. There would be no more commitment in his life, no more trying to save the world from itself. From that point on, he would start looking out for himself. Just himself.

He'd taken the money he'd inherited and had come home, to do as little as possible with the rest of his life. Sun and sea in the summer, roaring fires and howling winds in the winter. It wasn't so damn much to ask.

He'd been settling in, feeling pretty good about himself. Then she'd come along.

Hadn't it been bad enough that he'd looked at her and felt—Lord, the way he'd felt when he'd been twenty years old. Churned up and hungry. He was still hung up on her.

The lovely, and unattainable, Suzanna Calhoun of the Bar Harbor Calhouns. The princess in the tower. She'd lived high up in her castle on the cliffs. And he had lived in a cottage on the edge of the village. His father had been a lobsterman, and Holt had often delivered a catch to the Calhoun's back door—never going beyond the kitchen. But he'd sometimes heard voices or laughter or music. And he had wondered and wanted.

Now she had come to him. But he wasn't a love-struck boy any longer. He was a realist. Suzanna was out of his league, just as she had always been. Even if it had been different, he wasn't interested in a woman who had home and hearth written all over her.

As far as the emeralds went, there was nothing he could do to help her. Nothing he wanted to do.

He'd known about the emeralds, of course. That particular story had made national press. But the idea that his grandfather had been involved, had loved and been loved by a Calhoun woman. That was fascinating.

Even with the coincidence about the dogs, he wasn't sure he believed it. Holt hadn't known his grandmother, but his grandfather had been the hero of his childhood. He'd been the dashing and mysterious figure who had gone off to foreign places, come back with fabulous stories. He'd been the man who had been able to perform magic with a canvas and brush.

He could remember climbing up the stairs to the studio as a child to watch the tall man with the snow-white hair at work. Yet it had seemed more like combat than work. An elegant and passionate duel between his grandfather and the canvas.

They would take long walks, the young boy and the old man, along the shore, across the rocks. Up on the cliffs. With a sigh, Holt sat back. Very often they had walked to the cliffs just below The Towers. Even as a child he'd understood that as his grandfather had looked out to sea, he had gone someplace else.

Once, they had sat on the rocks there and his grandfather had told him a story about the castle on the cliffs, and the princess who'd lived there.

Had he been talking about The Towers, and Bianca?

Restless, Holt rose to go inside. Sadie glanced up, then settled her head on her front paws again as the screen door slammed.

The cottage suited him more than the home he'd grown up in. That had been a neat and soulless place with worn linoleum and dark paneled walls. Holt had sold it after his mother's death three years before. Recently he'd used the profits for some repairs and modernization of the cottage, but preferred keeping the old place much as it had been in his grandfather's day.

It was a boxy house, with plaster walls and wood floors. The original stone fireplace had been pointed up, and Holt looked forward to the first cool night when he could try it out.

The bedroom was tiny, almost an afterthought that jutted out from the main structure. He liked lying in bed at night and listening to rain drumming on the tin roof. The stairs to his grandfather's studio had been reinforced, as well as the railing that skirted along the open balcony. He climbed up now, to look at the wide, airy space, dim with twilight.

Now and then he thought about putting skylights in the angled roof, but he never considered refinishing the floor. The dark old wood was splattered with paint that had dripped from brush or palette. There were streaks of carmine and turquoise, drops of emerald green and canary yellow. His grandfather had preferred the vivid, the passionate, even the violent in his work.

Against one wall, canvases were stacked, Holt's legacy from a man who had only begun to find critical and financial success in his last years. They would, he knew, be worth a hefty sum. Yet as he never considered sanding the paint from the floors, he had never considered selling this part of his inheritance.

Crouching down, he began to look through the paintings. He knew them all, had studied them countless times, wondering how he could have come from a man with such vision and talent. Holt turned over the portrait, knowing that was why he had come up here.

The woman was as beautiful as a dream—the fine-featured oval face, the alabaster skin. Rich red-gold hair was swept up off a graceful neck. Full, soft lips were curved, just a little. But it was the eyes that drew Holt, as they always had. They were green, like a misty sea. It wasn't their color that pulled at him, but the expression in them, the look, the emotion that had been captured by his grandfather's brush and skill.

Such quiet sadness. Such inner grief. It was almost too painful to look at, because to look too long was to feel. He had seen that expression today, in Suzanna's eyes.

Could this be Bianca? he wondered. The resemblance was there, in the shape of the face, the curve of the mouth. The coloring was certainly wrong and the similarities slight. Except the eyes, he thought. When he looked at them, he thought of Suzanna.

Because he was thinking of her too much, he told himself. He rose, but he didn't turn the portrait back to the wall. He stood staring at it for a long time, wondering if his grandfather had loved the woman he'd painted.

It was going to be another hot one, Suzanna thought. Though it was barely seven, the air was already sticky. They needed rain, but the moisture hung in the air and stubbornly refused to fall.

Inside her shop, she checked on the refrigerated blooms and left a note for Carolanne to push the carnations by selling them at half price. She checked the soil in the hanging pots of impatiens and geraniums, then moved on to the display of gloxinia and begonias.

Satisfied, she took her sprayer out to drench the flats of annuals and perennials. The rosebushes and peonies were moving well, she noted. As were the yews and junipers.

By seven-thirty, she was checking on the greenhouse plants, grateful that her inventory was dwindling. What didn't sell, she would winter over. She would also take cuttings for next year's plants. But winter, and that quiet work, was months away.

By eight her pickup was loaded, and she was on her way to Seal Harbor. She would put in a full day's work there on the grounds of a newly constructed home. The buyers were from Boston, and wanted their summer home to have an established yard, complete with shrubs, trees and flower beds.

It would be hot, sweaty work, Suzanne mused. But it would also be quiet. The Andersons were in Boston this week, so she would have the yard to herself. She liked nothing better than working with the soil and living things, tending something she had planted and watching it grow and thrive.

Like her children, she thought with a smile. Her babies. Every time she put them to bed at night or watched them run in the sunlight, she knew that nothing that had happened to her before, nothing that would happen to her in the future would dim that glow of knowing they were hers.

The failed marriage had left her shaken and uncertain, and there were times she still had terrible doubts about herself as a woman. But not as a mother. Her children had the very best she could give them. The bond nourished her, as well as them.

Over the past two years, she'd begun to believe that she could be a success in business. Her flair for gardening had been her only useful skill and had been a kind of salvation during the last months of her dying marriage.

In desperation she had sold her jewelry, taken out a loan and had plunged into Island Gardens.

It had made her feel good to use her maiden name. She hadn't wanted any frivolous or clever name for the business, but something straightforward. The first year had been rough—particularly when she'd been pouring every cent she could spare into legal fees to fight a custody suit.

The thought of that, the memory of it, still made her blood run cold. She couldn't have lost them.

Bax hadn't wanted the children, but he'd wanted to make things difficult for her. When it had been over, she'd lost fifteen pounds, countless hours of sleep and had been up to her neck in debt. But she had her children. The ugly battle had been won, and the price meant nothing.

Gradually she was pulling out. She'd gained back a few of the pounds, had caught up a bit on her sleep and was slowly, meticulously hacking away at the debt. In the two years since she'd opened the business, she'd earned a reputation as dependable, reasonable and imaginative. Two of the resorts had tried her out, and it looked as though they'd be negotiating long-term contracts.

That would mean buying another truck, hiring on full-time labor. And maybe, just maybe, that trip to Disney World.

She pulled up in the driveway of the pretty Cape Cod house. Now, she reminded herself, it meant getting to work.

The grounds took up about a half acre and were gently sloped. She had had three in-depth meetings with the owners to determine the plan. Mrs. Anderson wanted plenty of spring flowering trees and shrubs, and the long-term privacy factor of evergreens. She wanted to enjoy a perennial bed that was carefree and full of summer color.

Mr. Anderson didn't want to spend his summers maintaining the yard, particularly the side portion, which fell in a more dramatic grade. There, Suzanna would use ground covers and rockeries to prevent erosion.

By noon, she had measured off each area with stakes and strings. The hardy azaleas were planted. Two long-blooming fairy roses flanked the flagstone walk and were already sweetening the air. Because Mrs. Anderson had expressed a fondness for lilacs, Suzanna placed a trio of compact shrubs near the master bedroom window, where the next spring's breezes would carry the scent indoors.

The yard was coming alive for her. It helped her ignore the aching muscles in her arms as she drenched the new plants with water. Birds were chirping, and somewhere in the near distance, a lawn mower was putting away.

One day, she would drive by and see that the fast-growing hedge roses she had planted along the fence had spread and bloomed until they covered the chain link. She would see the azaleas bloom in the spring and the maple leaves go red in the fall, and know that she'd been part of that.

It was important, more important than she could admit to anyone, that she leave a mark. She needed that to remind herself that she wasn't the weak and useless woman who had been so callously tossed aside.

Dripping with sweat, she picked up her water bottle and shovel and headed around to the front of the house again. She'd put in the first of the flowering almonds and was digging the hole for the second when a car pulled into the driveway behind her truck. Resting on her shovel, Suzanna watched Holt climb out.

She let out a little huff of breath, annoyed that her solitude had been invaded, and went back to digging.

"Out for a drive?" she asked when his shadow fell over her.

"No, the girl at the shop told me where to find you. What the hell are you doing?"

"Playing canasta." She shoveled some more dirt. "What do you want?"

"Put that shovel down before you hurt yourself. You've got no business digging ditches."

"Digging ditches is my business—more or less. Now, what do you want?"

He watched her dig for another ten seconds before he snatched the shovel away from her. "Give me that damn thing and sit down."

Patience had always been her strong point, but she was hard-pressed to find it now. Working at it, she adjusted the brim of the fielder's cap she wore. "I'm on a schedule, and I have six more trees, two rosebushes and twenty square feet of ground cover to plant. If you've got something to say, fine. Talk while I work."

He jerked the shovel out of her reach. "How deep do you want it?" She only lifted a brow. "How deep do you want the hole?"

She skimmed her gaze down, then up again. "I'd say a little more than six feet would be enough to bury you in."

He grinned, surprising her. "And you used to be so sweet." Plunging the shovel in, he began to dig. "Just tell me when to stop."

Normally she repaid kindness with kindness. But she was going to make an exception. "You can stop right now, I don't need any help. And I don't want the company."

"I didn't know you had a stubborn streak." He glanced up as he tossed dirt aside. "I guess I had a hard

time getting past that pretty face.'' That pretty face, he
noted, was flushed and damp and had shadows of fatigue under the eyes. It annoyed the hell out of him. ''I
thought you sold flowers.''

''I do. I also plant them.''

''Even I know that thing there is a tree.''

''I plant those, too.'' Giving up, she took out a bandanna and wiped at her neck. ''The hole needs to be
wider, not deeper.''

He shifted to accommodate her. Maybe he needed to
do a little reevaluating. ''How come you don't have any-
body doing the heavy work for you?''

''Because I can do it myself.''

Yes, there was stubbornness in the tone, and just a
touch of nastiness. He liked her better for it. ''Looks like
a two-man job to me.''

''It is a two-man job—the other man quit yesterday to
be a rock star. His band got a gig down in Brighton
Beach.''

''Big time.''

''Hmm. That's fine,'' she said, and turned to heft the
three-foot tree by its balled roots. As Holt frowned at her,
she lifted it, then set it carefully in the hole.

''Now I guess I fill it back in.''

''You've got the shovel,'' she pointed out. As he
worked, she dragged a bag of peat moss closer and began to mix it with the soil.

Her nails were short and rounded, he noted as she dug
her already grimed fingers into the soil. There was no
wedding ring on her finger. In fact, she wore no jewelry
at all, though she had hands that were meant to wear
beautiful things.

She worked patiently, her head down, her cap shield-
ing her eyes. He could see the nape of her neck and won-

dered what it would be like to press his lips there. Her skin would be hot now, and damp. Then she rose, switching on the garden hose to drench the dirt.

"You do this every day?"

"I try to take a day or two in the shop. I can bring the kids in with me." With her feet, she tamped down the damp earth. When the tree was secure, she spread a thick lawyer of mulch, her moves competent and practiced. "Next spring, this will be covered with blooms." She wiped the back of her wrist over her brow. The little tank top she wore had a line of sweat down the front and back that only emphasized her fragile build. "I really am on a schedule, Holt. I've got some aspens and white pine to plant out in back, so if you need to talk to me, you're going to have to come along."

He glanced around the yard. "Did you do all this today?"

"Yes. What do you think?"

"I think you're courting sunstroke."

A compliment, she supposed, would have been too much to ask. "I appreciate the medical evaluation." She put a hand on the shovel, but he held on. "I need this."

"I'll carry it."

"Fine." She loaded the bags of peat and mulch into a wheelbarrow. He swore at her, tossed the shovel on top then nudged her away to push the wheelbarrow himself.

"Where out back?"

"By the stakes near the rear fence."

She frowned after him when he started off, then followed him. He began digging without consulting her so she emptied the wheelbarrow and headed back to her truck. When he glanced up, she was pushing out two more trees. They planted the first one together, in silence.

He hadn't realized that putting a tree in the ground could be soothing, even rewarding work. But when it stood, young and straight in the dazzling sunlight, he felt soothed. And rewarded.

"I was thinking about what you said yesterday," he began when they set the second tree in its new home.

"And?"

He wanted to swear. There was such patience in the single word, as if she'd known all along he would bring it up. "And I still don't think there's anything I can do, or want to do, but you may be right about the connection."

"I know I'm right about the connection." She brushed mulch from her hands to her jeans. "If you came out here just to tell me that, you've wasted a trip."

She rolled the empty wheelbarrow to the truck. She was about to muscle the next two trees out of the bed when he jumped up beside her.

"I'll get the damn things out." Muttering, he filled the wheelbarrow and rolled it back to the rear of the yard. "He never mentioned her to me. Maybe he knew her, maybe they had an affair, but I don't see how that helps you."

"He loved her," Suzanna said quietly as she picked up the shovel to dig. "That means he knew how she felt, how she thought. He might have had an idea where she would have hidden the emeralds."

"He's dead."

"I know." She was silent a moment as she worked. "Bianca kept a journal—at least we're nearly certain she did, and that she hid it away with the necklace. Christian might have kept one, too."

Annoyed, he grabbed the shovel again. "I never saw it."

She suppressed the urge to snap at him. However much it might grate, he could be a link. "I suppose most people keep a private journal in a private place. Or he might have kept some letters from her. We found one Bianca wrote him and was never able to send."

"You're chasing windmills, Suzanna."

"This is important to my family." She set the white pine carefully in the hole. "It's not the monetary value of the emeralds. It's what they meant to her."

He watched her work, the competent and gentle hands, the surprisingly strong shoulders. The delicate curve of her neck. "How could you know what they meant to her?"

She kept her eyes down. "I can't explain that to you in any way you'd understand or accept."

"Try me."

"We all seem to have some kind of bond with her—especially Lilah." She didn't look up when she heard him digging the next hole. "We'd never seen the emeralds, not even a photograph. After Bianca died, Fergus, my great-grandfather, destroyed all pictures of her. But Lilah . . . she drew a sketch of them one night. It was after we'd had a séance."

She did look up then and caught his look of amused disbelief. "I know how it sounds," she said, her voice stiff and defensive. "But my aunt believes in that sort of thing. And after that night, I think she may be right to. My youngest sister, C.C. had an. . .experience during the séance. She saw them—the emeralds. That's when Lilah drew the sketch. Weeks later, Lilah's fiancé found a picture of the emeralds in a library book. They were exactly as Lilah had drawn them, exactly as C.C. had seen them."

He said nothing for a moment as he set the next tree in place. "I'm not much on mysticism. Maybe one of your sisters saw the picture before, and had forgotten about it."

"If any of us had seen a picture, we wouldn't have forgotten. Still, the point is that all of us feel that finding the emeralds is important."

"They might have been sold eighty years ago."

"No. There was no record. Fergus was a maniac about keeping his finances." Unconsciously she arched her back, rolled her shoulders to relieve the ache. "Believe me, we've been through every scrap of paper we could find."

He let it drop, mulling it over as they planted the last of the trees.

"You know the bit about the needle in the haystack?" he asked as he helped her spread mulch. "People don't really find it."

"They would if they kept looking." Curious, she sat back on her heels to study him. "Don't you believe in hope?"

He was close enough to touch her, to rub the smudge of dirt from her cheek or run a hand down the ponytail. He did neither. "No, only in what is."

"Then I'm sorry for you." They rose together, their bodies nearly brushing. She felt something rush along her skin, something race through her blood, and automatically stepped back. "If you don't believe in what could be, there isn't any use in planting trees, or having children or even watching the sun set."

He'd felt it, too. And resented and feared it every bit as much as she. "If you don't keep your eye on what's real, right now, you end up dreaming your life away. I don't believe in the necklace, Suzanna, or in ghosts, or in eternal love. But if and when I'm certain that my grandfather was involved with Bianca Calhoun, I'll do what I can to help you.''

She gave a half laugh. ''You don't believe in hope or love, or anything else apparently. Why would you agree to help us?''

''Because if he did love her, he would have wanted me to.'' Bending, he picked up the shovel and handed it back to her. ''I've got things to do.''

Chapter 3

Suzanna pulled up to the shop, pleased that she had to squeeze between a station wagon and a hatchback in the graveled parking area. There were a few people wandering around the flats of annuals, and a young couple deliberating over the climbing roses. A woman, hugely pregnant, strolled about, carrying a tray of mixed pots. The toddler by her side held a single geranium like a flag.

Inside, Carolanne was ringing up a sale and flirting with the young man who held a ceramic urn of pink double begonias. "Your mother will love them," she said, and swept her long lashes over doe-colored eyes. "There's nothing like flowers for a birthday. Or anytime. We're having a special on carnations." She smiled and tossed her long, curling brown hair. "If you have a girlfriend."

"Well, no..." He cleared his throat. "Not really. Right now."

"Oh." Her smile warmed several degrees. "That's too bad." She gave him his change and a long look. "Come back anytime. I'm usually here."

"Sure. Thanks." He shot a glance over his shoulder, trying to keep her in sight, and nearly ran over Suzanna. "Oh. Sorry."

"That's all right. I hope your mother enjoys them." Chuckling, she joined the pert brunette at the cash register. "You're amazing."

"Wasn't he cute? I love it when they blush. Well." She turned her smile on Suzanna. "You're back early."

"It didn't take as long as I thought." She didn't feel it was necessary to add she'd had unexpected and unwanted help. Carolanne was a hard worker, a skilled salesperson, and an inveterate gossip. "How are things here?"

"Moving along. All this sunshine must be inspiring people to beef up their gardens. Oh, Mrs. Russ was back. She liked the primroses so much, she made her husband build her another window box so she could buy more. Since she was in the mood, I sold her two hibiscus—and two of those terra-cotta pots to put them in."

"I love you. Mrs. Russ loves you, and Mr. Russ is going to learn to hate you." At Carolanne's laugh, Suzanna looked out through the glass. "I'll go and see if I can help those people decide which roses they want."

"The new Mr. and Mrs. Halley. They both wait tables over at Captain Jack's, and just bought a cottage. He's studying to be an engineer, and she's going to start teaching at the elementary school in September."

Shaking her head, Suzanna laughed. "Like I said, you're amazing."

"No, just nosy." Carolanne grinned. "Besides, people buy more if you talk to them. And boy, do I love to talk."

"If you didn't, I'd have to close up shop."

"You'd just work twice as hard, if that's possible." She waved a hand before Suzanna could protest. "Before you go, I asked around to see if anyone needed any part-time work." Carolanne lifted her hands. "No luck yet."

It wasn't any use moaning, Suzanna thought. "This late in the season, everyone's already working."

"If Tommy the creep Parotti hadn't jumped ship—"

"Honey, he had a chance to make a break and do something he's always wanted to do. We can't blame him for that."

"You can't," Carolanne muttered. "Suzanna, you can't keep doing all the site work yourself. It's too hard."

"We're getting by," she said absently, thinking of the help she'd had that day. "Listen, Carolanne, after we deal with these customers, I have another delivery to make. Can you handle things until closing?"

"Sure." Carolanne let out a sigh. "I'm the one with a stool and a fan, you're the one with the pick and the shovel."

"Just keep pushing the carnations."

An hour later, Suzanna pulled up at Holt's cottage. It wasn't just impulse, she told herself. And it wasn't because she wanted to pressure him. Lecturing herself, she climbed out of the truck. It certainly wasn't because she wanted his company. But she was a Calhoun, and Calhouns always paid their debts.

She walked up the steps to the porch, again thinking it was a charming place. A few touches—morning glories climbing up the railing, a bed of columbine and larkspur, with some snapdragons and lavender.

Day lilies along that slope, she thought as she knocked. A border of impatiens. Miniature roses under the windows. And there, where the ground was rocky and uneven, a little herb bed, set off with spring bulbs.

It could be a fairy-tale place—but the man who lived there didn't believe in fairy tales.

She knocked again, noting that his car was there. As she had before, she walked around the side, but he wasn't in the boat this time. With a shrug, she decided she would do what she'd come to do.

She'd already picked the spot, between the water and the house, where the shrub could be seen and enjoyed through what she'd determined was the kitchen window. It wasn't much, but it would add some color to the empty backyard. She wheeled around what she needed, then began to dig.

Inside his work shed, Holt had the boat engine broken down. Rebuilding it would require concentration and time. Which was just what he needed. He didn't want to think about the Calhouns, or tragic love affairs, or responsibilities.

He didn't even glance up when Sadie rose from her nap on the cool cement and trotted outside. He and the dog had an understanding. She did as she chose, and he fed her.

When she barked, he kept on working. As a watchdog, Sadie was a bust. She barked at squirrels, at the wind in the grass, and in her sleep. A year before there'd been an attempted burglary in his house in Portland. Holt had relieved the would-be thief of his stereo equipment while Sadie had napped peacefully on the living room rug.

But he did look up, he did stop working when he heard the low, feminine laughter. It skimmed along his skin, light and warm. When he pushed away from the workbench, his stomach was already in knots. When he stood in the doorway and looked at her, the knots yanked tight.

Why wouldn't she leave him alone? he wondered, and shoved his hands into his pockets. He'd told her he'd think about it, hadn't he? She had no business coming here again.

They didn't even like each other. Whatever she did to him physically was his problem, and so far he'd managed quite nicely to keep his hands off her.

Now here she was, standing in his yard, talking to his dog. And digging a hole.

His brows drew together as he stepped out of the shed. "What the hell are you doing?"

Her head shot up. He saw her eyes, big and blue and alarmed. Her face, flushed from the heat and her work, went very pale. He'd seen that kind of look before—the quick, instinctive fear of a cornered victim. Then it was gone, fading so swiftly he nearly convinced himself he'd imagined it. Color seeped slowly into her cheeks again as she managed to smile.

"I didn't think you were here."

He stayed where he was and continued to scowl. "So, you decided to dig a hole in my yard."

"I guess you could say that." Steady now, annoyed with herself for the instinctive jolt, she plunged the shovel in again, braced her foot on it and deepened the hole. "I brought you a bush."

Damned if he was going to take the shovel from her this time and dig the hole himself. But he did cross to her. "Why?"

"To thank you for helping me out today. You saved me a good hour."

"So you use it to dig another hole."

"Uh-huh. There's a breeze off the water today." She lifted her face to it for a moment. "It's nice."

Because looking at her made his palms sweat, he scowled down at the tidy shrub pregnant with sassy yellow blooms. "I don't know how to take care of a bush. You put it there, you're condemning it to death row."

With a laugh, she scooped out the last of the dirt. "You don't have to do much. This one's very hardy, even when it's dry, and it'll bloom for you into the fall. Can I use your hose?"

"What?"

"Your hose?"

"Yeah." He raked a hand through his hair. He hadn't a clue how he was supposed to react. It was certainly the first time anyone had given him flowers—unless you counted the batch the guys at the precinct had brought in when he'd been in the hospital. "Sure."

At ease with her task, she continued to talk as she went to the outside wall to turn on the water. "It'll stay neat. It's a very well behaved little bush and won't get over three feet." She petted Sadie, who was circling the bush and sniffing. "If you'd like something else instead..."

He wasn't going to let himself be touched by some idiotic plant or her misplaced gratitude. "It doesn't matter to me. I don't know one from the other."

"Well, this is a *hypericum kalmianum.*"

His lips quirked into what might have been a smile. "That tells me a lot."

Chuckling, she set it in place. "A sunshine shrub in layman's terms." Still smiling, she tilted her head back to look at him. If she didn't know better, she'd have thought he was embarrassed. Fat chance. "I thought you could use some sunshine. Why don't you help me plant it? It'll mean more to you then."

He'd said he wasn't going to get sucked in, and damn it, he'd meant it. "Are you sure this isn't your idea of a bribe? To get me to help you out?"

Sighing a little, she sat back on her heels. "I wonder what makes someone so cynical and unfriendly. I'm sure you have your reasons, but they don't apply here. You did me a favor today, and I'm paying you back. Very simple. Now if you don't want the bush, just say so. I'll give it to someone else."

He lifted a brow at the tone. "Is that how you keep your kids in line?"

"When necessary. Well, what's it to be?"

Maybe he was being too hard on her. She'd made a gesture and he was slapping it back in her face. If she could be casually friendly, so could he. "I've already got a hole in my yard," he pointed out then knelt beside her. The dog lay down in the sunlight to watch. "We might as well put something in it."

And that, she supposed, was his idea of a thank-you. "Fine."

"So how old are your kids?" Not that he cared, he told himself. He was just making conversation.

"Five and six. Alex is the oldest, then Jenny." Her eyes softened as they always did when she thought of them. "They're growing up so fast, I can hardly keep up."

"What made you come back here after the divorce?"

Her hands tensed in the soil, then began to work again. It was a small and quickly concealed gesture, but he had very sharp eyes. "Because it's home."

There was a tender spot, he thought and eased around it. "I heard you're going to turn The Towers into a hotel."

"Just the west wing. That's C.C.'s husband's business."

"It's hard to picture C.C. married. The last time I saw her she was about twelve."

"She's grown up now, and beautiful."

"Looks run in the family."

She glanced up, surprised, then back down again. "I think you've just said something nice."

"Just stating a fact. The Calhoun sisters were always worth a second look." To please himself, he reached out to toy with the tip of her ponytail. "Whenever guys got together, the four of you were definitely topics of conversation."

She laughed a little, thinking how easy life had been back then. "I'm sure we'd have been flattered."

"I used to look at you," Holt said slowly. "A lot."

Wary, she lifted her head. "Really? I never noticed."

"You wouldn't have." His hand dropped away again. "Princesses don't notice peasants."

Now she frowned, not only at the words but at the clipped tone. "What a ridiculous thing to say."

"It was easy to think of you that way, the princess in the castle."

"A castle that's been crumbling for years," she said dryly. "And as I recall, you were too busy swaggering around and juggling girls to notice me."

He had to grin. "Oh, between the swaggering and juggling, I noticed you all right."

Something in his eyes set off a little warning bell. It might have been some time since she'd heard that particular sound, but she recognized it and heeded it. She looked down again to firm the dirt around the bush.

"That was a long time ago. I imagine we've both changed quite a bit."

"Can't argue with that." He pushed at the dirt.

"No, don't shove at it, press it down—firm, but gentle." Scooting closer, she put her hands over his to show him. "All it needs is a good start, and then—"

She broke off when he turned his hands over to grip hers.

They were close, knees brushing, bodies bent toward each other. He noted that her hands were hard, callused, a direct and fascinating contrast to the soft eyes and tea rose complexion. There was a strength in her fingers that would have surprised him if he hadn't seen for himself how hard she worked. For reasons he couldn't fathom, he found it incredibly erotic.

"You've got strong hands, Suzanna."

"A gardener's hands," she said, trying to keep her voice light. "And I need them to finish planting this bush."

He only tightened his grip when she tried to draw away. "We'll get to it. You know, I've thought about kissing you for fifteen years." He watched the faint smile fade away from her face and the alarm shoot into her eyes. He didn't mind it. It might be best for both of them if she was afraid of him. "That's a long time to think about anything."

He released one hand, but before she could let out a sigh of relief, he had cupped the back of her neck. His fingers were firm, his grip determined. "I'm just going to get it out of my system."

She didn't have time to refuse. He was quick. Before she could deny or protest, his mouth was on hers, cov-

ering and conquering. There was nothing soft about him.
His mouth, his hands, his body when he pulled her
against him, were hard and demanding. The swift fris-
son of fear had her lifting a hand to push against his
shoulder. She might as well have tried to move a boul-
der.

Then the fear turned to an ache. She fisted her hand
against him, forced to fight herself now rather than him.

She was taut as a wire. He could feel her nerves sizzle
and snap as he clamped her against him. He knew it was
wrong, unfair, even despicable, but damn it, he needed
to wipe out this fever that continued to burn in him. He
needed to convince himself that she was just another
woman, that his fantasies of her were only remnants of a
boy's foolish dreams.

Then she shuddered. A soft, yielding sound followed.
And her lips parted beneath his in irresistible and avid
invitation. Swearing, he plunged, dragging her head back
by the hair so that he could take more of what she so
mindlessly offered.

Her mouth was a banquet, and he too racked with
hunger to stem the greed. He could smell her hair, fresh
as rainwater, her skin, seductively musky with heat and
labor, and the rich and primitive fragrance of earth newly
turned. Each separate scent slammed into his system,
pumping through his blood, roaring through his head to
churn a need he'd hoped to dispel.

She couldn't breathe, or think. All of the weighty and
worrisome cares she carried in her vanished. In their
place, rioting sensations sprinted. The tensed ripple of
muscle under her fingers, the hot and desperate taste of
his mouth, the thunder of her heartbeat that raced with
dizzying speed. She was wrapped around him now, her

fingers digging in, her body straining, her mouth as urgent and impatient as his.

It had been so long since she had been touched. So long since she had tasted a man's desire on her lips. So long since she had wanted any man. But she wanted now—to feel his hands on her, rough and demanding, to have his body cover hers on the soft, sunny grass. To be wild and willful and wanton until this clawing ache was soothed.

The sheer power of that want ripped through her, tearing through her lips in a sobbing moan.

His fingers were curled into her shirt, had nearly ripped it aside before he caught himself, cursed himself. And released her. Her shallow ragged breaths were both condemnation and seduction as he forced himself to pull away. Her eyes had gone to cobalt and were wide with shock.

Small wonder, he thought in livid self-disgust. The woman had nearly been shoved to the ground and ravished in broad daylight.

Her lashes lowered before he could see the shame.

"I hope you feel better now."

"No." His hands were far from steady, so he curled them into fists. "I don't."

She didn't look at him, couldn't. Nor could she afford to think, just at this moment, of what she had done. To comfort herself she began to spread mulch around the newly planted bush. "If it stays dry, you'll have to water this regularly until it's established."

For a second time, he gripped her hands. This time she jolted. "Aren't you going to belt me?"

Using well-honed control, she relaxed and looked up. There was something in her eyes, something dark and passionate, but her voice was very calm. "There doesn't seem to be much point in that. I'm sure you're of the opinion that a woman like me would be . . . needy.''

''I wasn't thinking about your needs when I kissed you. It was a purely selfish act, Suzanna. I'm good at being selfish.''

Because his grip was light, she slipped her hands from under his. ''I'm sure you are.'' She brushed her palms on her thighs before she rose. The only thought in her head was of getting away, but she made herself load the wheelbarrow calmly. Until he gripped her arm and whirled her around.

''What the hell is this?'' His eyes were stormy, his voice as rough as his hands. He wanted her to rage at him—needed it to soothe his conscience. ''I all but took you on the ground, without giving a hell of a lot of consideration to whether you'd have liked it or not, and now you're going to load up your cart and go away?''

She was very much afraid she would have liked it. That was why it was imperative that she stay very calm and very controlled. ''If you want to pick a fight or a casual lover, Holt, you've come to the wrong person. My children are expecting me home, and I'm very tired of being grabbed.''

Yes, her voice was calm, he thought, even firm, but her arm was trembling lightly under his hold. There was something here, he realized, some secrets she held behind those sad and beautiful eyes. The same stubbornness that had had him pursuing his gold shield made it essential that he discover them.

''Grabbed in general, or just by me?''

''You're the one doing the grabbing.'' Her patience was wearing thin. The Calhoun temper was always difficult to control. ''I don't like it.''

"That's too bad, because I have a feeling I'm going to be doing a lot more of it before we're through."

"Maybe I haven't made myself clear. We are through." She shook loose and grabbed the handles of the wheelbarrow.

He simply put his weight on it to stop her. He wasn't sure if she realized she'd just issued an irresistible challenge. His grin came slowly. "Now you're getting mad."

"Yes. Does that make you feel better?"

"Quite a bit. I'd rather have you claw at me than crawl off like a wounded bird."

"I'm not crawling anywhere," she said between her teeth. "I'm going home."

"You forgot your shovel," he told her, still grinning.

She snatched it up and tossed it into the wheelbarrow with a clatter. "Thanks."

"You're welcome."

He waited until she'd gone about ten feet. "Suzanna."

She slowed but didn't stop, and tossed a look over her shoulder. "What?"

"I'm sorry."

Her temper eased a bit as she shrugged. "Forget it."

"No." He dipped his hands into his pockets and rocked back on his heels. "I'm sorry I didn't kiss you like that fifteen years ago."

Swearing under her breath, she quickened her pace. When she was out of sight, he glanced back at the bush. Yeah, he thought, he was sorry as hell, but planned to make up for lost time.

She needed some time to herself. That wasn't a commodity Suzanna found very often in a house as filled with people as The Towers. But just now, with the moon on the rise and the children in bed, she took a few precious moments alone.

It was a clear night, and the heat of the day had been replaced by a soft breeze that was scented with the sea and roses. From her terrace she could see the dark shadow of the cliffs that always drew her. The distant murmur of water was a lullaby, as sweet as the call of a night bird from the garden.

Tonight it wouldn't ease her into sleep. No matter how tired her body was, her mind was too restless. It didn't seem to matter how often she told herself she had nothing to worry about. Her children were safely tucked into bed, dreaming about the day's adventures. Her sisters were happy. Each one of them had found her place in the world, just as each one of them had found a mate who loved her for who and what she was. Aunt Coco was happy and healthy and looking forward to the day when she would become head chef of The Towers Retreat.

Her family, always Suzanna's chief concern, was content and settled. The Towers, the only real home she'd ever known, was no longer in danger of being sold, but would remain the Calhoun home. It was pointless to worry about the emeralds. The family was doing all that could be done to find the necklace.

If they hadn't been exploring every avenue, she would never have gone to Holt Bradford. Her fingers curled on the stone wall. That, she thought, had been a useless exercise. He was Christian Bradford's grandson, but he didn't feel the connection. It was obvious that the past held no interest for him. He thought only about the moment, about himself, about his own comfort and pleasures.

Catching herself, Suzanna sighed and forced herself to relax her hands. If only he hadn't made her so angry. She despised losing her temper, and it had come dangerously close to breaking loose that day. It was her own fault, and her own problem that something else had broken loose.

Needs. She didn't want to need anyone but her family—the family she could love and depend on and worry about. She'd already learned a painful lesson about needing a man, one man. She didn't intend to repeat it.

He'd kissed her on impulse, she reminded herself. It had been a kind of dare to himself. There had certainly been no affection in it, no softness, no romance. The fact that it had stirred her was strictly chemical. She'd cut herself off from men for more than two years. And the last year or so of her marriage—well, there had been no affection, softness or romance there, either. She'd learned to do without those things when it came to men. She could continue to do without them.

If only she hadn't responded to him so...blatantly. He might as well have knocked her over the head with a club and dragged her into a cave by the hair for all the finesse he'd shown. Yet she had thrown herself into the moment, clinging to him, answering those hard and demanding lips with a fervor she'd never been able to show her own husband.

By doing so, she'd humiliated herself and amused Holt. Oh, the way he had grinned at her at the end had had her steaming for hours afterward. That was her problem, too, she thought now. Just as it was her problem that she could still taste him.

Perhaps she shouldn't be so hard on herself. As embarrassing as the moment had been, it had proved something. She was still alive. She wasn't the cold shell of a woman that Bax had tossed so carelessly aside. She could feel, and want.

Closing her eyes, she pressed a hand to her stomach. Want too much, it seemed. It was like a hunger, and the kiss, like a crust of bread after a long fast, had stirred the juices. She could be glad of that—to feel something again besides remorse and disillusionment. And feeling it, she could control it. Pride would prevent her from avoiding Holt. Just as pride would save her from any new humiliation.

She was a Calhoun, she reminded herself. Calhoun women went down fighting. If she had to deal with Holt again in order to widen the trail to the emeralds, then she would deal with him. She would never, never let herself be dismissed and destroyed by a man again. He hadn't seen the last of her.

"Suzanna, there you are."

Her thoughts scattered as she turned to see her aunt striding through the terrace doors. "Aunt Coco."

"I'm sorry, dear, but I knocked and knocked. Your light was on so I just peeked in."

"That's all right." Suzanna slipped an arm around Coco's sturdy waist. This was a woman she'd loved for most of her life. A woman who had been mother and father to her for more than fifteen years. "I was lost in the night, I guess. It's so beautiful."

Coco murmured an agreement and said nothing for a moment. Of all of her girls, she worried most about Suzanna. She had watched her ride away, a young bride radiant with hope. She had been there when Suzanna had come back, barely four years later, a pale, devastated woman with two small children. In the years since, she'd been proud to see Suzanna gain her feet, devoting herself to the difficult task of single parenthood, working hard, much too hard, to establish her own business.

And she had waited, painfully, for the sad and haunted look that clouded her niece's eyes, to finally fade forever.

"Couldn't you sleep?" Suzanna asked her.

"I haven't even thought about sleep yet." Coco let out a huff of breath. "That woman is driving me out of my mind."

Suzanna managed not to smile. She knew *that woman* was her Great-Aunt Colleen, the eldest of Bianca's children, and the sister of Coco's father. The rude, demanding and perpetually cranky woman had descended on them a week before. Coco was certain the move had been made with the sole purpose of making her life a misery.

"Did you hear her at dinner?" Tall and stately in her draping caftan, Coco began to pace. Her complaints were issued in an indignant whisper. Colleen might have been well past eighty, her bedroom may have been two dozen feet away, but she had ears like a cat. "The sauce was too rich, the asparagus too soft. The idea of her telling *me* how to prepare coq au vin. I wanted to take that cane and wrap it around her—"

"Dinner was superb, as always," Suzanna soothed. "She has to complain about something, Aunt Coco, otherwise her day wouldn't be complete. And as I recall, there wasn't a crumb left on her plate."

"Quite right." Coco drew in a deep breath, releasing it slowly. "I know I shouldn't let the woman get on my nerves. The fact is, she's always frightened me half to death. And she knows it. If it wasn't for yoga and meditation, I'm sure I'd have already lost my sanity. As long as she was living on one of those cruise ships, all I had to do was send her an occasional duty letter. But actually living under the same roof." Coco couldn't help it—she shuddered.

"She'll get tired of us soon, and sail off down the Nile or the Amazon or whatever."

"It can't be too soon for me. I'm afraid she's made up her mind to stay until we find the emeralds. Which is what this is all about anyway." Coco calmed herself enough to stand at the wall again. "I was using my crystal to meditate. So soothing, and after an evening with Aunt Colleen—" She broke off because she was clenching her teeth. "In any case, I was just drifting along, when thoughts and images of Bianca filled my head."

"That's not surprising," Suzanne put in. "She's on all of our minds."

"But this was very strong, dear. Very clear. There was such melancholy. I tell you, it brought tears to my eyes." Coco pulled a handkerchief out of her caftan. "Then suddenly, I was thinking of you, and that was just as strong and clear. The connection between you and Bianca was unmistakable. I realized there had to be a reason, and thinking it through, I believe it's because of Holt Bradford." Coco's eyes were shining now with discovery and enthusiasm. "You see, you've spoken to him, you've bridged the gap between Christian and Bianca."

"I don't think you can call my conversations with Holt a bridge to anything."

"No, he's the key, Suzanna. I doubt he understands what information he might have, but without him, we can't take the next step. I'm sure of it."

With a restless move of her shoulders, Suzanna leaned against the wall. "Whatever he understands, he isn't interested."

"Then you have to convince him otherwise." She put a hand on Suzanna's and squeezed. "We need him. Until we find the emeralds, none of us will feel completely safe. The police haven't been able to find that miserable

thief, and we don't know what he may try next time. Holt
is our only link with the man Bianca loved.''

"I know.''

"Then you'll see him again. You'll talk to him.''

Suzanna looked toward the cliffs, toward the shadows. "Yes, I'll see him again.''

*I knew she would come back. However unwise, however
wrong it might have been, I looked for her every afternoon. On the days she did not come to the cliffs, I would
find myself staring up at the peaks of The Towers, aching for her in a way I had no right to ache for another
man's wife. On the days she walked toward me, her hair
like melted flame, that small, shy smile on her lips, I
knew a joy like no other.*

*In the beginning, our conversations were polite and
distant. The weather, unimportant village gossip, art and
literature. As time passed, she became more at ease with
me. She would speak of her children, and I came to know
them through her. The little girl, Colleen, who liked
pretty dresses and yearned for a pony. Young Ethan who
only wanted to run and find adventure. And little Sean,
who was just learning to crawl.*

*It took no special insight to see that her children were
her life. Rarely did she speak of the parties, the musi-
cals, the social gatherings I knew she attended almost
nightly. Not at all did she speak of the man she had married.*

*I admit I wondered about him. Of course, it was com-
mon knowledge that Fergus Calhoun was an ambitious
and wealthy man, one who had turned a few dollars into
an empire during the course of his life. He commanded
both respect and fear in the business world. For that I
cared nothing.*

It was the private man who obsessed me. The man who had the right to call her wife. The man who lay beside her at night, who touched her. The man who knew the texture of her skin, the taste of her mouth. The man who knew how it felt to have her move beneath him in the dark.

I was already in love with her. Perhaps I had been from the moment I had seen her walking with the child through the wild roses.

It would have been best for my sanity if I had chosen another place to paint. I could not. Already knowing I would have no more of her, could have no more than a few hours of conversation, I went back. Again and again.

She agreed to let me paint her. I began to see, as an artist must see, the inner woman. Beyond her beauty, beyond her composure and breeding was a desperately unhappy woman. I wanted to take her in my arms, to demand that she tell me what had put that sad and haunted look in her eyes. But I only painted her. I had no right to do more.

I have never been a patient or a noble man. Yet with her, I found I could be both. Without ever touching me, she changed me. Nothing would be the same for me after that summer—that all too brief summer when she would come, to sit on the rocks and look out to sea.

Even now, a lifetime later, I can walk to those cliffs and see her. I can smell the sea that never changes, and catch the drift of her perfume. I have only to pick a wild rose to remember the fiery lights of her hair. Closing my eyes, I hear the murmur of the water on the rocks below and her voice comes back as clear and as sweet as yesterday.

I am reminded of the last afternoon that first summer, when she stood beside me, close enough to touch, as distant as the moon.

"We leave in the morning," she said, but didn't look at me. "The children are sorry to go."

"And you?"

A faint smile touched her lips but not her eyes. "Sometimes I wonder if I've lived before. If my home was an island like this. The first time I came here, it was as if I had been waiting to see it again. I'll miss the sea."

Perhaps it was only my own needs that made me think, when she glanced at me, that she would miss me, as well. Then she looked away again and sighed.

"New York is so different, so full of noise and urgency. It's hard to believe such a place exists when I stand here. Will you stay on the island through the winter?"

I thought of the cold and desolate months ahead and cursed fate for taunting me with what I could never have. "My plans change with my mood." I said it lightly, fighting to keep the bitterness out of my voice.

"I envy you your freedom." She turned away then to walk back to where her nearly completed portrait rested on my easel. "And your talent. You've made me more than what I am."

"Less." I had to curl my hands into fists to keep from touching her. "Some things can never be captured with paint and canvas."

"What will you call it?"

"Bianca. Your name is enough."

She must have sensed my feelings, though I tried desperately to hold them in myself. Something came into her eyes as she looked at me, and the look held longer than it should. Then she stepped back, cautiously, like a woman who had wandered too close to the edge of a cliff.

"One day you'll be famous, and people will beg for your work."

I couldn't take my eyes off her, knowing I might never see her again. "I don't paint for fame."

"No, and that's why you'll have it. When you do, I'll remember this summer. Goodbye, Christian."

She walked away from me—for what I thought was the last time—away from the rocks, through the wild grass and the flowers that fight through both for the sun.

Chapter 4

Coco Calhoun McPike didn't believe in leaving things up to chance—particularly when her horoscope that day had advised her to take a more active part in a family matter and to visit an old acquaintance. She felt she could do both by paying an informal call on Holt Bradford.

She remembered him as a dark, hot-eyed boy who had delivered lobster and loitered around the village, waiting for trouble to happen. She also remembered that he had once stopped to change a flat for her while she'd been struggling on the side of the road trying to figure out which end of the jack to put under the bumper. He'd refused—stiffly, she recalled—her offer of payment and had hopped back on his motorcycle and ridden off before she'd properly thanked him.

Proud, defiant, rebellious, she mused as she maneuvered her car into his driveway. Yet, in a grudging sort of way, chivalrous. Perhaps if she was clever—and Coco thought that she was—she could play on all of those traits to get what she wanted.

So this had been Christian Bradford's cottage, she mused. She'd seen it before, of course, but not since she'd known of the connection between the families. She paused for a moment. With her eyes closed she tried to *feel* something. Surely there was some remnant of energy here, something that time and wind hadn't washed away.

Coco liked to consider herself a mystic. Whether it was a true evaluation, or her imagination was ripe, she was certain she did feel some snap of passion in the air. Pleased with it, and herself, she trooped to the house.

She'd dressed very carefully. She wanted to look attractive, of course. Her vanity wouldn't permit otherwise. But she'd also wanted to look distinguished and just the tiniest bit matronly. She felt the old and classic Chanel suit in powder blue worked very well.

She knocked, putting what she hoped was a wise and comforting smile on her face. The wild barking and the steady stream of curses from within had her placing a hand on her breast.

Five minutes out of the shower, his hair dripping and his temper curdled, Holt yanked open the door. Sadie bounded out. Coco squeaked. Good reflexes had Holt snatching the amorous dog by the collar before she could send Coco over the porch railing.

"Oh my." Coco looked from dog to man, juggling the plate of double-fudge brownies. "Oh, goodness. What a very *large* dog. She certainly does look like our Fred, and I'd so hoped he'd stop growing soon. Why you could practically *ride* her if you liked, couldn't you?" She beamed a smile at Holt. "I'm so sorry, have I interrupted you?"

He continued to struggle with the dog, who'd gotten a good whiff of the brownies and wanted her share. Now. "Excuse me?"

"I've interrupted," Coco repeated. "I know it's early, but on days like this I just can't stay in bed. All this sun and twittering birds. Not to mention the sawing and hammering. Do you suppose she'd like one of these?" Without waiting for an answer, Coco took one of the brownies off the plate. "Now you sit and behave."

With what was certainly a grin, Sadie stopped straining, sat and eyed Coco adoringly.

"Good dog." Sadie took the treat politely then padded back into the house to enjoy it. "Well, now." Pleased with the situation, Coco smiled at Holt. "You probably don't remember me. Goodness, it's been years."

"Mrs. McPike." He remembered her, all right, though the last time he'd seen her, her hair had been a dusky blond. It had been ten years, he thought, but she looked younger. She'd either had a first-class face-lift or had discovered the fountain of youth.

"Why, yes. It's so flattering to be remembered by an attractive man. But you were hardly more than a boy the last time. Welcome home." She offered the plate of brownies.

And left him no choice but to accept it and ask her in.

"Thanks." He studied the plate as she breezed inside. Between plants and brownies, the Calhouns were making a habit of bearing gifts. "Is there something I can do for you?"

"To tell you the truth, I've just been dying to see the place. To think this is where Christian Bradford lived, and worked." She sighed. "And dreamed of Bianca."

"Well, he lived and worked here anyway."

"Suzanna tells me you're not quite convinced they loved each other. I can appreciate your reluctance to fall right in with the story, but you see, it's a part of my family history. And yours. Oh, what a glorious painting!"

She crossed the room to a misty seascape hung above the stone fireplace. Even through the haze of fog, the colors were ripe and vivid, as though the vitality and passion were fighting to free themselves from the thin graying curtain. Turbulent whitecaps, the black and toothy edge of rock, the gloom-crowned shadows of islands marooned in a cold, dark sea.

"It's powerful," she murmured. "And, oh, lonely. It's his, isn't it?"

"Yes."

She let out a shaky sigh. "If you'd like to see that view, you've only to walk on the cliffs beneath The Towers. Suzanna walks there, sometimes with the children, sometimes alone. Too often alone." Shaking off the mood, Coco turned back. "My niece seems to feel that you're not particularly interested in confirming Christian and Bianca's relationship, and helping to find the emeralds. I find that difficult to believe."

Holt set the plate aside. "It shouldn't be, Mrs. McPike. But what I told your niece was that if and when I was convinced there had been a connection of any importance, I'd do what I could to help. Which, as I see it, is next to nothing."

"You were a police officer, weren't you?"

Holt hooked his thumbs in his pockets, not trusting the change of subject. "Yeah."

"I have to admit I was surprised when I heard you'd chosen that profession, but I'm sure you were well suited to the job."

The scar on his back seemed to twinge. "I used to be."

"And you'd have solved cases, I suppose."

His lips curved a little. "A few."

"So you'd have looked for clues and followed them up until you found the right answer." She smiled at him. "I always admire the police on television who solve the mystery and tidy everything up before the end of the show."

"Life's not tidy."

On certain men, she thought, a sneer was not at all unattractive. "No, indeed not, but we could certainly use someone on our side who has your experience." She walked back toward him, and she was no longer smiling. "I'll be frank. If I had known what trouble it would cause my family, I might have let the legend of the emeralds die with me. When my brother and his wife were killed, and left their girls in my care, I was also left the responsibility of passing along the story of the Calhoun emeralds—when the time was right. By doing what I consider my duty, I've put my family in danger. I'll do anything in my power, and use anyone I can, to keep them from being hurt. Until those emeralds are found, I can't be sure my family is safe."

"You need the police," he began.

"They're doing what they can. It isn't enough." Reaching out, she put a hand on his. "They aren't personally involved, and can't possibly understand. You can."

Her faith and her obstinate logic made him uneasy. "You're overestimating me."

"I don't think so." Coco held his hand another moment, then gave it a brief squeeze before releasing it. "But I don't mean to nag. I only came so I could add my input to Suzanna's. She has such a difficult time pushing for what she wants."

"She does well enough."

"Well, I'm glad to hear it. But with her work and Mandy's wedding, and everything else that's been going on, I know she hasn't had time to speak with you again for the last couple of days. I tell you, our lives have been turned upside down for the last few months. First C.C.'s wedding, and the renovations, now Amanda and Sloan— and Lilah already setting a date to marry Max." She paused and hoped to look wistful. "If I could only find some nice man for Suzanna, I'd have all my girls set- tled."

Holt didn't miss the speculative look. "I'm sure she'll take care of that herself when she's ready."

"Not when she doesn't give herself a moment to look. And after what that excuse for a man did to her." She cut herself off there. If she started on Baxter Dumont, it would be difficult to stop. And it would hardly be proper conversation. "Well, in any case, she keeps herself too busy with her business and her children, so I like to keep my eye out for her. You're not married, are you?"

At least no one could accuse her of being subtle, Holt thought, amused. "Yeah. I've got a wife and six kids in Portland."

Coco blinked, then laughed. "It was a rude ques- tion," she admitted. "And before I ask another, I'll leave you alone." She started for the door, pleased that he had enough manners to accompany her and open it for her. "Oh, by the way, Amanda's wedding is Saturday, at six. We're holding the reception at the ballroom in The Tow- ers. I'd like for you to come."

The unexpected curve had him hesitating. "I really don't think it's appropriate."

"It's more than appropriate," she corrected. "Our families go back quite a long way, Holt. We'd very much like to have you there." She started toward her car then turned, smiling again. "And Suzanna doesn't have an escort. It seems a pity."

The thief called himself by many names. When he had first come to Bar Harbor in search of the emeralds, he had used the name Livingston and had posed as a successful British businessman. He had only been partially successful and had returned under the guise of Ellis Caufield, a wealthy eccentric. Due to bad luck and his partner's fumbling, he'd had to abandon that particular cover.

His partner was dead, which was only a small inconvenience. The thief now went under the name of Robert Marshall and was developing a certain fondness for this alter ego.

Marshall was lean and tanned and had a hint of a Boston accent. He wore his dark hair nearly shoulder length and sported a drooping mustache. His eyes were brown, thanks to contact lenses. His teeth were slightly bucked. The oral device had cost him a pretty penny, but it had also changed the shape of his jaw.

He was very comfortable with Marshall, and delighted to have signed on as a laborer on The Towers renovation. His references had been forged and had added to his overhead. But the emeralds would be worth it. He intended to have them, whatever the price.

Over the past months they had gone from being a job to an obsession. He didn't just want them. He needed them. He found the risk of working so close to the Calhouns only added spice to the game. He had, in fact, passed within three feet of Amanda when she had come into the west wing to talk to Sloan O'Riley. Neither of them, who had known him only as Livingston, had given him a second glance.

He did his job well, hauling equipment, cleaning up debris. And he worked without complaint. He was friendly with his co-workers, even joining them occasionally for a beer after work.

Then he would go back to his rented house across the bay and plan.

The security at The Towers posed no problem—not when it would be so easy for him to disengage it from the inside. By working for the Calhouns, he could stay close, he could be certain he would hear about any new developments in their search for the necklace. And with care and skill, he could do some searching on his own.

The papers he had stolen from them had offered no real clue as yet. Unless it came from the letter he'd discovered. One that had been written to Bianca and signed only "Christian." A love letter, Marshall mused as he stacked lumber. It was something he had to look into.

"Hey, Bob. Got a minute?"

Marshall looked up and gave his foreman an affable smile. "Sure, nothing but minutes."

"Well, they need some tables moved into the ballroom for that wedding tomorrow. You and Rick give the ladies a hand."

"Right."

Marshall strolled along, fighting back a trembling excitement at being free to walk through the house. He took his instructions from a flustered Coco, then hefted his end of the heavy hunt table to move it up to the next floor.

"Do you think he'll come?" C.C. asked Suzanna as they finished washing down the glass on the mirrored walls.

"I doubt it."

C.C. brushed back her short cap of black hair as she stood aside to search for streaks. "I don't see why he wouldn't. And maybe if we all gang up on him, he'll break down and join ranks."

"I don't think he's a joiner." Suzanna glanced around and saw the two men struggling in with the table. "Oh, it goes against that wall. Thanks."

"No problem," Rick managed through gritted teeth. Marshall merely smiled and said nothing.

"Maybe if he sees the picture of Bianca and hears the tape from the interview Max and Lilah had with the maid who used to work here back then, he'll pitch in. He's Christian's only surviving family."

"Hey!" Rick muffled a curse when Marshall bobbled the table.

"I don't think he's big on family feeling," Suzanna put in. "One thing that hasn't changed about Holt Bradford is that he's still a loner."

Holt Bradford. Marshall committed the name to memory before he called across the room. "Is there anything else we can do for you ladies?"

Suzanna glanced over her shoulder with an absent smile. "No, not right now. Thanks a lot."

Marshall grinned. "Don't mention it."

"Some lookers, huh?" Rick muttered as they walked back out.

"Oh, yeah." But Marshall was thinking of the emeralds.

"I tell you, bud, I'd like to—" Rick broke off when two other women and a young boy came to the top of the stairs. He gave them both a big, toothy smile. Lilah gave him a lazy one in return and kept walking.

"Man, oh, man," Rick said with a hand to his heart. "This place is just full of babes."

"Pardon the leers," Lilah said mildly. "Most of them don't bite."

The slim strawberry blonde gave a weak smile. At the moment a couple of leering carpenters were the least of her worries. "I really don't want to get in the way," she began in a soft Southwestern drawl. "I know what Sloan said, but I really think it would be best if Kevin and I checked into a hotel for the night."

"This late in the season, you couldn't check into a tent. And we want you here. All of us. Sloan's family is our family now." Lilah smiled down at the dark-haired boy who was gawking at everything in sight. "It's a wild place, isn't it? Your uncle's making sure it doesn't come crashing down on our heads." She walked into the ballroom.

Suzanna was standing on a ladder, polishing glass, while C.C. sat on the floor, hitting the low spots. Lilah bent to the boy. "I was supposed to be in on this," she whispered. "But I played hooky."

The idea made him laugh, and the laughter, so much like Alex's, had Suzanna glancing over.

She was expecting them. Their arrival had been anticipated for weeks. But seeing them here, knowing who they were, had her nerves jolting.

The woman wasn't just Sloan's sister, nor was the boy just his nephew. A short time before, Suzanna had learned that Megan O'Riley had been her husband's lover, and the boy his child. The woman who was staring at her now, the boy's hand gripped in hers, had been only seventeen when Baxter had charmed her into bed and seduced her with vows of love and promises of mar-

riage. And all the while, he had been planning to marry
Suzanna.

Which one of us, Suzanna wondered, had been the
other woman?

It didn't matter now, she thought, and she climbed
down. Not when she could see the nerves so clearly in
Megan O'Riley's eyes, the tension in the set of her body,
and the courage in the angle of her chin.

Lilah made introductions so smoothly that an outsider might have thought there was nothing but pleas-
antries in the ballroom. As Suzanna offered a hand, all
Megan could think was that she had overdressed. She felt
stiff and foolish in the trim bronze-colored suit, while
Suzanna seemed so relaxed and lovely in faded jeans.

This was the woman she had hated for years, for taking away the man she'd loved and stealing the father of
her child. Even after Sloan had explained Suzanna's innocence, even knowing the hate had been wasted, Megan couldn't relax.

"I'm so glad to meet you." Suzanna put both hands
over Megan's stiff one.

"Thank you." Feeling awkward, Megan drew her
hand away. "We're looking forward to the wedding."

"So are we all." After a bracing breath, Suzanna let
herself look down at Kevin, the half brother to her children. Her heart melted a little. He was taller than her son,
and a full year older. But they had both inherited their
father's dark good looks. Unconsciously Suzanna
reached out to brush back the lock of hair that fell, the
twin of Alex's, over Kevin's brow.

Megan's arm came around his shoulders in an instinctive move of defense. Suzanna let her hand drop to her
side.

"It's nice to meet you, Kevin. Alex and Jenny could hardly sleep last night knowing you'd be here today."

Kevin gave her a fleeting smile, then glanced up at his mother. She'd told him he was going to meet his half brother and sister, and he wasn't too sure he was happy about it. He didn't think his mother was, either.

"Why don't we go down and find them?" C.C. put a hand on Suzanna's shoulder, gently rubbing. Megan noted that Lilah had already flanked her sister's other side. She didn't blame them for sticking together against an outsider, and her chin came up to prove it.

"It might be best if we—"

She never got to finish. Alex and Jenny came clattering down the hall to burst into the room, breathless and flushed. "Is he here?" Alex demanded. "Aunt Coco said he was, and we want to see—" He cut himself off, skidding to a halt on the freshly polished floor.

The two boys eyed each other, interested and cautious, like two terriers. Alex wasn't sure he was pleased that his new brother was bigger than he was, but he'd already decided it would be neat to have something besides a sister.

"I'm Alex and this is Jenny," Alex said, taking over introductions. "She's only five."

"Five and a half," Jenny put in, and marched up to Kevin. "And I can beat you up if I have to."

"Jenny, I don't think that'll be necessary." Suzanna spoke mildly, but the lifted brows said it all.

"Well, I could," Jenny muttered, still sizing him up. "But Mom says we have to be nice 'cause we're family."

"Do you know any Indians?" Alex demanded.

"Yeah." Kevin was no longer gripping his mother's hand for dear life. "Lots of them."

"Want to see our fort?" Alex asked.

"Yeah." He sent a pleading glance at his mother. "Can I?"

"Well, I—"

"Lilah and I'll take them out." C.C. gave Suzanna's shoulder a final squeeze.

"They'll be fine," Suzanna assured Megan as her sisters hustled the children along. "Sloan designed the fort, so it's sturdy." She picked up her rag again to run it through her hands. "Does Kevin know?"

"Yes." Megan turned her purse over and over in restless hands. "I didn't want him to meet your children without understanding." She took a deep breath and prepared to launch into the speech she'd prepared. "Mrs. Dumont—"

"Suzanna. This is hard for you."

"I don't imagine it's easy, or comfortable for either of us. I wouldn't have come," she continued, "if it hadn't been so important to Sloan. I love my brother, and I won't do anything to spoil his wedding, but you must see that this is an impossible situation."

"I can see it's a painful one for you. I'm sorry." Her hands lifted then fell. "I wish I had known sooner, about you, about Kevin. It's unlikely that I could have made any difference as far as Bax is concerned, but I wish I had known." She glanced down at the rag she was gripping too tightly, then put it aside. "Megan, I realize that while you were giving birth to Kevin, alone, I was in Europe, honeymooning with Kevin's father. You're entitled to hate me for that."

Megan could only stare and shake her head. "You're nothing like I expected. You were supposed to be cool and remote and resentful."

"It would be hard to resent a seventeen-year-old girl who was betrayed and left alone to raise a child. I wasn't much older than that when I married Bax. I understand how charming he could be, how persuasive. And how cruel.''

"I thought we'd live happily ever after," Megan said with a sigh. "Well, I grew up quickly, and I learned fast." She let out another long breath as she studied Suzanna. "I hated you, for having everything I thought I wanted. Even when I'd stopped loving him, it helped get me through to hate you. And I was terrified of meeting you."

"That's something else we have in common."

"I can't believe I'm here, talking to you like this." To relieve her nerves she wandered around the ballroom. "I imagined it so many times all those years ago. I'd face you down, demand my rights." She gave a soft laugh. "Even today, I had a whole speech planned out. It was very sophisticated, very mature—maybe just a little vicious. I didn't want to believe that you hadn't known about Kevin, that you'd been a victim, too. Because it was so much easier to think of myself as the only one who'd been betrayed. Then your children came in." She closed her eyes. "How do you deal with the hurt, Suzanna?"

"I'll let you know when I figure it out."

Smiling a little, Megan glanced out of the window. "It hasn't affected them. Look."

Suzanna walked over. Down in the yard she could see her children, and Megan's son, climbing into the plywood fort.

Holt gave it a lot of thought. Up until the moment when he dragged the suit out of his closet, he'd been certain he wasn't going. What the devil was he supposed to do at a society wedding? He didn't like socializing or making small talk or picking at those tiny little canapés. You never knew what the hell was in them anyway.

He didn't like strangling himself with a tie or having to iron a shirt.

So why was he doing it?

He loosened the hated knot of the tie and frowned at himself in the dusty mirror over the bureau. Because he was an idiot and couldn't resist an invitation to the castle on the cliffs. Because he was twice an idiot and wanted to see Suzanna again.

It had been over a week since they had planted the yellow bush. A week since he'd kissed her. And a week since he'd admitted that one kiss, however turbulent, wasn't going to be enough.

He wanted to get a handle on her and thought the best way was to observe her in the midst of the family she seemed to love so much. He wasn't quite sure if she was the cool and remote princess of his youth, the hot-blooded woman he'd held in his arms or the vulnerable one whose eyes were haunting his dreams.

Holt was a man who liked to know exactly what he was up against, whether it was a suspect, a dinky motor or a woman. Once he had Suzanna pegged, he'd move at his own pace.

He didn't want to admit that she'd gotten to him with her fervent belief in the connection between his grandfather and her ancestor. More, he hated to admit that the visit by Coco McPike had made him feel guilty and responsible.

He wasn't going to the wedding to help anyone, he reminded himself. He wasn't making any commitments. He was going to please himself. This time he didn't have to stop at the kitchen door.

It wasn't a long drive, but he took his time, drawing it out. His first glimpse of The Towers bounced him back a dozen years. It was, as it had always been, a fanciful place, a maze of contrasts. It was built of somber stone, yet it was flanked with romantic towers. From one angle, it seemed formidable, from another graceful. At the moment, there was scaffolding on the west side, but instead of looking unsightly, it simply looked productive.

The sloped lawn was emerald green and guarded by gnarled and dignified trees, dashed with fragile and fragrant flowers. There was already a crowd of cars, and Holt felt foolish handing over the keys to his rusted Chevy to the uniformed valet.

The wedding was to take place on the terrace. Since it was about to begin, Holt kept well to the back of the crowd of people. There was organ music, very stately. He had to force himself not to drag at his tie and light a cigarette. There were a few murmured comments and sighs as the bridesmaids started down a long white runner spread over the lawn.

He barely recognized C.C. as the stunning goddess in the long rose-colored dress. Yeah, the Calhoun girls had always been lookers, he thought, and skimmed his gaze over the woman who walked behind her. Her dress was the color of sea foam, but he hardly noticed. It was the face—the face in the portrait in his grandfather's loft. Holt let out the breath between his teeth. Lilah Calhoun was a dead ringer for her great-grandmother. And Holt wasn't going to be able to deny the connection any longer.

He stuffed his hands into his pockets, wishing he hadn't come after all.

Then he saw Suzanna.

This was the princess of his youthful imagination. Her pale gold hair fell in soft curls to her shoulders under a fingertip veil of misty blue. The dress of the same color flowed around her, skirts billowing in the breeze as she walked. She carried flowers in her hands; more were scattered in her hair. When she passed him, her eyes as soft and dreamy as the dress, he felt a longing so deep, so intense, he could barely keep from speaking her name.

He remembered nothing about the brief and lovely ceremony except how her face had looked when the first tear slipped down her cheek.

As it had been so many years ago, the ballroom was filled with light and music and flowers. As for the food, Coco had outdone herself. The guests were treated to lobster croquettes, steamship round, salmon mousse and champagne by the bucket. Dozens of chairs had been set up in corners and along the mirrored walls, and the terrace doors had been thrown open to allow the guests to spill outside.

Holt held himself apart, sipping the cold, frothy wine and using the time to observe. As his first visit to The Towers, it was quite a show, he decided. Mirrors tossed back the reflection of women in pastel dresses as they stood or sat or were lured out to dance. Music and the scent of gardenias filled the air.

The bride was stunning, tall and regal in white lace, her face luminous as she danced with the big, bronzed man who was now her husband. They looked good together, Holt thought idly. The way people were meant to, he supposed, when they were in love. He saw Coco dancing with a tall, fair man who looked as if he'd been born in a tuxedo.

Then he looked back, as he already had several times, at Suzanna. She was leaning over now, saying something to a dark-haired little boy. Her son? Holt wondered. It was obvious the kid was on the verge of some kind of rebellion. He was shuffling his feet and tugging at the bow tie. He had Holt's sympathy. There couldn't be anything much worse for a kid on a summer evening then being stuck in a mini tuxedo and having to hang around with adults. Suzanna whispered something in his ear, then tugged on it. The boy's mutinous expression turned into a grin.

"Still brooding in corners, I see."

Holt turned and was once again struck by Lilah Calhoun's resemblance to the woman his grandfather had painted. "Just watching the show."

"It is worth the price of a ticket. Max." Lilah laid a hand on the arm of the tall, lanky man at her side. "This is Holt Bradford, whom I was madly in love with for about twenty-four hours some fifteen years ago."

Holt's brow lifted. "You never told me."

"Of course not. At the end of the day I decided I didn't want to be in love with the surly, dangerous sort after all. This is Max Quartermain, the man I'm going to love for the rest of my life."

"Congratulations." Holt took Max's offered hand. Firm grip, Holt mused, steady eyes and a slightly embarrassed smile. "You're the teacher, right?"

"I was. And you're Christian Bradford's grandson."

"That's right," Holt agreed, and his voice had cooled.

"Don't worry, we're not going to hound you as long as you're a guest." Studying him, Lilah ran a fingertip around the rim of her glass. "We'll do that later. I'll have Max show you the scar he got while we were having our little publicity stunt."

"Lilah." Max's voice was soft with an underlying command.

Lilah merely shrugged and sipped champagne. "You remember C.C." She gestured as her sister joined them.

"I remember a gangly kid with engine grease on her face." He relaxed enough to smile. "You look good."

"Thanks. My husband, Trent. Holt Bradford."

It was Coco's dance partner, Holt noted as the two men summed each other up during the polite introductions.

"And the bride and groom," Lilah announced, toasting the couple before she drank again.

"Hello, Holt." Though she was still glowing, Amanda's eyes were steady and watchful. "I'm glad you could come." As she introduced Sloan, Holt realized he'd been surrounded quite neatly. They didn't press. No, the emeralds were never mentioned. But they'd joined ranks, he thought, in a solid wall of determination he had to admire, even as he resented it.

"What is this, a family meeting?" Suzanna hurried up. "You're supposed to be mingling, not huddling in a corner. Oh. Holt." Her smile wavered a bit. "I didn't know you were here."

"Your aunt invited me."

"Yes, I know, but—" She broke off and put her hostess's smile back in place. "I'm glad you could make it."

Like hell, he thought and lifted his glass. "It's been... interesting so far."

At some unspoken signal, her family drifted away, leaving them alone in the corner beside a tub of gardenias. "I hope they didn't make you uncomfortable."

"I can handle it."

"That may be, but I wouldn't want you badgered at my sister's wedding."

"But it doesn't bother you if it's someplace else."

Before she could retort, small impatient hands were tugging at her skirt. "Mom, when can we have the cake?"

"When Amanda and Sloan are ready to cut it." She skimmed a finger down Alex's nose.

"But we're hungry."

"Then go over to the buffet table and stuff your little face."

He giggled at that but didn't relent. "The cake—"

"Is for later. Alex, this is Mr. Bradford."

Not particularly interested in meeting another adult who would pat his head and tell him what a big boy he was, Alex pouted up at Holt. When he was offered a very manly handshake, he perked up a bit.

"Are you the policeman?"

"I used to be."

"Did you ever get shot in the head?"

Holt muffled a chuckle. "No, sorry." For some reason he felt as though he'd lost face. "I did catch one in the leg once."

"Yeah?" Alex brightened. "Did it bleed and bleed?"

He had to grin. "Buckets."

"Wow. Did you shoot lots of bad guys?"

"Dozens of them."

"Okay! Wait a minute." He raced off.

"I'm sorry," Suzanna began. "He's going through a murder-and-mayhem stage."

"I'm sorry I didn't get shot in the head."

She laughed. "Oh, that's all right, you made up for it by telling him you shot lots of bad guys." She wondered, but didn't ask, if he'd been telling the truth.

"Suzanna, would—"

"Hey." Alex skidded to a halt, with two other children in tow. "I told them how you got shot in the leg."

"Did it hurt?" Jenny wanted to know.

"Some."

"It bled and bled," Alex said with relish. "This is Jenny, she's my sister. And this is my brother, Kevin."

Suzanna wanted to kiss him. She wanted to pull Alex up in her arms and smother him with kisses for accepting so easily what adults had made so complicated. Instead, she brushed a hand over his hair.

The three of them bombarded Holt with questions until Suzanna called a halt. "I think that's enough gore for now."

"But, Mom—"

"But, Alex," she mimicked. "Why don't you go get some punch?"

Since it seemed like a pretty good idea, they trooped off.

"Quite a brood," Holt murmured, then looked back at Suzanna. "I thought you had two kids."

"I do."

"Seems to me I just saw three."

"Kevin is my ex-husband's son," she said coolly. "Now, if you'll excuse me."

He put a hand on her arm. Another secret, he thought, and decided he would dig up that answer, as well. Not now. Now he was going to do something he'd thought about doing since he'd seen her walk down the white satin runner in the floaty blue dress.

"Would you like to dance?"

Chapter 5

She couldn't quite relax in his arms. She told herself it was foolish, that the dance was just a casual social gesture. But his body was so close, so firm, the hand at her back so possessive. It reminded her too clearly of the moment he had pulled her against him to send her soaring into a kiss.

"It's quite a house," he said, and gave himself the pleasure of feeling her hair against his cheek. "I always wondered what it was like inside."

"I'll have to give you a tour sometime."

He could feel her heart thud against his. Experimenting, he skimmed his hand up her spine. The rhythm quickened. "I'm surprised you haven't been back to nag me."

There was annoyance in her eyes as she drew her head back. "I have no intention of nagging you."

"Good." He brushed his thumb over her knuckles and felt her tremble. "But you will come back."

"Only because I promised Aunt Coco."

"No." He increased the pressure on her spine and brought her an inch closer. "Not only because of that. You wonder what it would be like, the same way I've wondered half my life."

A little line of panic followed his fingers up her spine. "This isn't the place."

"I choose my own ground." His lips hovered bare inches from hers. He watched her eyes darken and cloud. "I want you, Suzanna."

Her heart had leaped up to throb in her throat so that her voice was husky and uneven. "Am I supposed to be flattered?"

"No. You'd be smart to be scared. I won't make things easy on you."

"What I am," she said with more control, "is uninterested."

His lips curved. "I could kiss you now and prove you wrong."

"I won't have a scene at my sister's wedding."

"Fine, then come to my place tomorrow morning."

"No."

"All right then." He lowered his head. She turned hers away so that his lips brushed her temple, then nibbled on her ear.

"Stop it. My children—"

"Should hardly be shocked to see a man kiss their mother." But he did stop, because his knees were going weak. "Tomorrow morning, Suzanna. There's something I need to show you. Something of my grandfather's."

She looked up again, struggling to steady her pulse. "If this is some sort of game, I don't want to play."

"No game. I want you, and this time I'll have you. But there is something of my grandfather's you have the right to see. Unless you're afraid to be alone with me."

Her spine stiffened. "I'll be there."

The next morning, Suzanna stood on the terrace with Megan. They watched their children race across the lawn with Fred.

"I wish you could stay longer."

With a half laugh, Megan shook her head. "I'm surprised to say I wish I could, too. I have to be back at work tomorrow."

"You and Kevin are welcome here anytime. I want you to know that."

"I do." Megan shifted her gaze to meet Suzanna's. There was a sadness there she understood, though she rarely allowed herself to feel it. "If you and the kids decide to visit Oklahoma, you've got a home with us. I don't want to lose touch. Kevin needs to know this part of his family."

"Then we won't." She stooped to pick up a rose petal that had drifted from a bouquet to float to the terrace. "It was a beautiful wedding. Sloan and Mandy are going to be happy—and we'll have nieces and nephews in common."

"God, the world's a strange place." Megan took Suzanna's hand. "I'd like to think we can be friends, not only for our children's sakes or for Sloan and Amanda."

Suzanna smiled. "I think we already are."

"Suzanna!" Coco signaled from the kitchen door. "A phone call for you." She was chewing her lip when Suzanna reached her. "It's Baxter."

"Oh." Suzanna felt the simple pleasure of the morning drain. "I'll take it in the other room."

She braced herself as she walked down the hallway. He couldn't hurt her any longer, she reminded herself. Not physically, not emotionally. She slipped into the library, took a long, steadying breath, then picked up the phone.

"Hello, Bax."

"I suppose you considered it sly to keep me waiting on the phone."

And there it was again, she thought, that clipped, critical tone that had once made her shiver. Now she only sighed. "I'm sorry. I was outside."

"Digging in the garden, I suppose. Are you still pretending to make a living pruning rosebushes?"

"I'm sure you didn't call to see how my business is going."

"Your business, as you call it, is nothing to me but a slight embarrassment. Having my ex-wife selling flowers on the street corner—"

"Clouds your image, I know." She passed a hand over her hair. "We're not going to go through that again, are we?"

"Quite the little shrew these days." She heard him murmur something to someone else, then laugh. "No, I didn't call to remind you you're making a fool of yourself. I want the children."

Her blood turned to ice. "What?"

The shaky whisper pleased him enormously. "I believe it states quite clearly in the custody agreement that I'm entitled to two weeks during the summer. I'll pick them up on Friday."

"You . . . but you haven't—"

"Don't stammer, Suzanna. It's one of your more annoying traits. If you didn't comprehend, I'll repeat. I'm exercising my parental rights. I'll pick the children up on Friday, at noon."

"You haven't seen them in nearly a year. You can't just pick them up and—"

"I most certainly can. If you don't choose to honor the agreement, I'll simply take you back to court. It isn't legal or wise for you to try to keep the children from me."

"I've never tried to keep them from you. You haven't bothered with them."

"I have no intention of rearranging my schedule to suit you. Yvette and I are going to Martha's Vineyard for two weeks, and have decided to take the children. It's time they saw something of the world besides the little corner you hide in."

Her hands were shaking. She gripped the receiver more tightly. "You didn't even send Alex a card on his birthday."

"I don't believe there's anything in the agreement about birthday cards," he said shortly. "But it is very specific on visitation rights. Feel free to check with your lawyer, Suzanna."

"And if they don't want to go?"

"The choice isn't theirs—or yours." But his, he thought, which was exactly as he preferred it. "I wouldn't try to poison them against me."

"I don't have to," she murmured.

"See that they're packed and ready. Oh, and Suzanna, I've been reading quite a bit about your family lately. Isn't it odd that there wasn't any mention of an emerald necklace in our settlement agreement?"

"I didn't know it existed."

"I wonder if the courts would believe that."

She felt tears of frustration and rage fill her eyes. "For God's sake, didn't you take enough?"

"It's never enough, Suzanna, when you consider how very much you disappointed me. Friday," he said. "Noon." And hung up.

She was trembling. Even when she lowered carefully into a chair, she couldn't stop. She felt as though she'd been jerked back five years, into that terrible helplessness. She couldn't stop him. She'd read the custody agreement word for word before signing it, and he was within his rights. Oh, technically she could have demanded more notice, but that would only postpone the inevitable. If Bax had made up his mind, she couldn't change it. The more she fought, the more she argued, the harder he would twist the knife.

And the more difficult he would make it on the children.

Her babies. Rocking, she covered her face with her hands. It was only for a short time—she could survive it. But how would they feel when she shipped them off, giving them no choice?

She would have to make it sound like an adventure. With the right tone, the right words, she could convince them this was something they wanted to do. Pressing her lips together, she rose. But not now. She would never be able to convince them of anything but her own turmoil if she spoke with them now.

"Damn place is like Grand Central Station." The familiar thump of a cane nearly had Suzanna sinking back into the chair again. "People coming and going, phone ringing. You'd think nobody ever got married before." Suzanna's Great-Aunt Colleen, her magnificent white hair swept back and diamonds glittering at her ears, stopped in the doorway. "I'll have you know those little monsters of yours tracked dirt up the stairs."

"I'm sorry."

Colleen only huffed. She enjoyed complaining about the children, because she had grown so fond of them. "Hooligans. The one blessed day of the week there's not hammering and sawing every minute, and there's packs of children shrieking through the house. Why the hell aren't they in school?"

"Because it's July, Aunt Colleen."

"Don't see what difference that makes." Her frown deepened as she studied Suzanna. "What's the matter with you, girl?"

"Nothing. I'm just a little tired."

"Tired my foot." She recognized the look. She'd seen it before—the weary desperation and helplessness—in her own mother's eyes. "Who was that on the phone?"

Suzanna's chin came up. "That, Aunt Colleen, is none of your business."

"Well, you've climbed on your high horse." And it pleased her. She preferred that her grandniece bite back rather than take a slap. Besides, she'd just badger Coco until she learned what was going on.

"I have an appointment," Suzanna said as steadily as possible. "Would you mind telling Aunt Coco that I've gone out?"

"So now I'm a messenger boy. I'll tell her, I'll tell her," Colleen muttered, waving her cane. "It's high time she fixed me some tea."

"Thank you. I won't be long."

"Go out and clear your head," Colleen said as Suzanna started by. "There's nothing a Calhoun can't handle."

Suzanna sighed and kissed Colleen's thin cheek. "I hope you're right."

She didn't allow herself to think. She left the house and climbed into her pickup, telling herself she would handle whatever needed to be handled—but she would calm herself first.

She had become very skilled at pulling in her emotions. A woman couldn't sit in a courtroom with her children's futures hanging in the balance and not learn control.

It was possible to feel panic or rage or misery and function normally. When she was certain she could, she would speak with the children.

There was an appointment to be kept. Whatever Holt had to show her might distract her enough to help her keep control of her emotions until they leveled.

She thought she was calm when she pulled up at his house. As she got out of the truck, she combed a hand through her windblown hair. When she realized she was gripping her keys too hard she deliberately relaxed her fingers. She slid the keys into her pocket and knocked.

The dog sent up a din. Holt had one hand on Sadie's collar as he opened the door. "You made it. I thought I might have to come after you."

"I told you I'd be here." She stepped inside. "What do you have to show me?"

When he was sure Sadie would do no more than sniff and whine for attention, he released her. "Your aunt showed a lot more interest in the cottage."

"I'm a little pressed for time." After giving the dog an absent pat, she stuck her hands into the pockets of her baggy cotton slacks. "It's very nice." She glanced around, took in nothing. "You must be comfortable here."

"I get by," he said slowly, his eyes keen on her face. There wasn't a trace of color in her cheeks. Her eyes were too dark. He'd wanted to make her aware of him, maybe uncomfortably aware, but he hadn't wanted to make her sick with fear at the thought of seeing him again.

"You can relax, Suzanna." His voice was curt and dismissive. "I'm not going to jump you."

Her nerves stretched taut on the thin wire of control. "Can we just get on with this?"

"Yeah, we can get on with it, as soon as you stop standing there as if you're about to be chained and beaten. I haven't done anything—yet—to make you look at me that way."

"I'm not looking at you in any way."

"The hell you're not. Damn it, your hands are shaking." Furious, he grabbed them. "Stop it," he demanded. "I'm not going to hurt you."

"It has nothing to do with you." She yanked her hands away, hating the fact that she couldn't stop them from trembling. "Why should you think that anything I feel, any way I look depends on you? I have my own life, my own feelings. I'm not some weak, terrified woman who falls apart because a man raises his voice. Do you really think I'm afraid of you? Do you really think you could hurt me after—"

She broke off, appalled. She'd been shouting, and the furious tears were still burning her eyes. Her stomach was clenched so tight she could hardly breathe. Sadie had retreated to a corner and sat quivering. Holt stood a foot away, staring at her, eyes narrowed in speculation.

"I have to go," she managed, and bolted for the door. His hand slapped the wood and held it shut. "Let me go." When her voice broke, she bit down on her lip. She struggled with the door then whirled on him, eyes blazing. "I said let me go."

"Go ahead," he said with surprising calm, "take a punch at me. But you're not going anywhere while you're churned up like this."

"If I'm churned up, it's my own business. I told you, this has nothing to do with you."

"Okay, so you're not going to hit me. Let's try another release valve." He put his hands firmly on either side of her face and covered her mouth with his.

It wasn't a kiss meant to soothe or comfort. It did neither. This was raw and turbulent emotion and matched her own feelings completely.

Her arms were caught between them, her hands still fisted. Her body trembled; her skin heated. At the first flicker of response, he dived into the rough, desperate kiss until he was certain the only thing she was thinking about was him.

Then he took a moment longer, to please himself. She was a volcano waiting to erupt, a storm ready to blow. Her pent-up passion packed a punch more stunning than her fist could have. He intended to be around for the explosion, but he could wait.

When he released her, she leaned back against the door, her eyes closed, breath hitching. Watching her, he realized he'd never seen anyone fight so hard for control.

"Sit down." She shook her head. "All right, stand." With a dismissive shrug, he moved away to light a cigarette. "Either way you're going to tell me what set you off."

"I don't want to talk to you."

He sat on the arm of a chair and blew out a stream of smoke. "Lots of people haven't wanted to talk to me. But I usually find out what I want to know."

She opened her eyes. They were dry now, which relieved him considerably. "Is this an interrogation?"

With another shrug, he brought the cigarette to his lips again. It wouldn't do her any good if he caved in and offered soft words. He wasn't even sure he had them. "It can be."

She thought about pulling the door open and leaving. But he would only stop her. She'd learned the hard way that there were some battles a woman couldn't win.

"It isn't worth it," she said wearily. "I shouldn't have come while I was upset, but I thought I got myself under control."

"Upset about what?"

"It isn't important."

"Then it shouldn't be a problem to tell me."

"Bax called. My ex-husband." To comfort herself she began to roam the room.

Holt studied the tip of his cigarette, reminding himself that jealousy was out of place. "Looks like he can still stir you up."

"One phone call. One, and I'm back under his thumb." There was a bitterness in her voice he hadn't expected from her. He said nothing. "There's nothing I can do. Nothing. He's going to take the children for two weeks. I can't stop him."

Holt let out an impatient breath. "For God's sake, is that what all this hysteria's about? So the kids go off with Daddy for a couple of weeks." Disgusted, he crushed out his cigarette. And to think he'd been worried about her. "Save the vindictive-wife routine, babe. He's got a right."

"Oh yes, he's got the right." Her voice shook with an emotion so deep that Holt's head snapped up again. "Because it says so on a piece of paper. And he was there when they were conceived, so that makes him their father. Of course, that doesn't mean he has to love them, or worry about them or struggle to raise them without malice. It doesn't mean he has to remember Christmas or birthdays. It's just as Bax told me on the phone. There's nothing in the custody agreement that obligates him to send birthday cards. But it does obligate me to turn the children over to him when he has the whim."

There were tears threatening again, but she refused them. Tears in front of a man never brought anything but humiliation. "Do you think this is about me? He can't hurt me anymore. But my children don't deserve to be used so that he can try to pay me back for being so much less than he wanted."

Holt felt something hot and lethal spread in his gut. "He did a good job on you, didn't he?"

"That isn't the point. Alex and Jenny are the point. Somehow I have to convince them that the father who hasn't bothered to contact them in months, who could barely tolerate them when they lived under the same roof, is going to take them on a wonderful two-week vacation." Suddenly tired, she pushed her hands through her hair. "I didn't come here to talk about this."

"Yes, you did." Calmer, Holt lit another cigarette. If he didn't do something with his hands, he was going to touch her again, and he wasn't sure either of them could handle it. "I'm not family, so I'm safe. You can dump on me and figure I won't lose any sleep over it."

She smiled a little. "Maybe you're right. Sorry."

"I didn't ask for an apology. How do the kids feel about him?"

"He's a stranger."

"Then they probably don't have any preset expectations. Seems to me they might think of the whole thing as an adventure—and that you're letting him push your buttons. If he is using them to get to you, he hit bull's-eye."

"I'd already come to those same conclusions myself. I needed to vent some excess frustration." She tried a smile again. "Usually I just pull some weeds."

"I think kissing me worked better."

"It was different anyway."

He tapped out his cigarette and rose. The hell with what they could handle. "Is that the best description you can come up with?"

"Off the top of my head. Holt," she began when he slid his arms around her.

"Yeah?" He nipped at her chin, then her mouth.

"I don't want to be held." But she did, too much.

"That's too bad." His arms tightened, bringing her closer.

"You asked me to come here so you could..." She made a little sound of distress when he closed his teeth over her earlobe. "You could show me something of your grandfather's."

"That's right." Her skin smelled like the air high on the cliffs—laced with the sea and wildflowers and hot summer sunlight. "I also asked you here so I could get my hands on you again. We'll just take one thing at a time."

"I don't want to get involved." But even as she said it, her mouth was moving to meet his.

"Me, either." He changed the angle and sucked on her bottom lip.

"This is just—oh—chemistry." Her fingers tangled in his hair.

"You bet." His rough-palmed hands slipped under her shirt to explore.

"It can't go anywhere."

"It already is."

He was right about that, as well. For one brief moment she let herself fall into the kiss, into the heat. She needed something, someone. If she couldn't have comfort or compassion, she would take desire. But the more she took, the more her body strained for something just out of reach. Something she couldn't afford to want or need again.

"This is too fast," she said breathlessly, and struggled away. "I'm sorry, I realize it must seem as though I'm sending you mixed signals."

He was watching her eyes, just her eyes, as his body pulsed. "I think I can sort them out."

"I don't want to start something I won't be able to finish." She moistened her lips still warm from his. "And I have too many responsibilities, too much to worry about right now to even think about having..."

"An affair?" he finished. "You're going to have to think about it." With his eyes still on hers, he gathered her hair in his hand. "Go ahead, take a few days. I can afford to be patient as long as I get what I want. And I want you."

Nerves skittered along her spine. "Just because I find you attractive, physically, doesn't mean I'm going to jump into bed with you."

"I don't much care whether you jump, crawl or have to be dragged. We can decide on the method later." Before she could think of a name to call him, he grinned, kissed her then stepped back. "Now that that's settled, I'll take you up and show you the portrait."

"If you think it's settled because you—what portrait?"

"You take a look, then tell me."

He led the way up into the loft. Torn between curiosity and fury, Suzanna followed him. The only thing she was certain of at the moment was that since she'd met Holt Bradford again, her emotions had been on a roller coaster. All she wanted out of life was a nice smooth, uneventful ride.

"He worked up here."

The simple statement captured her attention and her interest. "Did you know him well?"

"I don't think anyone did." Holt moved over to open a tilt-out window. "He came and went pretty much as he pleased. He'd come back here for a few days, or a few months. I'd sit up here sometimes and watch him work. If he got tired of me hanging around, he'd send me out with the dog, or into the village for ice cream."

"There's still paint on the floor." Unable to resist, Suzanna bent down to touch. She glanced up, met Holt's eyes and understood.

He'd loved his grandfather. These splotches of paint, more than the cabin itself, were memories. She reached a hand out for his, rising when their fingers linked. Then she saw the portrait.

The canvas was tilted against the wall, its frame old and ornate. The woman looked back at her, with eyes full of secrets and sadness and love.

"Bianca," Suzanna said, and let her own tears come. "I knew he must have painted her. He'd have had to."

"I wasn't certain until I saw Lilah yesterday."

"He never sold it," Suzanna murmured. "He kept it, because it was all he had left of her."

"Maybe." He wasn't entirely comfortable that the exact thought had occurred to him. "I've got to figure there was something between them. I don't see how that helps you get any closer to the emeralds."

"But you'll help."

"I said I would."

"Thank you." She turned to face him. Yes, he would help, she thought. He wouldn't break his word no matter how much it annoyed him to keep it.

"The first thing I have to ask you, is if you'll bring the portrait to The Towers so my family can see it. It would mean a great deal to them."

At Suzanna's insistence, they took Sadie as well. She rode in the back of the pickup, grinning into the wind. When they arrived at The Towers, they saw Lilah and Max sitting out on the lawn. Fred, spotting the truck, tore across the yard, then came to a stumbling halt when Sadie leaped nimbly out of the back.

Body aquiver, he approached her. The dogs gave each other a thorough sniffing over. With a flick of her tail, Sadie pranced across the yard. She sent Fred one come-hither look over her shoulder that had him scrambling after her.

"Looks like love at first sight for old Fred," Lilah commented as she walked with Max to the truck. "We wondered where you'd gone." She ran a hand down Suzanna's arm, letting her know without words that she knew about the call from Bax.

"Are the kids around?"

"No, they went into the village with Megan and her parents to help Kevin pick out some souvenirs before they leave."

With a nod, Suzanna took her hand. "There's something you have to see." Stepping back, she gestured. Through the open door of the truck, Lila saw the painting. Her fingers tightened on her sister's.

"Oh, Suze."

"I know."

"Max, can you see?"

"Yes." Gently he kissed the top of her head and looked at the portrait of a woman who was the double for the one he loved. "She was beautiful. This is a Bradford." He glanced at Holt with a shrug. "I've been studying your grandfather's work for the past couple of weeks."

"You've had this all along," Lilah began.

Holt let the accusation in the tone roll off him. "I didn't know it was Bianca until I saw you yesterday."

She subsided, studying his face. "You're not as nasty as you'd like people to think. Your aura's much too clear."

"Leave Holt's aura alone, Lilah," Suzanna said with a laugh. "I want Aunt Coco to see this. Oh, I wish Sloan and Mandy hadn't left on their honeymoon."

"They'll only be gone two weeks," Lilah reminded her.

Two weeks. Suzanna struggled to keep the smile in place as Holt carried the portrait inside.

The moment she saw it, Coco wept. But that was only to be expected. Holt had propped the painting on the love seat in the parlor, and Coco sat in the wing chair, drenching her handkerchief.

"After all this time. To have part of her back in this house."

Lilah touched her aunt's shoulder. "Part of her has always been in the house."

"Oh, I know, but to be able to look at her." She sniffled. "And see you."

"He must have loved her so much." Damp eyed, C.C. rested her head on Trent's shoulder. "She looks just as I imagined her, just as I knew she looked that night when I felt her."

Holt kept his hands in his pocket. "Look, sentiment and séances aside, it's the emeralds you need. If you want my help, then I need to know everything."

"Séance." Coco dried her eyes. "We should hold another one. We'll hang the portrait in the dining room. With that to focus on we're bound to be successful. I've got to check the astrological charts." She got up and hurried out of the room.

"And she's off and running," Suzanna murmured.

Trent nodded. "Not to discredit Coco, but it might be best if I filled in Holt in a more conventional way."

"I'll make some coffee." Suzanna sent one last glance at the portrait before heading for the kitchen.

There wasn't so very much Trent could tell him, she thought as she ground beans. Holt already knew about the legend, the research they'd done, the danger her sisters had faced. It was possible that he might make more of it, with his training, than they had. But would he care, even a fraction of the amount her family did?

She understood that emotional motivation could change lives. And that without it, nothing worthwhile could be accomplished.

He had passion. But could his passions run deeper than a physical need? Not for her, she assured herself, measuring the coffee carefully. She'd meant what she'd said about not wanting to become involved. She couldn't afford to love again.

She was afraid he was right about an affair. If she couldn't be strong enough to resist him, she hoped she could be strong enough to hold her heart and her body separate. It couldn't be wrong to need to be touched and wanted. Perhaps by giving herself to him, in a physical way, she could prove to herself that she wasn't a failure as a woman.

God, she wanted to feel like a woman again, to experience that rush of pleasure and release. She was nearly thirty, she thought, and the only man with whom she'd been intimate had found her wanting. How much longer could she go on wondering if he was right?

She jolted when hands came down on her shoulders.

Slowly, aware of how easily she paled, Holt turned her to face him. "Where were you?"

"Oh. Up to my ears weeding pachysandra."

"That's a pretty good lie if you'd put more flare into it." But he let it go. "I'm going to run down and talk with Lieutenant Koogar. Rain check the coffee."

"All right, I'll drive you down."

"I'm hitching a ride with Max and Trent."

Her brow lifted. "Men only, I take it."

"Sometimes it works better that way." He rubbed a thumb over the line between her brows in a gentle gesture that surprised them both. Catching himself, he dropped his hand again. "You worry too much. I'll be in touch."

"Thank you. I won't forget what you're doing for us."

"Forget it." He hauled her against him and kissed her until she went limp. "I'd rather you remember that."

He strode out, and she sank weakly into a chair. She wouldn't have any choice but to remember it.

Chapter 6

He wasn't playing good samaritan, Holt assured himself. After getting a clearer handle on the situation, he was doing what he felt was best. Somebody had to keep an eye on her until Livingston was under wraps. The best way to keep an eye on her was to stick close.

Swinging into the graveled lot, he pulled up next to her pickup. He saw that she was outside the shop with customers, so amused himself by roaming around.

He'd driven by Island Gardens before but had never stopped in. There hadn't been any reason to. There were a lot of thriving blossoms crowded on wooden tables or sitting in ornamental pots. Though he couldn't tell one from the other, he could appreciate their appeal. Or maybe it was the fact that the air smelled like Suzanna.

It was obvious she knew what she was doing here, he reflected. There was a tidiness to the place, enhanced by a breezy informality that invited browsers to browse even as it tempted them to buy.

Colorful pictures were set up here and there, describing certain flowers, their planting instructions and maintenance. Along the side of the main building were stacks of fifty- and hundred-pound bags of planting medium and mulch.

He was looking over a tray of snapdragons when he heard a rustle in the bush behind him. He tensed automatically, and his fingers jerked once toward the weapon he no longer wore. Letting out a quiet breath, he cursed himself. He had to get over this reaction. He wasn't a cop anymore, and no one was likely to spring at his back with an eight-inch buck knife.

He turned his head slightly and spotted the young boy crouched behind a display of peonies. Alex grinned and popped up. "I got you!" He danced gleefully around the peonies. "I was a pygmy and I zapped you with my poison blow dart."

"Lucky for me I'm immune to pygmy poison. If it'd been Ubangi poison, I would've been a goner. Where's your sister?"

"In the greenhouse. Mom gave us seeds and stuff, but I got bored. It's okay for me to come out here," he said quickly, knowing how fast adults could make things tough for you. "As long as I don't go near the street or knock over anything."

He wasn't about to give the kid a hard time. "Have you killed many customers today?"

"It's pretty slow. 'Cause it's Monday, Mom says. That's why we can come to work with her and Carolanne can have the day off."

"You like coming here?"

Holt wasn't sure how it had happened, but he and the boy were walking among the flats of flowers, and Alex's hand was in his.

"Sure, it's neat. We get to plant things. Like, see those?" He pointed at an edging of multicolored flowers that sprang up beside the gravel. "Those are zinnias, and I planted them myself, so I get to water them and stuff. Sometimes we get to carry things to the car for people, and they give you quarters."

"Sounds like a good deal."

"And Mom closes up at lunchtime and we walk down the street and get pizza and play the video games. We get to come almost every Monday. Except—" He broke off and kicked at the gravel.

"Except what?"

"Next week we'll have to be on vacation, and Mom won't come."

Holt looked down at the boy's bent head and wondered what the hell to do. "I, ah, guess she's pretty busy here."

"Carolanne or somebody could work, and she could come. But she won't."

"Don't you figure she'd go with you if she could?"

"I guess." Alex kicked at the gravel again and, when Holt didn't scold, kicked a third time. "We have to go to somebody named Martha's yard, with my father and his new wife. Mom says it'll be fun, and we'll go to the beach and have ice cream."

"Sounds pretty good."

"I don't want to go. I don't see how come I have to. I want to go to Disney World with Mom."

When the little voice broke, Holt let out a deep breath and crouched down. "It's tough having to do things you don't want to. I guess you'll have to look after Jenny while you're gone."

Alex shrugged and sniffled. "I guess. She's scared to go. But she's only five."

"She'll be okay with you. Tell you what, I'll look after your mom while you're gone."

"Okay." Feeling better, Alex wiped his nose with the back of his hand. "Can I see on your leg where they shot you?"

"Sure." Holt pointed to a scar about six inches above his kneecap on his left leg.

"Wow." Since Holt didn't seem to mind, Alex ran a fingertip over it. "I guess since you were a policeman and all, you'll take good care of Mom."

"Sure I will."

Suzanna wasn't sure what she felt when she saw Holt and her son, dark heads bent close. But she knew something warm stirred when Holt lifted a hand and brushed it through Alex's hair.

"Well, what's all this?"

Both males looked over then back at each other to exchange a quick and private look before Holt rose. "Man talk," he said, and gave Alex's hand a squeeze.

"Yeah." Alex pushed out his chest. "Man talk."

"I see. Well, I hate to interrupt, but if you want pizza, you'd better go wash your hands."

"Can he come?" Alex asked.

"His name," Suzanna said, "is Mr. Bradford."

"His name is Holt." Holt sent Alex a wink and got a grin in return.

"Can he?"

"We'll see."

"She says that a lot," Alex confided, then raced off to find his sister.

"I suppose I do." Suzanna sighed then turned back to Holt. "What can I do for you?"

She was wearing her hair loose, with a little blue cap over it that made her look about sixteen. Holt suddenly felt as foolish and awkward as a boy asking for his first date.

"Do you still need part-time help?"

"Yes, without any luck." She began to pinch off begonias. "All the high school and college kids are set for the summer."

"I can give you about four hours a day."

"What?"

"Maybe five," he continued as she stared at him. "I've got a couple of repair jobs, but I call my own hours."

"You want to work for me?"

"As long as I only have to haul and plant the things. I ain't selling flowers."

"You can't be serious."

"I mean it. I won't sell them."

"No, I mean about working for me at all. You've already started up your own business, and I can't afford to pay more than minimum wage."

His eyes went very dark, very fast. "I don't want your money."

Suzanna blew the hair out of her eyes. "Now, I am confused."

"Look, I figured we could trade off. I'll do some of the heavy work for you, and you can fix up my yard some."

Her smile bloomed slowly. "You'd like me to fix up your yard?"

Women always made things complicated, he thought and stuffed his hands into his pockets. "I don't want you to go crazy or anything. A couple more bushes maybe. Now do you want to make a deal or don't you?"

Her smile turned to a laugh. "One of the Andersons' neighbors admired our team effort. I'm scheduled to start tomorrow." She held out a hand. "Be here at six."

He winced. "A.M.?"

"Exactly. Now, how about lunch?"

He put his hand in hers. "Fine. You're buying."

Good God, the woman worked like an elephant. She worked like two elephants, Holt corrected as the sweat poured down his back. He had a pick or shovel in his hand so often, he might as well be on a chain gang.

It should've been cooler up here on the cliffs. But the lawn they were landscaping—attacking, he thought as he brought the pick down again—was nothing but rock.

In the three days he'd worked with her, he'd given up trying to stop her from doing any of the heavy work. She only ignored him and did as she pleased. When he went home in the midafternoon, every muscle twinging, he wondered how in holy hell she kept it up.

He couldn't put in more than four or five hours and juggle his own jobs. But he knew she worked eight to ten every day. It wasn't difficult to see that she was throwing herself into her work to keep from thinking about the fact that the kids were leaving the next day.

He brought the pick down again, hit rock. The shock sang up his arms. At the low, steady swearing, Suzanna glanced up from her own work. "Why don't you take a break. I can finish that."

"Did you bring the dynamite?"

The smile touched her lips for only a moment. "No, really. Go get a drink out of the cooler. We're nearly ready to plant."

"Fine." He hated to admit that the whole business was wearing him out. There were blisters on top of his blisters, his muscles felt as though he'd gone ten rounds with the champ—and lost. Wiping his face and neck dry, he walked over to the cooler they'd set in the shade of a beech tree. As he pulled out a ginger ale, he heard the pick ring against the rocky soil. It was no use telling her she was crazy, he thought as he guzzled down the cold liquid. But he couldn't help it.

"You're a lunatic, Suzanna. This is the kind of work they give to people with numbers across their chest."

"What we have here," she said in a thick Southern drawl, "is a failure to communicate."

Her quote of the line from *Cool Hand Luke* made him grin, but only for an instant. "Stark, raving mad," he continued, watching her swing the pick. "What the hell do you think's going to grow in that rock?"

"You'd be surprised." She took a moment to wipe at the sweat that was dripping in her eyes. "See those lilies on the bank there?" She gave a little grunt as she dislodged a rock. "I planted them two years ago in September."

He glanced at the profusion of tall, colorful flowers with grudging admiration. He had to admit that they were an improvement over the rough, rocky soil, but was it worth it?

"The Snyders gave me my first real job." She hefted a rock and tossed it into the wheelbarrow. Stretching her back, she listened to the fat bees buzzing in the gaillardia. "A sympathy job, seeing as they were friends of the family and poor Suzanna needed a break." Her breath whooshed out as she struck soil, and she blinked away the little red dots in front of her eyes. "Surprised them that I knew what I was doing, and I've been working here on and off ever since."

"Great. Would you put that damn thing down a minute?"

"Almost done."

"You won't be done until you keel over. Who's going to see a few posies wilting all the way up here?"

"The Snyders will see them, their guests will see them." She shook her head to clear a haze brought on by the heat. "The photographer from *New England Gardens* will see them." Lord, the bees were loud, she thought as the buzzing filled her head. "And nothing's going to wilt. I'm putting in pinks and campanula and some coreopsis, some lavender for scent and monarda for the hummingbirds." She pressed a hand to her head, ran it over her eyes. "In September we'll plant some bulbs. Dwarf irises and windflowers. Some tuberoses and..." She staggered under a hot wave of dizziness. Holt made the dash from shade to sun as the pick slid out of her hands. When he grabbed her she seemed to melt into his arms.

Cursing her helped relieve the fright as he carried her over and laid her down under the tree. Her body was like hot wax he could all but pour onto the cool grass. "That's it." He plunged his hand into the cooler then rubbed icy water over her face. "You're finished, do you understand? If I see a pick in your hands again, I'll murder you."

"I'm all right." Her voice was weak, but the irritation was clear enough. "Just a little too much sun." The water on her face felt heavenly, even if his hands were a bit rough. She took the ginger ale from him and drank carefully.

"Too much sun," he was ranting, "too much work. And not enough food or sleep from the look of you. You're a mess, Suzanna, and I'm tired of it."

"Thank you very much." She pushed his hands away and leaned back against the tree. She needed a minute, she'd admit. But she didn't need a lecture. "I should have taken a break," she said in disgust. "I know better, but I've got things on my mind."

"I don't care what you've got on your mind." God, she was white as a sheet. He wanted to hold her until the color came back into her cheeks, to stroke her hair until she was strong and rested again. But the concern came out in fury. "I'm taking you home and you're going to bed."

Steadier, she set the bottle aside. "I think you're forgetting who works for whom."

"When you pass out on me, I take over."

"I didn't pass out," she said irritably. "I got dizzy. And nobody takes over for me, not now, not ever again. Stop splashing water in my face, you're going to drown me."

She was recovering fast enough, he thought, but it didn't cool his temper. "You're stubborn, hardheaded and just plain stupid."

"Fine. If you've finished yelling at me, I'm going to take my lunch break." She knew she had to eat. She didn't mind being stubborn or hardheaded, but she did mind being stupid. Which, she thought as she snatched a sandwich out of the cooler, was exactly what she had been to skip breakfast.

"Maybe I haven't finished yelling."

She shrugged as she unwrapped the sandwich. "Then you can yell while I eat. Or you can stop wasting time and have some lunch."

He considered dragging her to the truck. He liked the idea, but the benefits would only be short-term. Short of tying her up and locking her in a room, he couldn't stop her from working herself into the ground.

At least she was eating, he reflected. And the color had seeped back into her cheeks. Maybe there was another tack to getting his way. Casually he took out a sandwich.

"I've been thinking about the emeralds."

The change in topic and attitude surprised her. "Oh?"

"I read the transcript Max put together from the interview with Mrs. Tobias, the maid. And I listened to the tape."

"What do you think?"

"I think she's got a good memory, and that she was impressed by Bianca. From her viewpoint, the setup was that Bianca was unhappy in her marriage, devoted to her children and in love with my grandfather. She and Fergus were already on shaky ground when they had the blowout over the dog. We'll figure that was the straw that broke it. She decided to leave him, but she didn't go that night. Why?"

"Even if she'd finally made the decision," Suzanna said slowly, "there would have been arrangements to make. She'd have had to consider the children." This she understood all too well. "Where could she take them, how could she be certain she could provide for them. Even if the marriage was a disaster, she would have to plan carefully how to tell them she was taking them away from their father."

"So when Fergus left for Boston after they fought, she started to work it out. We have to figure she went to my grandfather, because he ended up with the dog."

"She loved him," Suzanna murmured. "She would have gone to him first. And he loved her, so he would have wanted to go away with her and the children."

"If we go with that, we take it to the next step. She went back to The Towers to pack, to get the kids together. But instead of meeting my grandfather and riding off into the sunset, she takes a jump out of the tower window. Why?"

"She was in turmoil." With her eyes half-closed, Suzanna stared into the sunlight. "She was about to take a step that would end her marriage, separate her children from their father. Break her vows. It's so difficult, so frightening. Like dying. Maybe she thought she was a failure, and when her husband came home, and she had to face him and herself, she couldn't."

Holt ran a hand over her hair. "Is that what it was like for you?"

Her shoulders stiffened. "We're talking about Bianca. And I don't see what her reasons for killing herself have to do with the emeralds."

Holt took his hand away. "First we decide why she hid them, then we go for where."

Slowly she relaxed again. "Fergus gave them to her when their first son was born. Not their first child. A girl didn't rate." She took another sip of her ginger ale and washed away some of her own bitterness. "She would have resented that, I think. To be rewarded—like a prize mare—for producing an heir. But, they were hers because the child was hers."

Because her eyes were heavy, she let them drift closed. "Bax gave me diamonds when Alex was born. I didn't feel guilty about selling them to start the business. Because they were mine. She might have felt the same way. The emeralds would have bought a new life for her, for the children."

"Why did she hide them?"

"To make certain he didn't find them if he stopped her from leaving. So that she knew she'd have something of her own."

"Did you hide your diamonds, Suzanna?"

"I put them in Jenny's diaper bag. The last place Baxter would look." With a half laugh, she plucked at the grass. "That sounds so melodramatic."

But he wasn't smiling or sneering, she noted. He was frowning out at the dianthiums where the bees hovered and hummed. "It sounds damn smart to me. She spent a lot of time in the tower, right?"

"We've looked there."

"We'll look again, and take her bedroom apart."

"Lilah will love that." Suzanna closed her eyes again. The food and the shade were making her sleepy. "It's her bedroom now. And we've looked there, too."

"I haven't."

"No." She decided it wouldn't hurt to stretch out while they finished talking it through. The grass was blissfully cool and soft. "If we found her journal, we'd know the answers. Mandy went through every book in the library, just in case it got mixed in like the purloined letter."

He began to stroke her hair again. "We'll take another look."

"Mandy wouldn't have missed anything. She's too organized."

"I'd rather check over old ground than depend on a séance."

She made a sound that was half laugh and half sigh. "Aunt Coco'll talk you into it." Her voice grew heavy with fatigue. "We need to plant the pinks first."

"Okay." He'd moved his hands down and was gently massaging her shoulders.

"It'll trail right over the rocks and down the bank. It doesn't give up," she murmured, and was asleep.

"You're telling me."

He left her there in the shade and walked back into the sunlight.

* * *

The grass was tickling her cheek when she woke. She'd rolled over onto her stomach and had slept like a stone. Groggy, she opened her eyes. She saw Holt sitting back against the tree, his legs crossed at the ankles. He was watching her as he brought a cigarette to his lips.

"I must have dozed off."

"You could say that."

"Sorry." She pushed herself up on her elbow. "We were talking about the emeralds."

He flicked the cigarette away. "We've talked enough for now." In one swift move, he hooked his hands under her arms and pulled her against him. Before she was fully awake, she was in his lap and his mouth was on hers.

He'd watched her sleep. And as he had watched her sleep, the need to touch her had boiled inside him until his blood was like lava. She'd looked so perfect, the sleeping princess, creamy skin dappled by hazy shade, her cheek resting on her hand, her hand on the grass.

He'd wanted those soft, warm lips under his, to feel that long, fragile body molded to him, to hear that quick little catch in her breathing. So he took, feverishly.

Disarmed, disoriented, she struggled back. Her blood had gone from slow and cool to rapid and hot. Her body, relaxed by sleep, was now taut as a bow. She dragged in a single ragged breath. All she could see was his face, his eyes dark and dangerous, his mouth hard and hungry. Then all was a blur as his lips brushed down on hers again.

She let him take what he seemed to need to take so desperately. Under the shade of the beech she pressed against him, answering each demand. When the dizziness came again, she reveled in it. This was not a weakness she had to fight. It was one she had wanted to feel as long as she could remember.

On an oath, he buried his face at her throat where her pulse jackhammered. Nothing and no one had ever made him feel like this. Frantic and shaky. Each time his mouth came back to hers it was with a new edge of desperation, each keener than the last. Dozens of sensations knifed into him, all sharp and deadly. He wanted to shove her aside, walk away before they cut him to ribbons. He wanted to roll with her on the cool, soft grass and drive out all the aches and jagged needs.

But her arms were around him, her hands moving restlessly through his hair while her body trembled. Then her cheek was against his, nuzzling there in a gesture that was almost unbearably sweet.

"What are we going to do?" she murmured. Wanting comfort, she turned her lips to his skin and sighed.

"I think we both know the answer to that."

Suzanna closed her eyes. It was so simple for him. She rested against him a moment, listening to the bees buzz in the flowers. "I need time."

He put his hands on her shoulders, pushing her back until they were face-to-face. "I may not be able to give it to you. We're not children anymore, and I'm tired of wondering what it would be like."

She let out a shaky breath. The turmoil wasn't only hers, she realized. She could feel it, shimmering out of him. "If you ask for more than I can give, we'll both be disappointed. I want you." She bit back a gasp when his fingers tightened. "But I can't make another mistake."

His eyes darkened and narrowed. "Do you want promises?"

"No," she said quickly. "No, I don't. But I have to keep the ones I made to myself. If I come to you, I have to be sure it's not just something I want, but something I can live with." Reaching out, she laid a hand on his cheek. "The one thing I can promise you is that if we're lovers, I won't regret it."

He couldn't argue, not when she looked at him that way. "When," he corrected.

"When," she said with a nod, then rose. Her legs weren't as shaky as she'd thought they would be. She felt stronger. *When,* she thought again. Yes, she'd already accepted that it was only a matter of time. "But for now, we'll have to take things as they come. We've got a job to finish."

"It's finished." He pulled himself to his feet as she turned.

The plants were in place, the ground smoothed and mulched. Where there had only been rocks and thin, thirsty soil were bright hopeful young flowers and tender green leaves.

"How?" she began, already hurrying over to study his work.

"You slept three hours."

"Three—" Appalled, she looked back at him. "You should have woken me up."

"I didn't," he said simply. "Now I've got to get back, I'm running late."

"But you shouldn't have—"

"It's done." Impatience shimmered around him. "Do you want to rip the damn things out and do it yourself?"

"No." As she studied him she realized he wasn't just angry, he was embarrassed. Not only had he done something sweet and considerate, but he'd spent three hours planting what he still sneeringly called posies.

So he stood there, she thought, looking very male and ruffled in the streaming sun, the charming rockery at his feet and his rough, clever hands stuffed in his pockets. Thank me and I'll snarl, he seemed to say.

It was then, facing him on the rocky slope, that she realized what she had refused to admit in his arms. What she had insisted was only passion and need. She loved him. Not just for the hot-blooded kisses or the demanding hands. But for the man beneath. The man who would run a careless hand over her son's hair or answer her little girl's incessant questions. The man who would leave paint splattered on the floor in memory of his grandfather.

The one who would plant flowers for her while she slept.

As she continued to stare, Holt shifted uncomfortably. "Look, if you're going to faint again, I'm going to leave you where you fall. I haven't got time to play nursemaid."

A smile moved slowly, beautifully over her face, confusing him. She loved him for that, too—that snapping impatience that covered the compassion. She would need time to think, of course. Time to adjust. But for now, for this moment, she could simply hold tight to this rush of feeling and be content.

"You did a good job."

He glanced back at the flowers, certain he'd rather cut out his tongue than admit how much he'd enjoyed the work. "You stick them in and cover them up." He moved his shoulders in dismissal. "I put the tools and stuff in the truck. I've got to go."

"I put the Bryce job off until Monday. Tomorrow—I have to be home tomorrow."

"All right. See you later."

As he walked off to his car, Suzanna knelt down to touch the fragile new blooms.

In the cottage near the water, the man who called himself Marshall completed a thorough search. He found a few things of minor interest. The ex-cop liked to read and didn't cook. There were shelves of well-worn books in the bedroom, and only a few scattered supplies in the kitchen. He kept his medals in a box tossed in the bottom of a drawer, and a loaded .32 at the ready in the nightstand.

After rifling through a desk, Marshall discovered that Christian's grandson had made a few shrewd investments. He found it amusing that a former Vice cop had had the sense to create a tidy nest egg. He also found it interesting that training had caused Holt to write up a detailed report on everything he knew about the Calhoun emeralds.

His temper threatened as he read of the interview with the former servant—the servant that Maxwell Quartermain had located. That grated. Quartermain should have been working for him. Or he should have been dead. Marshall was tempted to wreck the place, to toss furniture, break lamps. To give in to an orgy of destruction.

But he forced himself to stay calm. He didn't want to tip his hand. Not yet. Perhaps he hadn't found anything particularly enlightening, but he knew as much as the Calhouns did.

Very carefully, he put the papers back in place, shut the drawers. The dog was beginning to bark out in the yard. He detested dogs. Sneering at the sound, he rubbed at the scar on his leg where the little Calhoun mutt had bitten him. They would have to pay for that. They would all have to pay.

And so they would, he thought. When he had the emeralds.

He left the cottage precisely as he had found it.

I will not write of the winter. That is not a memory I wish to relive. But I did not leave the island. Could not leave it. She was never out of my mind in those months. In the spring, she remained with me. In my dreams.

And then, it was summer.

It isn't possible for me to write how I felt when I saw her running to me. I could paint it, but I could never find the words. I haunted those cliffs, waiting for her, hoping for her. It had become easy to convince myself that it would be enough just to see her, just to speak with her again. If she would only walk down the slope, through the wildflowers and sit on the rocks with me.

Then all at once, she was calling my name, running, her eyes so filled with joy. She was in my arms, her mouth on mine. And I knew she had suffered as I had suffered. She loved as I loved.

We both knew it was madness. Perhaps I could have been stronger, could have convinced her to go and leave me. But something had changed in her over the winter. No longer would she be content with only emptiness, as I learned her marriage was for her. Her children, so dear to her, could not forge a bond between her and the husband who wanted only obedience and duty. Yet I could not allow her to give herself to me, to take the step that could cause her guilt or shame or regret.

So we met, day after day on the cliffs, in all innocence. To talk and laugh, to pretend the summer was endless. Sometimes she brought the children, and it was almost as if we were a family. It was reckless, but somehow we didn't believe anything could touch us while we stood, cupped between sky and sea, with the peaks of the house far up at our backs.

We were happy with what we had. There have been no happier days in my life before or since. Love like that has no beginning or end. It has no right or wrong. In those bright summer days, she was not another man's wife. She was mine.

A lifetime later, I sit here in this aging body and look out at the water. Her face, her voice, come so clearly to me.

She smiled. "I used to dream of being in love."

I had taken the pins from her hair so that my hands could lose themselves in it. A small, precious pleasure. "Do you still?"

"Now I don't have to." She bent toward me, to touch her lips to mine. "I'll never have to dream again. Only wish."

I took her hand to kiss it, and we watched an eagle soar. "There's a ball tonight. I'll wish you were there, to waltz with me."

I got to my feet, drew her to hers and began to dance with her through the wild roses. "Tell me what you'll wear, so I can see you."

Laughing, she lifted her face to mine. "I shall wear ivory silk with a low bodice that bares my shoulders and a draped beaded skirt that catches the light. And my emeralds."

"A woman shouldn't look sad when she speaks of emeralds."

"No." She smiled again. "These are very special. I've had them since Ethan was born, and I wear them to remind me."

"Of what?"

"That no matter what happens, I've left something behind. The children are my real jewels." As a cloud came over the sun she pressed her head to my shoulder. "Hold me closer, Christian."

Neither of us spoke of the summer that was so quickly coming to an end, but I know we both thought of it at that moment when my arms held her tight and our hearts beat together in the dance. The fury of what I was soon to lose again rushed through me.

"I would give you emeralds, and diamonds, sapphires." I crushed my mouth to hers. "All that and more, Bianca, if I could."

"No." She brought her hands to my face, and I saw the tears sparkling in her eyes. "Only love me," she said.

Only love me.

Chapter 7

Holt was home for less than three minutes when he knew someone had broken in. He might have turned in his shield, but he still had cop's eyes. There was nothing obviously out of place—but an ashtray was closer to the edge of the table, a chair was pulled at a slightly different angle to the fireplace, a corner of the rug was turned up.

Braced and at alert, he moved from the living room into the bedroom. There were signs here, as well. He noted them—the fractional rearrangement of the pillows, the different alignment of the books on the shelves—as he crossed to get his gun from the drawer. After checking the clip, he took his weapon with him as he searched the house.

Thirty minutes later, he replaced the gun. His face was set, his eyes flat and hard. His grandfather's canvases had been moved, not much, but enough to tell Holt that someone had touched them, studied them. And that was a violation he couldn't tolerate.

Whoever had tossed the place had been a pro. Nothing had been taken, little had been disturbed, but Holt was certain every inch of the cottage had been combed.

He was also certain who had done the combing. That meant that Livingston, by whatever guise he was using, was still close. Close enough, Holt thought, that he had discovered the Bradford connection to the Calhouns. And the emeralds.

Now, he decided as he dropped a hand on the head of the dog who whined at his feet, it was personal.

He went through the kitchen door to sit on the porch with his dog and a beer and watch the water. He would let his temper cool and his mind drift, sorting through all the pieces of the puzzle, arranging and rearranging until a picture began to form.

Bianca was the key. It was her mind, her emotions, her motivations he had to tap into. He lit a cigarette, resting his crossed ankles on the porch rail as the light began to soften and pearl toward twilight.

A beautiful woman, unhappily married. If the current crop of Calhoun women were anything to go by, Bianca would also have been strong willed, passionate and loyal. And vulnerable, he added. That came through strongly in the eyes of the portrait, just as it came through strongly in Suzanna's eyes.

She'd also been on the upper rungs of society's ladder, one of the privileged. A young Irishwoman of good family who had married extremely well.

Again, like Suzanna.

He drew on the cigarette, absently stroking Sadie's ears when she nuzzled her head into his lap. His gaze was drawn toward the little yellow bush, the slice of sunshine

Suzanna had given him. According to the interview with the former maid, Bianca had also had a fondness for flowers.

She had had children, and by all accounts had been a good and devoted mother, while Fergus had been a strict and disinterested father. Then Christian Bradford had come into the picture.

If Bianca had indeed taken him as a lover, she had also taken an enormous social risk. Like Caesar's wife, a woman in her position was expected to be unblemished. Even a hint of an affair—particularly with a man beneath her station—and her reputation would have been in tatters.

Yet she had become involved.

Had it all grown to be too much for her? Holt wondered. Had she been eaten up by guilt and panic, hidden the emeralds away as some kind of last-ditch show of defiance, only to despair at the thought of the disgrace and scandal of divorce. Unable to face her life, she had chosen death.

He didn't like it. Shaking his head, Holt blew out a slow stream of smoke. He just didn't like the rhythm of it. Maybe he was losing his objectivity, but he couldn't see Suzanna giving up and hurling herself onto the cliffs. And there were too many similarities between Bianca and her great-granddaughter.

Maybe he should try to get inside Suzanna's head. If he understood her, maybe he could understand her starcrossed ancestor. Maybe, he admitted with a pull on the beer, he could understand himself. His feelings for her seemed to undergo radical changes every day, until he no longer knew exactly what he felt.

Oh, there was desire, that was clear enough. But it wasn't simple. He'd always counted on it being simple.

What made Suzanna Calhoun Dumont tick? Her kids, Holt thought immediately. No contest there, though the rest of her family ran a dead heat. Her business. She would work herself ragged making it run. But Holt suspected that her thirst to succeed in business doubled right back around to her children and family.

Restless, he rose to pace the length of the porch. A whippoorwill came to roost in the old wind-bent maple and lifted its voice in its three-note call. Roused, the insects began to whisper in the grass. The first firefly, a lone sentinel, flickered near the water that lapped the bank.

This, too, was something he wanted. The simple quiet of solitude. But as he stood, looking out into the night, he thought of Suzanna. Not just the way she had felt in his arms, the way she made his blood swim. But what it would be like to have her beside him now, waiting for moonrise.

He needed to get inside her head, to make her trust him enough to tell him what she felt, how she thought. If he could make the link with her, he would be one step closer to making it with Bianca.

But he was afraid he was already in too deep. His own thoughts and feelings were clouding his judgment. He wanted to be her lover more than he had ever wanted anything. To sink into her, to watch her eyes darken with passion until that sad, injured look was completely banished. To have her give herself to him the way she had never given herself to anyone—not even the man she had married.

Holt pressed his hands to the rail, leaned out into the growing dark. Alone, with night to cloak him, he admitted that he was following the same pattern as his grandfather.

He was falling in love with a Calhoun woman.

It was late before he went back inside. Later still before he slept.

Suzanna hadn't slept at all. She had lain awake all night trying not to think about the two small suitcases she had packed. When she managed to get her mind off that, it had veered toward Holt. Thoughts of him only made her more restless.

She'd been up at dawn, rearranging the clothes she'd already packed, adding a few more things, checking yet again to be sure she had included a few of their favorite toys so that they wouldn't feel homesick.

She'd been cheerful at breakfast, grateful that her family had been there to add support and encouragement. Both children had been whiny, but she'd nearly joked them out of it by noon.

By one, her nerves had been frayed and the children were cranky again. By two she was afraid Bax had forgotten the entire thing, then was torn between fury and hope.

At three the car had come, a shiny black Lincoln. Fifteen horrible minutes later, her children were gone.

She couldn't stay home. Coco had been so kind, so understanding, and Suzanna had been afraid they would both dissolve into puddles of tears. For her aunt's sake as much as her own, she decided to go to work.

She would keep herself busy, Suzanna vowed. So busy that when the children got back, she hardly would have noticed they'd been gone.

She stopped by the shop, but Carolanne's sympathy and curiosity nearly drove her over the edge.

"I don't mean to badger you," Carolanne apologized when Suzanna's responses became clipped. "I'm just worried about you."

"I'm fine." Suzanna was selecting plants with almost obsessive care. "And I'm sorry for being short with you. I'm feeling a little rough today."

"And I'm being too nosy." Always good-natured, Carolanne shrugged. "I like the salmon-colored ones," she said as Suzanna debated over the group of New Guinea impatiens. "Listen, if you want to blow off some steam, just call me. We can have a girls' night out."

"I appreciate that."

"Anytime," Carolanne insisted. "It'll be fine. That's a really nice grouping," she added as Suzanna began to load her choices into the truck. "Are you putting in another bed?"

"Paying off a debt." Suzanna climbed into the truck, gave a wave then drove off. On the way to Holt's, she busied her mind by designing and redesigning the arrangement for the flower bed. She'd already scouted out the spot, bordering the front porch so he could enjoy it whenever he came or went from the cottage. Whether he wanted to or not.

The job would take her the rest of the day, then she would unwind by walking along the cliffs. Tomorrow she would put in a full day at the shop, then spend the cool of the evening working the gardens at The Towers.

One by one, the days would pass.

She didn't bother to announce herself after she'd parked the truck, but set right to work staking out the bed. The result was not what she'd hoped for. As she dug and hoed and worked the soil there was no soothing response. Her mind didn't empty of worries and fill with the pleasure of planting. Instead a headache began to work nastily behind her eyes. Ignoring it, she wheeled over a load of planting medium and dumped it. She was raking it smooth when Holt stepped out.

He'd watched her from the window for nearly ten minutes, hating the fact that the strong shoulders were slumped and her eyes dull with sadness.

"I thought you were taking the day off."

"I changed my mind." Without glancing up, she rolled the wheelbarrow back to the truck and loaded it with flats of plants.

"What the hell are all of those?"

"Your paycheck." She started with snapdragons, delphiniums and bright shasta daisies. "This was the deal."

Frowning, he came down a couple of steps. "I said maybe you could put in a couple of bushes."

"I'm putting in flowers." She packed down the soil. "Anyone with an ounce of imagination can see that this place is crying for flowers."

So she wanted to fight, he noted, rocking back on his heels. Well, he could oblige her. "You could have asked before you dug up the yard."

"Why? You'd just sneer and make some nasty macho remark."

He came down another step. "It's my yard, babe."

"And I'm planting flowers in it. *Babe.*" She tossed her head up. Yeah, she was mad enough to spit nails, he noted. And she was also miserable. "If you don't want to bother to give them any water or care, then I will. Why don't you go back inside and leave me to it?"

Without waiting for a response, she went back to work. Holt took a seat while she added lavender and larkspur, dahlias and violas. He smoked lazily, noting that her hands were as sure and graceful as usual.

"Planting posies doesn't seem to be improving your mood today."

"My mood is just fine. In fact, it's dandy." She snapped a sprig off some freesia and swore. "Why shouldn't it be, just because I had to watch Jenny get in that damn car with tears running down her cheeks? Just because I had to stand there and smile when Alex looked back at me, his little mouth quivering and his eyes begging me not to make him go."

When her eyes filled, she shook the tears away. "And I had to stand there and take it when Bax accused me of being an overprotective, smothering mother who was turning his children, *his* children into timid weaklings."

She hacked her spade into the dirt. "They're not timid or weak," she said viciously. "They're just children. Why shouldn't they be afraid to go with him, when they hardly know him? And with his wife who stood there in her silk suit and Italian heels looking distressed and helpless. She won't have a clue what to do if Jenny has a bad dream or Alex gets a stomachache. And I just let them go. I just stood there and let them get in that awful car with two strangers. So I'm feeling just fine. I'm feeling terrific."

She sprang up to shove the wheelbarrow back to the truck. When she came back to do the mulching, he was gone. She forced herself to do the work carefully, reminding herself that at least here, over this one thing, she had control.

Holt came back, dragging the hose from around the other side of the house and holding two beers. "I'll water them. Have a beer."

Swiping a hand over her brow, she frowned at the bottles. "I don't drink beer."

"That's all I've got." He shoved one into her hand, then pushed the lever for the sprayer. "I think I can handle this part by now," he said dryly. "Why don't you have a seat?"

Suzanna walked to the steps and sat. Because she was thirsty she took one long sip, then rested her chin on her hand and watched him. He'd learned not to drown the plants, or pound them with a heavy spray. She let out a little sigh, then sipped again.

No words of sympathy, she thought. No comforting pats or claims to understand just how she felt. Instead, he'd given her exactly what she'd needed, a silent wall to hurl her misery and anger against. Did he know he'd helped her? She couldn't be sure. But she knew she had come here, to him, not only to plant flowers, not only to get out of the house, but because she loved him.

She hadn't given herself time to think about that, not since the feeling had opened and bloomed inside of her. Nor had she given herself a chance to wonder what it would mean to either of them.

It wasn't something she wanted. She wanted never to love again, never to risk hurt and humiliation at a man's hands again. But it had happened.

She hadn't looked for it. She had looked only for peace of mind, for security for her children, for simple contentment for herself. Yet she had found it.

And what would his reaction be if she told him. Would it please his ego? Would it shock or appall or amuse? It didn't matter, Suzanna told herself as she slipped an arm around the dog who had come to join her. For now, perhaps for always, the love was hers. She no longer expected emotions to be shared.

Holt shut off the spray. The colorful bed added charm to the simple wooden cottage. It even pleased him that he recognized some of the blooms by name. He wasn't going to ask her about the ones that were unfamiliar. But he'd look them up.

"It looks pretty good."

"They're mostly perennials," she said in the same casual tone. "I thought you might find it rewarding to see them come back year after year."

He might, but he also thought he would remember, much too vividly, how hurt and unhappy she'd looked when she'd planted them. He didn't dare dwell on how much it upset him to picture Alex and Jenny climbing tearfully into a car and driving away.

"They smell okay."

"That's the lavender." She took a deep breath of it herself before rising. "I'll go around and turn off the hose." She'd nearly turned the corner when he called her name.

"Suzanna. They'll be all right."

Not trusting her voice, she nodded and continued around back. She was crouched down, the dog's face in hers when he joined her.

"You know, if you put some day lilies and some sedum on that bank, you'd solve most of the erosion problem."

He cupped a hand under her elbow to pull her to her feet. "Is working the only thing you use to take your mind off things?"

"It does the job."

"I've got a better idea."

Her heart gave a quick jolt. "I really don't—"

"Let's go for a ride."

She blinked. "A ride?"

"In the boat. We've got a couple of hours before dark."

"A ride in the boat," she said, unaware that she amused him with her long, relieved sigh. "I'd like that."

"Good." He took her hand and pulled her to the pier. "You cast off." When the dog jumped in beside him,

Suzanna realized this was an old routine. For a man who didn't want to appear to have any sentiment, it was a telling thing that he took a dog along for company when he set out to sea.

The engine roared to life. Holt waited only until Suzanna had climbed on board before he headed into the bay.

The wind slapped against her face. Laughing, she clapped a hand to her cap to keep it from flying off. After she'd pulled it on more securely, she joined him at the wheel.

"I haven't been out on the water in months," she shouted over the engine.

"What's the use of living on an island if you never go out on the water?"

"I like to watch it."

She turned her head and caught the bright glint of window glass from the secluded houses on Bar Island. Overhead gulls wheeled and screamed. Sadie barked at them, then settled on the boat cushions with her head on the side so that the wind could send her ears flying.

"Has she ever jumped out?" Suzanna asked him.

He glanced back at the dog. "No. She just looks stupid."

"You'll have to bring her by the house again. Fred hasn't been the same since he met her."

"Some women do that to a man." The salt breeze was carrying her scent to him, wrapping it around his senses so that he drew her in with every breath. She was standing close, braced against the boat's motion. The expression in her eyes was still far off and troubled, and he knew she wasn't thinking of him. But he thought of her.

He moved expertly through the bay traffic, keeping the speed slow and steady as he maneuvered around other boats, passed a hotel terrace where guests sat under striped umbrellas drinking cocktails or eating an early dinner. Far to starboard, the island's three-masted schooner streamed into port with its crowd of waving tourists.

Then the bay gave way to the sea and the water became less serene. The cliffs roared up into the sky. Arrogantly, defiantly, The Towers sat on its ridge overlooking village and bay and sea. Its somber gray stone mirrored the tone of the rain clouds out to the west. Its old, wavy glass glinted with fanciful rainbows. Like a mirage, there were streaks and blurs of color that was Suzanna's garden.

"Sometimes when I went lobstering with my father, I'd look up at it." And think of you. "Castle Calhoun," Holt murmured. "That's what he called it."

Suzanna smiled, shading her eyes with the flat of her hand as she studied the imposing house on the cliffs. "It's just home. It's always been home. When I look up at it I think of Aunt Coco trying out some new recipe in the kitchen and Lilah napping in the parlor. The children playing in the yard or racing down the stairs. Amanda sitting at her desk and working her meticulous way through the mounds of bills it takes to hold a home together. C.C. diving under the hood of the old station wagon to see if she could make a miracle happen and get one more year out of the engine. Sometimes I see my parents laughing at the kitchen table, so young, so alive, so full of plans." She turned around to keep the house in sight. "So many things have changed, and will change. But the house is still there. It's comforting. You'd understand that or you wouldn't have chosen to live in Christian's cottage, with all his memories."

He understood exactly, and it made him uneasy. "Maybe I just like having a place on the water."

Suzanna watched Bianca's tower disappear before she shifted to face him. "Sentiment doesn't make you weak, Holt."

He frowned out over the water. "I could never get close to my father. We came at everything from different directions. I never had to explain or justify anything I felt or wanted to my grandfather. He just accepted. I guess I figured there was a reason he left me the place when he died, even though I was only a kid."

It moved her in a very soft, very lovely way that he had shared even that much with her. "So you came back to it. We always come back to what we love." She wanted to ask him more, what his life had been like during the span of years he'd been away. Why he had turned his back on police work to repair boat motors and props. Had he been in love, or had his heart broken? But he hit the throttle and sent the boat streaking out over the wide expanse of water.

He hadn't come out to think deep thoughts, to worry or to wonder. He had come to give her, and himself, an hour of relaxation, a respite from reality. Wind and speed worked that particular miracle for him. It always had. When he heard her laugh, when she tossed her face up into the sun, he knew he'd chosen well.

"Here, take the wheel."

It was a challenge. She could hear the dare in his voice, see it in his eyes when he grinned at her. Suzanna didn't hesitate, but took his place at the helm.

She gloried in the control, in the power vibrating under her fingertips. The boat sliced through the water like a blade, racing to nowhere. There was only sea and sky and unlimited freedom. The Atlantic roughened, adding a dash of danger. The air took on a bite that shivered along the skin and made each breath a drink of icy wine.

Her hands were firm and competent on the wheel, her body braced and ready. The wistful look in her eyes had been replaced by a bright fearlessness that quickened his blood. Her face was flushed with excitement, dampened by the spray. She didn't look like a princess now, but like a queen who knew her own power and was ready to wield it.

He let her race where she chose, knowing that she would end where he had wanted her for most of his life. He wouldn't wait another day. Not even another hour.

She was breathless and laughing when she gave him the wheel again. "I'd forgotten what it was like. I haven't handled a boat in five years."

"You did all right." He kept the speed high as he turned the boat in a wide half circle.

Still laughing, she rubbed her hands over her arms. "Lord, it's freezing."

He glanced toward her and felt the punch low in his gut. She was glowing—her eyes as blue as the sky and only more vital, the thin cotton pants and blouse plastered against her slender body, her hair streaming out from under the cap.

When his palms grew damp and unsteady on the wheel, he looked away. Not falling in love, he realized. He'd stopped falling and had hit the ground with a fatal smack. "There's a jacket in the cabin."

"No, it feels wonderful." She closed her eyes and let the sensations hammer her. The wild wind, the golden evening sun, the smell of salt and sea and the man beside her, the roar of the motor and the churning wake. They might have been alone, completely, with nothing but excitement and speed, with either of them free to take the wheel and spear off into that fabulous aloneness.

She didn't want to go back. Suzanna drank deeply of the tangy air and thought how liberating it would be to race and race in no direction at all, then to drift wherever the current took her.

But the air was already warming. They were no longer alone. She heard the long, droning horn of a tourist boat as Holt cut the speed and glided toward the harbor.

This too was lovely, she thought. Coming home. Knowing your place, certain of your welcome. She let out a little sigh at the simple familiarity. The blue water of Frenchman Bay deepening now with evening, the buildings crowded with people, the clang of buoys. It was all the more comforting after the frantic race to nowhere.

They said nothing as he navigated across the bay and circled around to drift to his pier. But she was relaxed when she jumped out to secure the lines, when she ran her hands over the dog who leaned against her legs, begging for attention.

"You're quite the sailor, aren't you, girl?" She crouched down to give the dog a good rub. "I think she wants to go again."

Holt stepped nimbly to the dock and stood a foot apart. "There's a storm coming in."

Suzanna glanced up and saw that the clouds were blowing slowly but determinedly inland. "You're right. We can certainly use the rain." Foolish, she thought, to feel awkward now and start talking of the weather. She rose, uncertain of her moves now that he was standing here, tension in every line of his body, his eyes dark and intent on hers. "Thanks for the ride. I really enjoyed it."

"Good." The pier swayed when he started forward. Suzanna took two steps back and felt better when her feet hit solid ground.

"If you get a chance, maybe you can bring Sadie to visit Fred this weekend. He'll be lonely without the kids around."

"All right."

She was halfway across the yard, and he was still a foot away. If it hadn't seemed so paranoid, she would have said he was stalking her. "The bush is doing well." She ran her fingers over it as she passed. "But you really need to feed this lawn. I could recommend a simple and inexpensive program."

His lips curved slightly, but his eyes stayed on hers. "You do that."

"Well, I . . . it's getting late. Aunt Coco—"

"Knows you're a big girl." He took her arm to hold her still. "You're not going anywhere tonight, Suzanna."

Perhaps if she'd been wiser or more experienced, she would have gauged his mood before he touched her. There was no mistaking it now, not when his fingers had closed over her with taut possession, not when his needs, and his intention of satisfying them, were so clear in those deep gray eyes.

She wished she could have been so certain of her own mood and her own needs.

"Holt, I told you I needed time."

"Time's up," he said simply, with an underlying edge that had her pulse jerking.

"This isn't something I intend to take casually."

Heat flashed into his eyes. From miles away came the violent rumble of thunder. "There's nothing casual about it. We both know that."

She did know it, and the knowledge was terrifying. "I think—"

He swore and swept her into his arms. "You think too much."

The moment the shock wore off she began to struggle. By then he had already carried her onto the back porch. "Holt. I won't be pressured." The screen door slammed behind them. Didn't he know she was afraid? That she was so afraid if she took this step he would find her dull, shrug her off and leave her shattered? "I'm not going to be rushed into this."

"If you had your way, it would take another fifteen years." He kicked open the door to the bedroom then dropped her onto the bed. It wasn't what he had planned, but he was too knotted up with terror and longings to struggle with soft words.

She was off the bed in a shot to stand beside it, slim and straight as an arrow. The lowering light, already gathering gloom, crept through the window at her back. "If you think you can cart me in here and throw me on the bed—"

"That's exactly what I've done." His eyes stayed hard on hers as he pulled his shirt over his head. "I'm tired of waiting, Suzanna, and I'm damn tired of wanting you. We're going to do this my way."

It had been like this for her before, she thought as her heart sank to her stomach like a stone. Only then it had been Bax, ordering her into bed, peeling off his clothes before he climbed on top of her to take his marital rights, quick and hard and without affection. And after, there would come his derision and disgust for her.

"Your way's hardly new," she said tightly. "And it doesn't interest me. I'm not obligated to go to bed with you, Holt. To let you demand and take and tell me I'm not good enough to satisfy. I'm not going to be used again, by anyone."

He caught her arms before she could storm from the room, dragged her struggling and swearing against him to crush his heated mouth to hers. The force of it sent her reeling. She would have stumbled away if his arms hadn't banded her so tightly.

Over the fear and the anger her own needs swelled. She wanted to scream at him for pulling them from her, for leaving her raw and naked and defenseless. But she could only hold on.

He yanked her away, arm's length, his breath already ragged and shallow. Her eyes were dark as midnight and held as many secrets. He would uncover them, that he promised himself. One by one he would learn them all. And tonight, he would begin.

"No one is going to be used here, and I'm only going to take what you give." His tensed fingers flexed on her arms. "Look at me, Suzanna. Look at me and tell me you don't want me, and I'll let you go."

Her lips parted on a shaky breath. She loved him, and she was no longer a girl who could hold love to herself like a comforting pillow in the night. If she was not as strong as she hoped and able to hold her heart and body separate, then she had no choice but to unite them. If that heart was broken, she would survive.

Hadn't she promised them both there would be no regrets?

She lifted a hand to his gently though she expected no gentleness in return. The choice was one she made freely.

"I can't tell you I don't want you. There's no need to wait any longer."

Chapter 8

If his nerves hadn't been so tangled, if the need hadn't been so acute, he might have been able to show her tenderness. If his blood hadn't been so hot, desire so greedy, he would have tried to give her some romance. But he was certain if he didn't possess now, possess quickly, he would shatter into hundreds of jagged shards of desperation.

So his mouth was fevered with impatience, his hands rough with urgency. At the first potent taste he understood she was already his. But it wasn't enough. Maybe it could never be enough.

She didn't tremble or hesitate. The vulnerability was cloaked inside a generosity that urged him to take his fill. As her hands roamed restlessly over his back he felt only her hunger, and none of her doubt.

He pushed the cap from her hair, then yanked the band from it so that his hands could take fistfuls of honey-colored silk. And the hands that gripped were unsteady, even as his mouth ruthlessly devoured hers.

She opened for him, releasing a soft and sultry moan of pleasure as his tongue plunged to duel with hers. He wanted so badly, and that want vibrating from him aroused her own. She had risen on her toes, unaware that she was fighting to meet him flare for flare. Her body was quaking with passions long suppressed.

And there was fear in that, fear in not knowing what would become of her if she lost that last toehold on control. She had to show him that she could give pleasure, make him enjoy and continue to want. If she fumbled now, lessened her grip on proving herself a woman, might he not find her less than his fantasy?

Yet she had never been wanted like this. Not like this with the violence of desire pulsing in the air so that every breath was like breathing temptation. She strained against him, hoping what she had to give would be enough while her system jolted along the battering tide of sensations.

His mouth raced over her face, down her throat where his teeth and the rough stubble of beard scraped. And his hands—Lord, his hands were fast and lethal.

She had to keep her head, but her knees were watery and her mind was spinning from the onslaught. Desperately she dug her nails into his back as she struggled away from the edge and tried to remember what a man would like.

She was quivering like a plucked bow, so tensed and wired he thought she might snap in two in his hands. She was holding back. The knowledge that she could do so when he was half-crazed brought on a kind of virulent fury. He tore the blouse aside as he pushed her onto the bed.

"Damn you, I want it all." Breath heaving, he encircled her wrists and dragged her arms over her head. "I'll have it all." When his mouth swooped down to capture hers, her hands strained under his grip, her pulse jittering in quick, rabbit jumps under his fingers.

His body was like a furnace, hot damp flesh fusing with hers in a way that made her shudder from the sheer wonder of it. Like iron, his fingers clamped hers still while his free hand raked over her in a merciless assault. She could feel the anger, taste the frustrated and furious desire. Desperate, she tried to pull in a breath to beg him to wait, to give her a moment, but all she could manage were jagged moans.

The wind kicked the curtains aside, letting dusk pour through. The first drops of rain hit the roof, sounding to her sensitized ears like gunshots that echoed the war he was waging on her. Again thunder rumbled, closer now, warning of a reckless power.

When his mouth found her breast, he let out a hot groan of pleasure. Here she was as soft as a summer breeze and as potent as whiskey. As she writhed beneath him, he dampened and tugged on the taut nipple, losing himself in the taste and texture while her heartbeat hammered against his mouth.

And she wanted as he wanted. He could feel the urgent excitement raging through her, hear it in her quick, sobbing breaths. Her hips arched and plunged against his until he was senseless. He ranged lower, his teeth nipping at her rib cage, his tongue laying a line of wet heat over her belly.

Her hands were free now and her fingers gripped his hair, then tore at the bedspread. She couldn't breathe. She needed to tell him. Her body was too full of aches and heat. She needed . . .

She needed.

Someone cried out. Suzanna heard the quick desperate sound, felt it tear from her own throat as her body arched up. Whole worlds exploded inside of her with a roar more huge than the thunder that stalked just overhead. Stunned, she lay shuddering under him as he lifted his head to stare at her.

Her eyes were dark, her face flushed with fresh fever. Beneath his, her body shook with aftershocks even as her hands slipped limply from his back to the ravaged bed. He hadn't guessed what it would do to him to see that kind of dazed pleasure on her face.

But he knew he wanted more.

He was driving her up again before she could recover. Now she could only embrace the speed and the thrill of danger. As the rain began to pound, she rolled with him, too giddy to be shocked by her own greed. Her hands were as rough and ready as his now, her mouth as merciless. When he dragged the slacks down her legs, her quick gasp was one of triumph. Her fingers were equally impatient as they yanked the denim over his hips, as they streaked and pressed over slick, heated flesh.

She wanted to touch as urgently as she needed to be touched. To possess even as she was possessed. She craved the madness, the turbulent hunger she hadn't known she could feel, and this tempestuous desire that reared up like a wild wolf to consume.

There was no thought of control now, not from either of them. When he sent her racing up again, then again, she rode each slashing crest only frantic for more. More was what he wanted to give her, and what he wanted to take. As the blood fired through his veins he drove himself into her, claiming possession in a frenzy of speed and heat. She matched him, beat for wild beat, the long, nurturing fingers digging into his hips.

They were alone again, but this time the sea was violently churning and the air was flaming hot. Here, at last was the power and the freedom. The speed was reckless, the journey a glorious risk. She felt him shudder, bury his face in her hair as he reached the end. Suzanna locked tight around him, and followed.

He'd wondered what it would be like for fifteen years. From boy to man he had dreamed about her, imagined her, wanted her. None of his fantasies had come close. She had been like a volcano, smoldering and shuddering, then erupting hot. Now she lay like warm wax beneath him, her body meltingly soft with passions spent. Her hair smelled of sun and sea. He thought he could stay just so for eternity, molded against her with the rain drumming on the roof and the wind blowing the curtains.

But he wanted to see her.

When he shifted, she made a small sound of protest and reached out. He said nothing, only kissed her until she relaxed again. Her eyes were drifting shut when he turned the lamp beside the bed on low.

Lord, she was beautiful, with her hair fanned out on the pillows, her skin glowing, her mouth soft and full. She tensed, but he ignored her discomfort as he took a long, silent study of the rest of her.

"Like I said," he murmured when his eyes came back to hers. "The Calhoun women are all lookers."

She didn't know what she was supposed to say or how she was expected to act. She knew that he had taken her to a new place, an extraordinary place, but she had no idea if he had experienced the same mind-spinning ride.

Then he frowned and her stomach twisted. With his eyes narrowed, he traced a finger down her throat, over the swell of her breasts.

"I should have shaved," he said abruptly, hating the fact that he'd scraped and reddened her skin. "You could have told me I was hurting you."

"I guess I didn't notice."

"Sorry." He touched his lips gently to her throat. Her look of dazed surprise made him feel like an idiot. When he rolled away, she reached out tentatively for his hand.

"You didn't hurt me," she said softly. "It was wonderful." And she waited, hopeful that he would tell her the same.

"I've got to let the dog in." His voice was rough, but he gave her fingers a quick squeeze before he left the room.

Suzanna heard it now, the whining howls, the scratching at the screen. She told herself it wasn't a rejection. It only meant that he could go from passion to practicality more quickly than she. They had shared something, something vital. She could cling to that. She sat up, more than a little amazed to see the state of the bed. The spread was a heap on the floor, the sheets a tangled knot at the foot. Her clothes—what was left of them—were scattered with his.

She rose and, uncomfortable naked, tugged on his shirt before she lifted her own. One button out of five remained, hanging by a thread. Laughing, she hugged it to herself. To have been wanted like that. With a little sigh, she bent down to search for her buttons. Maybe now he could be cool and collected, maybe his life hadn't been changed as hers had, but she had been wanted, desperately. She would never forget it.

"What are you doing?"

She looked up to see him standing in the doorway. Obviously walking around buck naked didn't concern him in the least, she thought and felt her steady pulse jerk and dance again. He looked angry. She wished she understood what she had done, or hadn't done, to put that scowl on his face.

"My blouse," she said. "I found the buttons." She gripped them in one hand, the thin cotton in the other. "Do you have a needle and thread?"

"No." Didn't she know what she did to him, standing there in nothing but his shirt, her hair tousled, her eyes heavy? Did she want him to get down on his knees and beg?

"Oh." She swallowed and tried to smile. "Well, I can fix it at home. If I could just borrow your shirt. I'd better get back."

He closed the door behind him. "No," he said again, and crossed the room to take her.

The rain stopped at dawn, leaving the air washed clean. Suzanna awoke to the lazy music of water dripping from the gutters. Before her mind had adjusted to where she was, her mouth was captured in a hot, hungry kiss. Her body catapulted from sleep to desire in one breathless leap.

He'd awakened wanting her. That burning need wouldn't ease no matter how much he took, how willingly she gave. There were no words, none he knew, that could express what she had come to mean to him. From a boy's fantasy to a man's salvation.

He could only show her.

He covered her. He filled her. Watching her face in the watery morning sunlight, he knew he would never be content unless she was with him.

"You're mine." He threw the words out like a curse as her body shuddered beneath his. "Say it." His hands fisted on the sheets and he buried his face against her throat. "Damn it, Suzanna, say it."

She could say nothing but his name as he dragged her over the edge.

When her hands slid limply from his back, he rolled over, locking her close so that she lay over him. He could be content with her head resting on his heart. He told himself that he'd already pushed her hard and fast enough. But he'd wanted badly to hear the words.

His hands were fisted in her hair. As if, she thought dizzily, he would yank her back if she tried to move. Her body felt achy and bruised and glorious. She smiled, listening to the rapid thud of his heart and the liquid beauty of morning bird song.

Her eyes flew open, her head up. He did pull her hair, but more from reflex than intent. "It's morning," Suzanna said.

"That usually happens when the sun comes up."

"No, I—ouch."

"Sorry," he muttered, and reluctantly released her hair.

"I must have fallen asleep."

"Yeah." He ran his hands up and down her back. He liked the long, smooth feel of it. "You dozed off before I could interest you in another round."

Her color fluctuated, but when she tried to scramble up, he held her firmly in place.

"Going somewhere?"

"I have to get home. Aunt Coco must be frantic."

"She knows where you are." Because it was easier to keep her in place, he reversed positions again and began to nibble at her throat. Nothing could have pleased him more than feeling the instant quickening of her pulse under his lips. "And in all likelihood, she's got a pretty good idea what you've been up to."

Without much hope of dislodging him, she pushed at his shoulder. "I didn't tell her where I was going."

"I called her last night when I let Sadie in. Scratch my back, will you? Base of the spine."

She obliged automatically, even while her thoughts spun. "You—you told my aunt that I . . ."

"I told her you were with me. I figure she could put the rest together. That's good. Thanks."

Suzanna let out a long breath. Oh yes, Aunt Coco wouldn't have any trouble adding two and two. And there was absolutely no reason to feel uncomfortable or embarrassed. But she was both. Not only relating to her aunt but to the man whose naked body was spread over hers.

It had been one thing to face him at night. But the morning . . .

He lifted his head to study her. "What's the problem?"

"Nothing." When he lifted a brow she shifted in what passed for a shrug. "It's just that I'm not sure what to do now. I've never done this before."

He grinned at her. "How'd you get two kids?"

"I don't mean that I've never . . . I mean I've never . . ."

His grin only widened. "Well, get used to it, babe." Considering, he trailed a finger over her jawline. "Want me to help you out with morning-after etiquette?"

"I want you to stop leering at me."

"No, you see that's part of the form." He replaced his trailing finger with a light nip of his teeth. "I'm supposed to leer at you in the morning so you don't start feeling that you look like a hag."

"A—" The word caught in her throat. "A hag?"

"And you're supposed to tell me I was incredible."

Her brow lifted. "I am?"

"That, and any other superlatives you can come up with. Then—" he rolled her over again "—you're supposed to go fix me breakfast, to show me your talents are versatile."

"I can't tell you how grateful I am that you're filling me in on the procedure."

"No problem. And after you fix me breakfast, you should seduce me back into bed."

She laughed and pressed her cheek to his in a move that disarmed and delighted him. "I'll have to practice up on that, but I could probably handle a couple of scrambled eggs."

"Let me know if you find any."

"Have you got a robe?"

"What for?"

She looked up again. He was still leering. "Never mind." Sliding away, she instinctively turned her back as she groped on the floor for his shirt. "And what do you do while I'm fixing breakfast?"

He caught the ends of her hair, let them shift through his fingers. "I watch you."

And he enjoyed it, seeing her move around his kitchen, his shirt skimming her thighs with the scent of coffee ripening the air and her voice low and amused as she spoke to the dog.

She felt more at ease here, with familiar chores. The bush they had planted was a cloud of sunlight outside the window, and the breeze still smelled of rain.

"You know," she said as she grated cheese into the eggs, "you could use more than a toaster, one pot and a skillet."

"Why?" He kicked back in the chair and took a comfortable drag on his cigarette.

"Well, some people actually use this room to prepare entire meals."

"Only if they haven't heard of take-out." He saw that the coffee had dripped through and rose to pour them both a cup. "What do you take in this?"

"Just black. I need the kick."

"If you ask me, what you need is more sleep."

"I have to be at work in an hour or so." With the bowl of eggs in her hands, she stopped to stare out of the window. He recognized the look in her eyes and rubbed a hand over her shoulder.

"Don't."

"I'm sorry." She turned to the stove to pour the beaten eggs into the skillet. "I can't help but wonder what they're doing, if they're having a good time. They've never been away before."

"Hasn't he taken them for a weekend?"

"No, just a couple of afternoons that weren't terribly successful." She made an effort to shake the mood as she stirred the eggs. "Well, there's only thirteen days left to go."

"You're not helping them or yourself by getting worked up." His impotence grated as he fought to massage the tension from her shoulders.

"I'm fine. I will be fine," she corrected. "I've got more than enough to keep me busy for the next couple of weeks. And with the kids gone, I can put in more time trying to find the emeralds."

"You leave that to me."

She glanced over her shoulder. "This is a team effort, Holt. It always has been."

"I'm involved now, and I'll handle it."

She dished the eggs up as carefully as she chose her words. "I appreciate your help. All of us do. But they're called the Calhoun emeralds for a reason. Two of my sisters have been threatened because of them."

"Exactly my point. You're out of your league with Livingston, Suzanna. He's smart and he's brutal. He won't ask you nicely to get out of his way."

Turning, she handed him his plate. "I'm accustomed to smart, brutal men, and I've already spent enough of my life being afraid."

"What's that supposed to mean?"

"Just what I said." She lifted her plate, and the mug of coffee. "I won't let some thief intimidate me or make me afraid to do what's best for myself and my family."

But Holt was shaking his head. That wasn't the answer he'd wanted. "Are you afraid of Dumont? Physically?"

Her gaze wavered then leveled. "We're talking about the emeralds." She tried to move by him, but Holt blocked her path. His eyes had gone dark, but when he spoke his voice was softer, more controlled than she had ever heard it.

"Did he hit you?"

Her color deepened, then raced away from her cheeks. "What?"

"I want to know if Dumont ever hit you."

Nerves were tightening her throat. No matter how quiet his voice, there was a terrible gleam of violence in his eyes. "The eggs are getting cold, Holt, and I'm hungry."

He fought back the urge to hurl the plate against the wall. He sat, waited for her to take the seat across from him. She looked very frail and very composed in the stream of sunlight. "I want an answer, Suzanna." He picked up his coffee and sipped as she toyed with her food. He knew how to wait and how to push.

"No." Her voice was flat as she took the first bite. "He never hit me."

"Just knocked you around?" He kept his voice casual and ate without tasting. Her gaze flicked up to his, then away.

"There are a lot of ways to intimidate and demoralize, Holt. After that, humiliation is a snap." Picking up a slice of toast, she buttered it carefully. "You're nearly out of bread."

"What did he do to you?"

"Let it go."

"What," he repeated slowly, "did he do to you?"

"He made me face facts."

"Such as?"

"That I was pitifully inadequate as a wife of a corporate lawyer with social and political ambitions."

"Why?"

She slammed down the knife. "Is this how you interrogate suspects?"

Anger, he thought. That was better. "It's a simple question."

"And you want a simple answer? Fine. He married me because of my name. He thought there was a bit more money as well as prestige attached to it, but the Calhoun name was more than adequate. Unfortunately it became quickly apparent that I wasn't the social boon he'd imagined. My dinner party conversation was pedestrian at best. I could be dressed up to look the part of the prominent wife of a politically ambitious attorney, but I could never quite pull it off. It was, as he told me often, a huge disappointment that I couldn't get it through my head what was expected of me. That I was boring, in the drawing room, the dining room and the bedroom.''

She sprang up to scrape the rest of her meal into Sadie's bowl. "Does that answer your question?''

"No." Holt pushed his plate away and pulled out a cigarette. "I'd like to know how he convinced you that you were at fault."

Keeping her back to him, she straightened. "Because I loved him. Or I loved the man I thought I'd married, and I wanted, very badly, to be the woman he'd be proud of. But the harder I tried, the more I failed. Then I had Alex, and it seemed . . . I had done something so incredible. I'd brought that beautiful baby into the world. And it was so easy, so natural for me to be a mother. I never had any doubts, any missteps. I was so happy, so focused on the child and the family we'd begun, that I didn't realize that Bax was discreetly finding more exciting companionship. Not until I found out I was going to have Jenny."

"So he cheated on you." His voice was deceptively mild. "What did you do about it?"

She didn't turn around, but began to run water in the sink to wash the dishes. "You can't understand what it's like to be betrayed that way. To already feel as though you're inadequate. To be carrying a man's child and find out that you've already been replaced."

"No, I can't. But it seems to me I'd be ticked off."

"Was I angry?" She nearly laughed. "Yes, I was angry, but I was also . . . wounded. I don't like to remember how easy it was for him to shatter me. Alex was only a few months old, and Jenny hadn't been planned. But I was so happy to be pregnant. He didn't want her. Nothing he'd done to me before had hurt or shocked me the way his reaction did when I told him I was pregnant again. He wasn't angry so much as...irked." She decided on a half laugh and plunged her hands into the soapy water.

"He had a son," she continued, "so the Dumont name would continue. He didn't intend to clutter up his life with children, and he certainly didn't want to have to drag me around the social wheel a second time while I was fat and tired and unattractive. The most practical solution was to terminate the pregnancy. We fought horribly about that. It was the first time I'd had the nerve to stand up to him—which only made it worse. Bax was used to getting his own way, he always had. Since he couldn't force me to do what he wanted, he paid me back, expertly."

Calmer now, she set the dish aside to drain and began to wash out the skillet. "He was still discreet publicly with his affairs, but he made sure I knew about them, and how sadly I compared to the women he slept with. He took my name off the checking and charge accounts so that I had to ask him whenever I needed money. That was one of his more subtle humiliations. The night Jenny was born, he was with another woman. He made certain I knew about that when he came to the hospital so the press could snap his picture while he played the proud father."

Holt hadn't moved. He didn't trust himself to move. "Why did you stay with him?"

"At first, because I kept hoping I would wake up beside the man I'd fallen in love with. Then, when I started to consider that my marriage was a failure, I had one child and was pregnant with another." She picked up a cloth and began to dry the dishes. "And I stayed because for a long time, a very long time I was convinced he was right about me. I wasn't clever and witty and sharp. I wasn't sexy or seductive. So the least I could be was loyal. When I realized I couldn't even be that, I had to consider the effect on the children. They weren't to be hurt. I couldn't have stood it if dissolving my marriage to Bax had hurt them. One day, I suddenly understood that it was all for nothing, that I was not only wasting my life but probably doing more harm to Alex and Jenny by pretending there was a marriage. Bax paid little attention to his son, and none at all to his daughter. He spent a great deal more time with his lover than he did with his family.''

She sighed, set the dishes down. ''So I hid my diamonds in Jenny's diaper bag and asked for a divorce.'' When she turned, the weariness was back on her face. ''Does that answer your question?''

Very slowly, his eyes on hers, he rose. ''Did it ever occur to you, did it ever once cross your mind that he was inadequate, that he was a failure? That he was a spoiled, selfish bastard?''

Her lips curved a little. ''Well, the last part certainly occurred to me. It also occurs to me that my little story is one-sided. I imagine Bax's view of our relationship would differ from mine, and not without some merit.''

''He's still pushing your buttons,'' Holt said with barely suppressed fury. ''So you're not clever? I guess anyone could manage to raise two kids and run a business. Dull, too?'' He took a step toward her, only more furious when he saw her instinctive move to brace. ''Yeah, I don't know when I've been so bored by anyone, but then most men are bored with women with brains and guts, especially when they're softhearted and hardheaded. Nothing puts me to sleep faster than a woman who'll sweat all day to make sure her kids are provided for. God knows you're not sexy. I just didn't have anything better to do last night than to spend it going crazy over you."

He'd trapped her against the sink with his body and with an anger so ripe she could almost taste it. "You asked and I answered. I don't know what you want me to say now."

"I want you to say you don't give a damn about him." He grabbed her by the shoulders, his face close to hers. "I want you to tell me what I told you to tell me when I was inside you, when I was so full of you I couldn't breathe. You're mine, Suzanna. Nothing that happened before counts because you're mine now. That's what I want to hear."

His hands slipped down to clamp over her wrists. Even as she opened her mouth to speak he saw the quick wince of pain. Swearing, he looked down and saw the bruises he'd already put on her. He jerked back as if she'd slapped him.

"Holt—"

He raised a hand to silence her, turning away until he could clear the red haze of fury from his mind. He'd put marks on her skin. It had been done in passion and without intention, but that didn't erase them. By putting them there, he was no better than the man who had bruised her soul.

He jammed his hands into his pockets before he turned. "I've got things to do."

"But—"

"We got off the track, Suzanna. My fault. I know you have to get to work, and so do I."

So that was that, she thought. She'd bared her soul, now he would walk away. "All right. I'll see you on Monday."

With a nod, he headed for the back door, then swore, stopping with his hand on the screen. "Last night meant something to me. Do you understand that?"

She let out a quiet breath. "No."

His hand curled into a fist on the screen. "You're important to me. I care about you, and having you here, this way, is . . . I need you. Is that clear enough?"

She studied him—a fist on the door, impatience in his eyes, his body rigid with passions she couldn't quite understand. It was enough, she realized. For now it was more than enough.

"Yes, I think it's clear."

"I don't want it to end there." He turned his head, and his eyes were dark and fierce again. "It's not going to end there."

She continued to study his face, keeping her voice calm. "Are you asking me to come back?"

"You know damn well—" He cut himself off and closed his eyes. "Yes, I'm asking you to come back. And I'm asking you to think about spending time with me that isn't at work or in bed. If that doesn't spell it out for you, then—"

"Would you like to come to dinner?"

He gave her a blank stare. "What?"

"Would you like to come to dinner, tonight? Maybe we could take a drive after."

"Yeah." He dragged a hand through his hair, not sure if he was relieved or uneasy that it had been so simple. "That would be good."

Yes, it would be good, she thought and smiled. "I'll see you about seven then. Bring Sadie if you like."

Chapter 9

It wasn't candlelight and moonbeams, Suzanna thought, but it was a romance. She hadn't believed she would find it again, or want it. Flexing her back as she drove up the curving road to The Towers, she smiled.

Of course, a relationship with Holt Bradford was lined with rough edges, but it had its softer moments. She'd had a lovely time discovering them over the past few days. And nights.

There was the way he'd shown up at the shop once or twice, just before lunchtime. He hadn't said anything about the children, or her missing the routine—just that he'd come into the village for some parts and felt like eating.

Or how he'd come up behind her at odd moments to rub the tension out of her shoulders. The evening he'd surprised her after a particularly grueling day by dragging her and a wicker basket filled with cold chicken into the boat.

He was still demanding, often abrupt, but he never made her feel less than what she wanted to be. When he loved her, he loved her with an urgency and ferocity that left no doubt as to his desire.

No, she hadn't been looking for romance, she thought as she parked the truck behind Holt's car. But she was terribly glad she'd found it.

The moment she opened the door, Lilah pounced. "I've been waiting for you."

"So I see." Suzanna lifted a brow. Lilah was still in her park service uniform. Knowing her schedule, Suzanna was sure her sister had been home nearly an hour. As a matter of routine, Lilah should have been in her most comfortable clothes and spread out dozing on the handiest flat surface. "What's up?"

"Can you do anything with that surly hulk you've gotten tangled up with?"

"If you mean Holt, not a great deal." Suzanna pulled off her cap to run her hands through her hair. "Why?"

"Right now, he's upstairs, taking my room apart inch by inch. I couldn't even change my clothes." She aimed a narrowed glance up the steps. "I told him we'd already looked there, and that if I'd been sleeping in the same room as the emeralds all these years, I'd know it."

"And he ignored you."

"He not only ignored me, he kicked me out of my own bedroom. And Max." She let out a hiss of breath and sat on the stairs. "Max grinned and said it was a damn good idea."

"Want to gang up on them?"

A wicked gleam came into Lilah's eyes. "Yeah." She rose then swung an arm over Suzanna's shoulders as they started up. "You're really serious about him, aren't you?"

"I'm taking it one step at a time."

"Sometimes when you love someone it's better to take it by leaps and bounds." Then she yawned and swore. "I missed my nap. It'd be satisfying if I could say I disliked that pushy jerk, but I can't. There's something too solid and steady under the bad manners."

"You've been looking at his aura again."

Lilah laughed and stopped at the top of the stairs. "He's a good guy, as much as I'd like to belt him right now. It's good to see you happy again, Suze."

"I haven't been unhappy."

"No, just not happy. There's a difference."

"I suppose there is. Speaking of happy, how are the wedding plans coming?"

"Actually, Aunt Coco and the relative from hell are in the kitchen arguing over them right now." She turned laughing eyes to her sister. "And having a delightful time. Our Great-Aunt Colleen is pretending she simply wants to make certain the event will live up to the Calhoun reputation, but the fact is, she's getting a big kick out of making guest lists and shooting down Aunt Coco's menus."

"As long as she's entertained."

"Wait until she gets hold of you," Lilah warned. "She has some very creative ideas for floral arrangements."

"Terrific." Suzanna stopped in Lilah's doorway. Holt was definitely hard at work. Never particularly ordered, Lilah's room looked as though someone had scooped up every piece of furniture and dropped it down again like pick-up sticks. At the moment, he had his head in the fireplace, and Max was crawling on the floor.

"Having fun, boys?" Lilah said lazily.

Max looked up and grinned. She was mad, all right, he thought. He'd learned to handle and enjoy her temper. "I found that other sandal you've been looking for. It was under the cushion of the chair."

"There's good news." She lifted a brow, noting that Holt was now sitting on Lilah's hearth, looking at Suzanna. And Suzanna was looking at him. "You need a break, Max."

"No, I'm fine."

"You definitely need a break." She walked in to take his hand and pull him to his feet. "You can come back and help Holt invade my privacy later."

"I told you she wouldn't like it," Suzanna said when Lilah dragged Max from the room.

"That's too bad."

With her hands on her hips she surveyed the damage. "Did you find anything?"

"Not unless you count the two odd earrings and one of those lacy things we found behind the dresser." He tilted his head. "You got any of those lacy things?"

"Not really." She looked down at her sweaty T-shirt. "Up until a few days ago, I didn't think I'd need any."

"You've got a real nice way of wearing denim, babe." He rose, and since she wasn't coming any closer, moved to her. "And..." He ran his hands over her shoulders, down her back to her hips. "I get a real charge out of taking it off you." He kissed her hard, in the deep and urgent way she'd come to expect. Then he nipped her bottom lip and grinned. "But anytime you want to borrow one of those lacy things from Lilah..."

She laughed and gave him a quick, affectionate hug, the kind she gave so freely that never failed to warm him from the inside out. "Maybe I'll surprise you. How long have you been here?"

"I came straight from the site. Did you get the rest of those whatdoyoucallits in?"

"Russian olives, yes." And her back was still aching. "You were a lot of help on the retaining wall."

"You were out of your mind to think you could build that thing on your own."

"I had a part-time laborer when I contracted."

He shook his head and went back to searching the fireplace. "You may be tough, Suzanna, but you're not equipped to haul around lumber and swing a sledge-hammer."

"I'd have done it—"

"Yeah." He glanced around. "I know." He tested another brick. "It did look pretty good."

"It looked terrific. And since you didn't swear at me more than half a dozen times when you were hefting landscape timbers, why don't I reward you?"

"Oh, yeah?" He lost his interest in the bricks.

"I'll go get you a beer."

"I'd rather have—"

"I know." She laughed as she walked out. "But you'll have to settle for a beer. For now."

It felt good, she thought, to be able to joke like that. Not to be embarrassed or edgy. There was no need to feel anything but content, knowing he cared for her. In time, they might have something deeper.

Full of energy and hope, she rounded the last step and turned into the hall. All at once, there was chaos. She heard the dogs first, Fred and Sadie, barking fiendishly, then the clatter of feet on the porch and two high bellowing shouts.

"*Mom!*" Both Jenny and Alex yelled the single syllable as they burst into the house.

The rich and fast joy came first as she bent to scoop them up in her arms. Laughing, she smothered them both with kisses as the dogs dashed in mad circles.

"Oh, I missed you. I missed you both so much. Let me look at you." When she drew them back arm's length, her smile faltered. They were both on the edge of tears. "Baby?"

"We wanted to come home." Jenny's voice trembled as she buried her face against her mother's shoulder. "We hate vacation."

"Shh." She stroked Jenny's hair as Alex rubbed a fist under his eyes.

"We were unmanageable and bad," he said in a trembly voice. "And we don't care, either."

"Just the attitude I've come to expect," Bax said as he walked through the open front door. Jenny's arms tightened around Suzanna's neck, but Alex turned and threw out his Calhoun chin.

"We didn't like the dumb party, and we don't like you, either."

"Alex!" Her tone sharp, she dropped a hand on his shoulder. "That's enough. Apologize."

His lips quivered, but the stubborn gleam remained in his eyes. "We're sorry we don't like you."

"Take your sister upstairs," Bax said tightly. "I want to speak with your mother in private."

"You and Jenny go in the kitchen." Suzanna brushed a hand over Alex's cheek. "Aunt Coco's there."

Bax took a careless swipe at Fred with his foot. "And take these damn mutts with you."

"Chéri?" This from the svelte brunette who continued to hover in the doorway.

"Yvette." Keeping her arms around the children, Suzanna rose. "I'm sorry, I didn't see you."

The Frenchwoman waved distracted hands. "I beg your pardon, it's so confusing, I see. I just wondered— Bax, the children's bags?"

"Have the driver bring them in," he snapped. "Can't you see I'm busy?"

Suzanna sent the frazzled woman a look of sympathy. "He can just leave them here in the hall. If you'd like to come into the parlor...go see Aunt Coco," she told the children. "She'll be so happy you're back."

They went, holding each other's hand, with the dogs prancing at their heels.

"If you could spare a moment of your time," Bax said, then cast a glance up and down her work clothes, "out of your obviously fascinating day."

"The parlor," she repeated and turned. She struggled for calm, knowing it was essential. Whatever had caused him to change his plans and bring the children home a full week early was undoubtedly going to fall on her head. That she could handle. But the fact that the children had been upset was a different matter.

"Yvette—" Suzanna gestured to a chair "—can I get you something?"

"Oh, if you would be so kind. A brandy?"

"Of course. Bax?"

"Whiskey, a double."

She went to the liquor cabinet and poured, grateful her hands were steady. As she served Yvette, she thought she caught a glance of apology and embarrassment.

"Well, Bax, would you like to tell me what happened?"

"What happened began years ago when you had the mistaken idea you could be a mother."

"Bax," Yvette began, and was rounded on.

"Get out on the terrace. I prefer to do this privately."

So that hadn't changed, Suzanna thought. She gripped her hands together as Yvette crossed the room and exited through the glass doors.

"At least this little experiment should have rid her of the notion of having a child."

"Experiment?" Suzanna repeated. "Your visit with the children was an experiment?"

He sipped at the whiskey and watched her. He was still a striking man with a charmingly boyish face and fair hair. But temper, as it always had, added an edge to his looks that was anything but appealing.

"My reasons for taking the children are my concern. Their unforgivable behavior is yours. They haven't any conception of how to act in public and in private. They have the manners and dispositions of heathens and as little control. You've done a poor job, Suzanna, unless it was your intention to raise two miserable brats."

"Don't think you can stand here and speak about them that way in my house." Eyes dangerously bright, she walked toward him. "I don't give a damn if they fit your standards or not. I want to know why you've brought them back this way."

"Then listen," he suggested, and shoved her into a chair. "Your precious children don't have a clue what's expected of a Dumont. They were loud and unmanageable in restaurants, whiny and fidgety on the drive. When corrected they became defiant or sulky. At the resort, among several of my acquaintances, their behaviour was an embarrassment."

Too incensed for fear, Suzanna pulled herself out of the chair. "In other words, they were children. I'm sorry your plans were upset, Baxter, but it's difficult to expect a five- and six-year-old to present themselves as socially correct on all occasions. Even more difficult when they're thrust into a situation that wasn't any of their doing. They don't know you."

He swirled whiskey, swallowed. "They're perfectly aware that I'm their father, but you've seen to it that they have no respect for that relationship."

"No, you've seen to it."

Deliberately he set the whiskey aside. "Do you think I don't know what you tell them? Sweet, harmless little Suzanna." She stepped back automatically, pleasing him.

"I don't tell them anything about you," she said, furious with herself for retreating.

"Oh, no? Then you didn't mention the fact that they had a bastard brother out in Oklahoma?"

So that was it, she realized, struggling to settle. "Megan O'Riley's brother married my sister. There was no way to keep the situation a secret, even if I had wanted to."

"And you just couldn't wait to sling my name around." He gave her another shove that sent her stumbling back.

"The boy's their half brother. They accept that, and they're too young to understand what a despicable thing you did."

"My affairs are mine. Don't you forget it." Gripping her shoulders, he pushed her up against the wall. "I have no intention of letting you get away with your pitiful plots for revenge."

"Take your hands off me." She twisted, but he forced her back again.

"When I'm damn good and ready. Let me warn you, Suzanna. I won't have you spreading my private business around. If even a hint of this gets out, I'll know where it started, and you know who'll pay for it."

She kept herself rigid, kept her eyes steady. "You can't hurt me anymore."

"Don't count on it. You make sure your children keep this business of half brothers to themselves. If it's mentioned again—" he tightened his grip and jerked her up on her toes "—ever, you'll be very sorry."

"Take your threats and get out of my house."

"Yours?" He closed a hand around her throat. "Remember, it's only yours because I didn't want this crumbling anachronism. Push me, and I'll have you back in court in a heartbeat. And I'll have it all this time. Those children might benefit from a nice, Swiss boarding school, which is exactly where they'll be if you don't watch your step."

He saw her eyes change, but it wasn't the fear he'd expected. It was fury. She lifted a hand, but before she could strike out, he was jerked away and tumbling to the floor. She watched Holt drag him up again by the collar then send him crashing into a Louis Quinze table.

She'd never seen murder in a man's eyes before, but she recognized it in Holt's as he pounded a fist into Baxter's face.

"Holt, don't—"

She started forward only to have her arm gripped with surprising strength. "Let him alone," Colleen said, her mouth grim, her eyes bright.

He wanted to kill him, and might have, if the man had fought back. But Bax slumped in his hold, nose and mouth seeping blood. "You listen to me, you bastard." Holt slammed him against the wall. "Put your hands on her again, and you're dead."

Shaken, hurting, Bax fumbled for a handkerchief. "I can have you arrested for assault." Holding the cloth to his nose, he looked around and saw his wife standing inside the terrace doors. "I have a witness. You assaulted me and threatened my life." It was his first taste of humiliation, and he detested it. His glance veered toward Suzanna. "You'll regret this."

"No, she won't," Colleen put in before Holt could give in to the satisfaction of smashing his fist into the sneering mouth. "But you will, you miserable, quivering, spineless swine." She leaned heavily on her cane as she walked toward him. "You'll regret it for what's left of your worthless life if you ever lay hands on any member of my family again. Whatever you think you can do to us, I can do only more viciously to you. If you're unclear about my abilities, my name is Colleen Theresa Calhoun, and I can buy and sell you twice over."

She studied him, a pitiful man in a rumpled suit, bleeding into a silk handkerchief. "I wonder what the governor of your state—who happens to be my godchild—will have to say if I mention this scene to him." She gave a slow, satisfied nod when she saw she was understood. "Now get your miserable hide out of my house. Young man—" she inclined her head to Holt "—you'll be so kind as to show our guest to the door."

"My pleasure." Holt dragged him into the hall. The last thing Suzanna saw when she ran from the house was Yvette's fluttering hands.

"Where did she go?" Holt demanded when he found Colleen alone in the parlor.

"To lick her wounds, I suppose. Get me a brandy. Damn it, she'll keep a minute," she muttered when he hesitated. Colleen eased herself into a chair and waited for her heart rate to settle. "I knew she'd had a difficult time, but I wasn't fully aware of the extent of it. I've had this Dumont looked into since the divorce." She took the brandy and drank deeply. "Pitiful excuse for a man. I still wasn't aware he had abused her. I should have been, the first time I saw that look in her eyes. My mother had the same look." She closed her own and leaned back. "Well, if he doesn't want to see his political ambitions go up in smoke, he'll leave her be." Slowly she opened her eyes and gave Holt a steely look. "You did well for yourself—I admire a man who uses his fists. I only regret I didn't use my cane on him."

"I think you did better. I just broke his nose, you scared the—"

"I certainly did." She smiled and drank again. "Damn good feeling, too." She noted that Holt was staring at the open terrace doors, his hands still fisted. Suzanna could do worse, she thought and swirled the remaining brandy. "My mother used to go to the cliffs. You might find Suzanna there. Tell her the children are having cookies and spoiling their dinner."

She had gone to the cliffs. She didn't know why when she'd needed to run, that she had run there. Only for a moment, she promised herself. She would only need a moment alone.

She sat on a rock, covered her face and wept out the bitterness and shame.

He found her like that, alone and sobbing, the wind carrying off the sounds of her grief, the sea pounding restlessly below. He didn't know where to begin. His mother had always been a sturdy woman, and whatever tears she had shed, had been shed in private.

Worse, he could still see Suzanna pushed against the wall, Dumont's hand on her throat. She'd looked so fragile, and so brave.

He stepped closer, laid a hesitant hand on her hair. "Suzanna."

She was up like a shot, choking back tears, wiping them from her damp face. "I have to get back in. The children—"

"Are in the kitchen stuffing themselves with cookies. Sit down."

"No, I—"

"Please." He sat, easing her down beside him. "I haven't been here in a long time. My grandfather used to bring me. He used to sit right here and look out to sea. Once he told me a story about a princess in the castle up on the ridge. He must have been talking about Bianca, but later, when I remembered it, I always thought of you."

"Holt, I'm so sorry."

"If you apologize, you're only going to make me mad."

She swallowed another hot ball of tears. "I can't stand that you saw, that anyone saw."

"What I saw was you standing up to a bully." He turned her face to his. When he saw the fading red marks on her throat, he had to force back an oath. "He's never going to hurt you again."

"It was his reputation. The children must have talked about Kevin."

"Are you going to tell me?"

She did, as clearly as she was able. "When Sloan told me," she finished, "I knew it was important that the children understand they had a brother. What Bax doesn't realize is that I never thought about him, never cared. It was the children who mattered, all of them. The family."

"No, he wouldn't understand that. Or you." He brought her hand to his lips to kiss it gently. The stunned look on her face had him scowling out to sea. "I haven't been Mr. Sensitivity myself."

"You've been wonderful."

"If I had you wouldn't look like I hit you with a rock when I kiss your hand."

"It just isn't your style."

"No." He shrugged and dug out a cigarette. "I guess it's not." Then he changed his mind and slipped an arm around her shoulders instead. "Nice view."

"It's wonderful. I've always come here, to this spot. Sometimes..."

"Go ahead."

"You'll just laugh at me, but sometimes it's as if I can almost see her. Bianca. I can feel her, and I know she's here, waiting." She rested her head on his shoulder and shut her eyes. "Like right now. It's so warm and real. Up in the tower, her tower, it's bittersweet, more of a longing. But here, it's anticipation. Hope. I know you think I'm crazy."

"No." When she started to shift, he pulled her closer so that her head nestled back on his shoulder. "No, I can't. Not when I feel it, too."

From the west tower, the man who called himself Marshall watched them through field glasses. He didn't worry about being disturbed. The family no longer came above the second floor in the west wing, and the crew had knocked off thirty minutes before. He'd hoped to take advantage of the time that Sloan O'Riley was away with his new bride on his honeymoon to move more freely around the house. The Calhouns were so accustomed to seeing men in tool belts that they rarely gave him a second glance.

And he was interested, very interested in Holt Bradford, finding it fascinating that he was being drawn into this generation of Calhouns. It pleased him that he could continue his work right under the nose of an ex-cop. Such irony added to his vanity.

He would continue to keep tabs, he thought, while the cop completed his search. And he would be there to take what was his the moment the treasure was found. Whoever was in the way would simply be eliminated.

Suzanna spent all evening with her children, soothing ruffled feathers and trying to turn their unhappy experience into a silly misadventure. By the time she got them tucked into bed, Jenny was no longer clinging and Alex had rebounded like a rubber ball.

"We had to ride in the car for hours and hours." He bounced on his sister's bed while Suzanna smoothed Jenny's sheets. "And they had dumb music on the radio the *whole* time. People were singing like this." He opened his mouth wide and let out what he thought passed for an operatic aria. "And you couldn't understand a word."

"Not like that, like this." Jenny let out a screech that could have shattered crystal. "And we had to be quiet and appreciate."

Suzanna held her temper and tweaked her daughter's nose. "Well, you appreciated that it was awful, didn't you?"

That made Jenny giggle and reach up for another kiss. "Yvette said we could play a word game, but he said it gave him a headache, so she went to sleep."

"And that's what you should do, right now."

"I liked the hotel," Alex continued, hoping to postpone the inevitable. "We got to jump on the beds when nobody was looking."

"You mean like you do in your room?"

He grinned. "They had little bars of soap in the bathroom, and they put candy on your pillow at night."

Suzanna cocked her head. "You can forget that idea, toadface."

After Jenny was settled with her nightlight and army of stuffed animals, Suzanna carried Alex to his room. He didn't let her pick him up and cuddle often anymore, but tonight, he seemed to need it as much as she did.

"You've been eating bricks again," she murmured, and nuzzled his neck.

"I had five bricks for lunch." He flew out of her arms and onto the bed. She wrestled with him until he was breathless. He flopped back, laughing, then leaped out of bed again.

"Alex—"

"I forgot."

"You've already stretched it tonight, kid. In the bed or I'll have you cooked over a slow fire."

He pulled something out of the jeans he'd been wearing when he'd come home. "I saved it for you."

Suzanna took the flattened, broken chocolate wrapped in gold paper. It was more than a little melted, certainly inedible and more precious than diamonds.

"Oh, Alex."

"Jenny had one, too, but she lost it."

"That's all right." She brought him close for a fierce hug. "Thanks. I love you, you little worm."

"I love you, too." It didn't embarrass him to say it as it sometimes did, and he cuddled against her a moment longer. When his mother tucked him into bed, he didn't complain when she stroked his hair. "Night," he said, ready to sleep.

"Good night." She left him alone, weeping a little over the smashed mint. In her room, she opened the little case that had once held her diamonds, and tucked her son's gift inside.

She undressed then slipped into a thin white night-gown. There was paperwork waiting on her desk in the corner, but she knew her mind and nerves were still too rattled. To soothe herself, she opened the terrace doors and, taking her brush, walked outside to feel the night.

There was an owl hooting, crickets singing, the quiet whoosh of the sea. Tonight the moon was gilded and its light clear as glass. Smiling to herself, she lifted her face to it and skimmed the brush lazily through her hair.

Holt had never seen anything more beautiful than Suzanna brushing her hair in the moonlight. He knew he made a poor Romeo and was deathly afraid he'd make a fool of himself trying, but he had to give her something, to somehow show her what it meant to have her in his life.

He came out of the garden and started up the stone steps. He moved quietly, and she was dreaming. She didn't know he was there until he said her name.

"Suzanna."

She opened her eyes and saw him standing only a foot away, his hair ruffled by the breeze, his eyes dark in the shimmering light. "I was thinking about you. What are you doing here?"

"I went home, but . . . I came back." He wanted her to go on brushing her hair, but was certain the request would sound ridiculous. "Are you all right?"

"I'm fine, really."

"The kids?"

"They're fine, too. Sleeping. I didn't even thank you before. Maybe it's petty, but now that I've had a chance to settle, I can admit I really enjoyed seeing Bax's nose bleed."

"Anytime," Holt said, and meant it.

"I don't think it'll be necessary again, but I appreciate it." She reached out to touch his hand, and pricked her finger on a thorn. "Ow."

"That's a hell of a start," he mumbled, and thrust the rose at her. "I brought you this."

"You did?" Absurdly touched, she brushed the petals to her cheek.

"I stole it out of your garden." He stuck his hands into his pockets and wished for a cigarette. "I don't guess it counts."

"It certainly does." She had had two gifts that night, she thought, from the two men she loved. "Thank you."

He shrugged and wondered what to do next. "You look nice."

She smiled and glanced down at the simple white gown. "Well, it's not lacy."

"I watched you brushing your hair." His hand came out of his pocket of its own volition to touch. "I just stood there, down at the edge of the garden and watched you. I could hardly breathe. You're so beautiful, Suzanna."

Now it was she who couldn't breathe. He'd never looked at her just this way. His voice had never sounded so quiet. There was a reverence in it, as in the hand that stroked over her hair.

"Don't look at me like that." His fingers tightened in her hair and he had to force them to relax again. "I know I've been rough with you."

"No, you haven't."

"Damn it, I have." He fought against a welling impatience as she only stared at him. "I've pushed you around and grabbed on. I ripped your blouse."

A smile touched her lips. "When I sewed the buttons back on I remembered that night, and what it felt like to be needed that way.'' More than a little baffled, she shook her head. "I'm not fragile, Holt."

Couldn't she see how wrong she was? Didn't she know how she looked right now, her hair smooth and shining in the moonlight, the thin white gown flowing down?

"I want to be with you tonight." He slid his hand down to touch her cheek. "Let me love you tonight."

She couldn't have denied him anything. When he lifted her to carry her in, she pressed her lips to his throat. But his mouth didn't turn hot and ready to hers. He laid her down carefully, took the brush and rose from her to set it on the nightstand. Then he turned the lights low.

When his mouth came to hers at last, it was soft as a whisper. His hands didn't race to excite, but moved with exquisite patience to seduce.

He felt her confusion, heard it in the unsteady murmur of his name, but he only rubbed his lips over hers, tracing the shape with his tongue. His strong hands moved with an artist's grace over the tensed slope of her shoulders.

"Trust me." He took his mouth on a slow, quiet journey over her face. "Let go and trust me, Suzanna. There's more than one way." Over her jaw, down the line of her throat, back to her trembling lips his mouth whispered. "I should have showed you before."

"I can't..." Then his kiss had her sinking, deep, deeper still into some thick velvet haze. She couldn't right herself. Didn't want to. Surely this endless, echoing tunnel was paradise.

He touched, hardly touching at all, and left her weak. His mouth, gliding like a cool breeze over her flesh was rapture. She could hear him murmur to her, incredible promises, soft, lovely words. There was passion in them, in the fingertips that seemed designed only to bring her pleasure, yet this was a passion to give she had never expected.

He stroked her through the thin cotton, delighting in the liquid movements of her body beneath his hands. He could watch her face in the lamplight, feed on that alone, knowing she was steeped in him, in what he offered her. There was no need to strap down greed, desire was no less, but it had taken a different hue.

When she sighed, he brought his lips back to hers to swallow the flavor of his name.

He undressed her slowly, bringing the gown down inch by inch, wallowing in the delight of warming newly bared skin. Fascinated with each tremor he brought her, he lingered. Then took her gently over the first crest.

Unbearably sweet. Each movement, each sigh. Exquisitely tender. Every touch, every murmur. He had imprisoned her in a world of silk, gently bringing dozens of pulses to a throbbing ache that was like music. Never had she been more aware of her body than now as he explored it so thoroughly, so patiently.

At last she felt his flesh against hers, the warm, hard body she had come to crave. Opening heavy eyes, she looked. Lifting weighted limbs, she touched.

He hadn't known a need could be so strong yet so quiet. She enfolded him. He slipped into her. For both, it was like coming home.

I could not have foreseen that the day would be my last with her. Would I have looked more closely, held more tightly? The love could have been no greater, but could it have been treasured more completely?

There is no answer.

We found the little dog, cowering and half-starved in the rocks by our cliffs. Bianca found such pleasure in him. It was foolish, I suppose, but I think we both felt this was something we could share, since we had found him together.

We called him Fred, and I must admit I was sad to see him go when it was time for her to return to The Towers. Of course it was right that she take the orphaned pup to her children so that they could make him a family. I went home alone, to think of her, to try to work.

When she came to me, I was stunned that she should have taken such a risk. Only once before had she been to the cottage, and we had not dared chance that again. She was frantic and overwrought. Under her cloak, she carried the puppy. Because she was pale as a ghost, I made her sit and poured her brandy.

She told me, as I sat, hardly daring to speak, of the events that had taken place since we'd parted.

The children had fallen in love with the dog. There had been laughter and light hearts until Fergus had returned. He refused to have the dog, a stray mutt, in his home. Perhaps I could have forgiven him for that, thought of him only as a rigid fool. Bianca told me that he had ordered the dog destroyed, holding firm even on the tears and pleas of his children.

On the girl, young Colleen, he had been the hardest. Fearing a harsher, perhaps a physical reprisal, Bianca had sent the children and the dog up to their nanny.

The argument that had followed was bitter. She did not tell me all, but her tremors and the flash of fear in her eyes said enough. In his fury, he had threatened and abused her. It was then I saw in the light of my lamp, the marks on her throat where his hands had squeezed.

I would have gone then. I would have killed him. But her terror stopped me. Never before and never again in my life have I felt a rage such as that. To love as I loved, to know that she had been hurt and frightened. There are times I wish to God I had gone, and had killed. Perhaps things would have been different. But I'll never be sure.

I didn't leave her, but stayed while she wept and told me that he had gone to Boston, and that when he returned he intended to bring a new governess of his choosing. He had accused her of being a poor mother, and would take the care and control of the children from her.

If he had threatened to cut out her heart, he could not have done more damage. She would not see her children raised by a paid servant, overseen by a cold, ambitious father. She feared most for her daughter, knowing if nothing was done, Colleen would one day be bartered off into marriage—even as her mother had been.

It was this great fear that forced her decision to leave him.

She knew the risks, the scandal, the position she would be giving up. Nothing could sway her. She would take her children away where she knew they would be safe. Her wish was for me to go with them, but she did not beg or call upon my love.

She did not need to.

I would make the arrangements the next day, and she would prepare the children. Then she asked me to make her mine.

For so long I had wanted her. Yet I had promised myself I would not take her. That night I broke one promise, and I made another. I would love her eternally.

I still remember how she looked, her hair unbound, her eyes so dark. Before I touched her I knew how she would feel. Before I laid her in my bed, I knew how she would look there. Now it is only a dream, the sweetest memory of my life. The sound of the water and the crickets, the smell of wildflowers.

In that timeless hour, I had everything a man could want. She was beauty and love and promise. Seductive and innocent, shy and wanton. Even now, I can taste her mouth, smell her skin. And ache for her.

Then she was gone. What I had thought was a beginning was an end.

I took what money I had, sold paints and canvases for more and bought four tickets on the evening train. She did not come. There was a storm brewing. Hot lightning, vicious thunder, heavy wind. I told myself it was the weather that turned my blood so cold. But God help me, I think I knew. There was such a sharp, terrifying pain, such unreasonable fear. It consumed me.

For the first time, and the last, I went to The Towers. The rain began to slash as I beat on the door. The woman who answered was hysterical. I would have pushed past her, run through the house calling for Bianca, but at that moment, the police arrived.

She had jumped from the tower, thrown herself through the window onto the rocks. This is unclear now, as it was even then. I remember running, shouting for her over the howling wind. The lights of the house were blinding, slashing through the gloom. Men were already scrambling on the ridge and below with lanterns. I stood, looking down at her. My love. Taken from me. Not by her own hand. I could never accept that. But gone. Lost.

I would have leaped off that ridge myself. But she stopped me. I will swear it was her voice that stopped me. Instead, I sat on the ground, the rain pouring over me.

I could not join her then. Somehow I would have to live out my life without her. I have done so, and perhaps some good has come from the time I have spent here. The boy, my grandson. How Bianca would have loved him. There are times I take him to our cliffs and I'm sure she's there with us.

There are still Calhouns in The Towers. Bianca would have wanted that. Her children's children, and theirs. Perhaps one day another lonely young woman will walk those cliffs. I hope her fate is a kinder one.

I know, in my heart, that it is not ended yet. She waits for me. When my time comes at last, I will talk with Bianca again. I will love her as I once promised. Eternally.

Chapter 10

Holt waited for Trent in the pergola along the seawall. Lighting a cigarette, he looked over the wide lawn to The Towers. One of the gargoyles along the center peak had lost its head while the other sat grinning down, more charming than ferocious. There were clematis—he recognized it now—and roses climbing up to the first terrace. The old stone glowered in the hazy sunlight. There was really no other word for it, but the flowers gave it a kind of magical, Sleeping Beauty aura. Towers and turrets speared up, arrogant of form, dignified with age.

Scaffolding bracketed the west end, and the high whine of a power saw cut the air. A lift truck was parked under the balcony, its mechanism groaning as it hefted its load of equipment to a trio of bare-backed men. A radio jolted out tough rock.

Maybe it was right and just that the house held so tenaciously to the past even while it accepted the present, Holt mused. If it was possible for stone and mortar to absorb emotion and memory, The Towers had done so. Already he felt as though it harbored some of his.

The windows of the room where he had spent most of the night with Suzanna winked back at him. He remembered every second of those hours, every sigh, every movement. He also remembered that he had confused her. No, tenderness wasn't his style, he thought, but it had been easy with her.

She hadn't asked him for softness. She hadn't asked him for anything. Was that why he felt compelled to give? Without trying, she had tapped into something inside him he hadn't known was there—and was still more than a little uncomfortable with. Finding it, feeling it left him as vulnerable as she. He'd yet to work out the right way to tell her.

She deserved the music, the candlelight, the flowers. She deserved the soft poetic words. He was going to try to give them to her, no matter how big a fool it made him feel.

In the meantime, he had a job to do. He was going to find those damn emeralds for her. And he was going to put Livingston behind bars.

Holt tossed the cigarette away as he saw Trent come out of the house. In the pergola, they would have relative privacy. The clatter of construction echoed in countertime to the beat and drum of waves. Whatever they said wouldn't carry above ten feet. Anyone looking out of the house would see two men sharing a late-afternoon beer, away from the women.

Trent stepped inside and offered a bottle.

"Thanks." Holt leaned negligently against a post and lifted the beer. "Did you get the list?"

"Yeah." Trent took a seat on one of the stone benches so that he could watch the house as he drank. "We've only signed on four new men in the last month."

"References?"

"Of course." The faint annoyance in his tone was instinctive. "Sloan and I are well aware of security."

Holt merely shrugged. "A man liked Livingston wouldn't have any problem getting references. They'd cost him." Holt drank deeply. "But he'd get them."

"You'd know more about that sort of thing than I." Trent's eyes narrowed as he watched two of the men replacing shingles on the roof of the west wing. "But I have a hard time buying that he could be here, working right under our noses."

"Oh, he's here." Holt took out another cigarette, lighted it, then took a thoughtful drag. "Whoever tossed my place knew about the connection almost as soon as you did. Since none of you go around talking about the situation at cocktail parties, he'd have heard something here, in the house. He didn't sign on at the start of the job, because he was busy elsewhere. But the last few weeks…" He paused as the children ran out, dogs in tow, to race to their fort. "He wouldn't just sit and wait, not as long as there's a possibility you could knock out a wall and have the emeralds fall into your hand. And where better to keep an eye on things than inside?"

"It fits," Trent admitted. "But I don't like the idea of my wife, or any of the others, being that close." He thought of C.C., the baby she carried, and his eyes darkened. "If there's a chance you're right, I want to move on it."

"Give me the list, and I'll check it out. I've still got connections." Holt's gaze remained on the children. "He's not going to hurt any of them. That's a fact."

Trent nodded. He was a businessman and had never done anything more violent than a little boxing in college. But he would do whatever it took to protect his wife and unborn child. "I filled Max in, and Sloan and Amanda decided to break off their honeymoon. They should be here in a couple of hours."

That was good, Holt thought. It was best having the family all in one place. "What did Sloan tell her?"

"That there was some problem with the job." More comfortable now that wheels were in motion, Trent grinned a little. "If she finds out he's stringing her along, there'll be hell to pay."

"The less the women know, the better."

This time Trent laughed. "If any of them heard you say that, you'd lose three layers of skin. They're a tough bunch."

Holt thought of Suzanna. "They think they are."

"No, they are. It took me quite a while to accept it. Individually they're strong—velvet-coated steel. Not to mention stubborn, impulsive and feverishly loyal. Together..." Trent smiled again. "Well, I'll admit I'd rather face a pair of sumo wrestlers than the Calhoun women on a roll."

"When it's over, they can be as mad as they want."

"As long as they're safe," Trent finished, and noted that Holt was watching the children. "Great kids," he commented.

"Yeah. They're okay."

"They've got a hell of a mother." Trent drank contemplatively. "Too bad they don't have a real father."

Even the thought of Baxter Dumont made Holt's blood boil. "How much do you know about him?"

"More than I like. I know he put Suzanna through hell. He nearly broke her with the custody suit."

"Custody suit?" Stunned, Holt looked back. "He went after the kids?"

"He went after her," Trent corrected. "What better way? She doesn't talk about it. I got the story from C.C. Apparently he was annoyed that she filed for the divorce. Not good for his image, particularly since he's got his eye on a senate seat. He dragged her through a long, ugly court battle, trying to prove she was unstable and unfit."

"Bastard." Choking on rage, Holt turned away to flick the cigarette onto the rocks.

"He didn't want them. The idea was to ship them off to a boarding school. Or that was the threat. He backed off when Suzanna made the settlement."

His hands were on the stone rail now, fingers digging in. "What settlement?"

"She gave him damn near everything. He dropped the case so the arrangements could be made privately. He got the house, all the property, along with a chunk of her inheritance. She could have fought it, but she and the kids were already an emotional mess. She didn't want to take any chances with them, or put them through any more stress."

"No, she wouldn't." Holt drank in a futile attempt to wash the bitterness from his throat. "He's not going to hurt her or the kids anymore. I'll see to it."

"I thought you would." Trent rose, satisfied. He pulled a list out of his pocket and exchanged it for Holt's empty bottle. "Let me know what you find out."

"Yeah."

"The séance tonight." Trent saw Holt grimace and laughed again. "It may surprise you."

"The only thing that surprises me is that Coco talked me into it."

"If you plan on sticking around, you'll have to get used to being talked into all manner of things."

He was going to stick around, all right, Holt thought as Trent walked away. He just needed to find the right way to tell Suzanna. After glancing at the names on the list, Holt tucked it away. He'd make a couple of calls and see what he could dig up.

As he started across the lawn, the dogs galloped up to him, Fred devotedly pressing to Sadie's side. When they stopped jumping long enough to be petted, Fred lapped frantically at her face. Sadie tolerated it, then turned away and ignored him.

"They've got a name for women like you," Holt told her.

"Remember the Alamo!" Alex shouted. He stood spread legged on the roof of his fort, a plastic sword in his hand. Because he counted on his challenge being answered, his eyes gleamed as they met Holt's. "You'll never take us alive."

"Oh yeah?" Unable to resist, Holt moved closer. "What makes you think I want you, monkey brain?"

"'Cause we're the patriots and you're the evil invaders."

Jenny popped her head through an opening that served as a window. Before Holt could evade it, he was hit dead center of the chest with a splat of water from her pistol. Alex let out a triumphant hoot as Holt scowled down at his shirt.

"I suppose you know," Holt said slowly, "this means war."

As Jenny shrieked, he grabbed her and pulled her through the window. To her delight, he held her upside down so that her two blond ponytails brushed the grass.

"He's taken a hostage!" Alex bellowed. "Death to the last man." He scrambled inside then burst out of the doorway, brandishing his sword. Holt barely had time to right Jenny before the little missile plowed into him. "Off with his head," Alex chanted, echoed by his sister. Holt let his body go lax and took them both to the ground with him.

There were screams and giggles as he wrestled with them. It wasn't as easy as he'd supposed. They were both agile and slick, wriggling out of his hold to attack. He found himself at a disadvantage as Alex sat on his chest and Jenny found a spot on his ribs to tickle.

"I'm going to have to get rough," he warned them. When he took a spray of water in the face, he swore, making them both howl with laughter. A quick roll and he dislodged the pistol, then snatched it up to drench them both. With shrieks and giggles, they fell on him.

It was a wet and messy battle, and when he finally managed to pin them, they were all out of breath.

"I massacred you both," Holt managed. "Say uncle." Jenny poked a finger in his ribs, making him twitch. In defense he lowered his cheek to her neck and rubbed a day's worth of stubble over her skin.

"Uncle, uncle, uncle!" She screamed, gurgling with laughter. Satisfied, he used the same weapon on Alex until victorious, he rolled over and lay stomach down on the grass.

"You killed us," Alex admitted, not displeased. "But you're morally wounded."

"Yeah, but I think you mean mortally."

"Are you going to take a nap?" Jenny climbed onto his back to bounce. "Lilah sleeps in the grass sometimes."

"Lilah sleeps anywhere," Holt muttered.

"You can take a nap in my bed if you want," she invited, then pressed a curious finger on the edge of the scar she saw beneath his hitched-up T-shirt. "You have a hurt on your back."

"Uh-huh."

Alex was already scrambling to look. "Can I see?"

Holt tensed automatically, then forced himself to relax. "Sure."

As Alex pushed up the shirt, both children's eyes widened. It wasn't like the neat little scar they had both admired on his leg. This was long and jagged and mean, slashing from the waist so high up on his back they couldn't push the shirt up enough to see the end of it.

"Gee," was all Alex could think to say. He swallowed, then gamely touched a finger to the scar. "Did you get in a big fight?"

"Not exactly." He remembered the pain, the incredible flash of white heat. "One of the bad guys got me," he said, and hoped it would satisfy. When he felt Jenny's little mouth lower to his back, he went very still.

"Does it feel better now?" she asked.

"Yeah." He had to let out a long breath to steady his voice. "Thanks." Turning over, he sat up to brush a hand through her hair.

Suzanna stood a few feet away, watching them with her heart in her throat. She'd seen the battle from the kitchen doorway. It had touched her to see how easily Holt had joined in the game with her children. She'd been smiling when she'd started out to join them—then she had watched Jenny and Alex examining the scar on Holt's back, and Jenny's kiss to make it better. She had seen the look of ragged emotion on Holt's face when he'd turned to sweep his hand over her little girl's hair.

Now the three of them were on the grass, Jenny cuddled on his lap, Alex's arm slung affectionately around his shoulder. She took a moment to make certain her eyes were dry before she continued toward them.

"Is the war over?" she asked, and three pair of eyes lifted.

"He won," Alex told her.

"It doesn't look as though it was an easy victory." She scooped Jenny up when the girl lifted her arms. "You're all wet."

"He blasted us—but I got him first."

"That's my girl."

"And he's ticklish," Jenny confided. "*Real* ticklish."

"Is that so?" Suzanna sent Holt a slow smile. "I'll keep that in mind. Now you two scat. I noticed nobody put away the game you were playing."

"But, Mom—" Alex had his excuses ready, but she stopped them with a look.

"If you don't clean it up, I will," she said mildly. "But then I'll have your share of strawberry shortcake tonight."

That was a tough one. Alex agonized over it for a minute, then caved in. "I'll do it. Then I get Jenny's share."

"Do not." Jenny sprinted toward the house with her brother giving chase.

"Very smooth, Mom," Holt commented as he rose.

"I know their weaknesses." She put her arms around him, surprising and pleasing him. It was very rare for her to make the first move. "You're all wet, too."

"Sniper fire, but I picked them off like flies." Bringing her closer, he rested his cheek on her hair. "They're terrific kids, Suzanna. I'm, ah . . ." He didn't know how to tell her he'd fallen in love with them, any more than he knew how to tell her he'd fallen in love with their mother. "I'm getting you wet." Feeling awkward, he drew away.

Smiling, she touched a hand to his cheek. "Want to take a walk?"

He thought of the list in his pocket. It could wait an hour, he decided, and took her hand.

He'd known she would head to the cliffs. It seemed right that they would walk there as the shadows lengthened and the air cooled toward evening. She talked a little of the job she'd finished that day, he of the hull he'd repaired. But their minds weren't on work.

"Holt." She looked out to sea, her hand in his. "Will you tell me why you resigned from the force?" She felt his fingers stiffen, but didn't turn.

"It's done," he said flatly. "There's nothing to tell."

"The scar on your back—"

"I said it's done." He withdrew and pulled out a cigarette.

"I see." She absorbed the rejection. "Your past and your personal feelings about it are none of my business."

He took an impatient drag. "I didn't say that."

"You certainly did. You have the right to know all there is to know about me. I'm supposed to trust you with everything, unquestioningly. But I'm not to pry into what's yours."

He turned angry eyes on her. "What is this, some kind of test?"

"Call it what you like," she tossed back. "I'd hoped you trusted me by now, that you cared enough to let me in."

"I do care, damn it. Don't you know it still rips me up to remember it? Ten years of my life, Suzanna. Ten years." He whirled away to flick the cigarette over the edge.

"I'm sorry." Instinctively she put her hands on his shoulders to soothe. "If anyone knows how painful it is to dredge up old wounds, it's me. Why don't we go back? I'll see if I can find you a clean shirt."

"No." His jaw was clenched, his body tight as a spring. "You want to know, you've got a right. I tossed it in because I couldn't handle it. I spent ten years telling myself I could make a difference, that none of the crap I had to wade through would affect me. I could rub shoulders with dealers and pimps and victims all day and not lose any sleep at night. If I had to kill somebody, it was line of duty. Not something you want to think about too much, but something you live with. I saw a few cops burn out along the way, but it wasn't going to happen to me."

She said nothing, just continued to rub at the knotted muscles of his shoulders while she waited for him to go on. He kept looking out to sea, smelling her, and the dusky scent of the wild roses that were at peak.

"Vice takes you into the pits, Suzanna. You get so you understand the people you're trying to wipe out. You think like them. You have to when you go under, or you don't come out again. There are things I'm never going to tell you, because I do care. Ugly things, and I just…" He closed his eyes, and jammed his hands into his pockets. "I just didn't want to see it anymore. I was already thinking about coming back here—just sort of kicking it around."

Suddenly weary, he lifted his hands to rub the heels over his eyes. "I was tired, Suzanna, and I wanted to live like a normal person again. The kind who doesn't strap on a gun every day or make deals with slime in back rooms. We were on a routine investigation, looking for a small-time dealer who we thought we could pressure information out of. Doesn't matter why," he said impatiently. "Anyway, we got a tip where to find him, and when we cornered him in this little dive, he snapped. Turned out the jerk had about twenty thousand in coke strapped under his clothes, and more than a couple lines in his system. He panicked. He dragged some half-stoned woman with him and bolted."

His palms were beginning to sweat, so he wiped them against his jeans. "My partner and I separated to cut him off. He pulled the woman out in the alley. With us on either end, he didn't have any hope of getting away. I had my weapon out. It was dark. The garbage had turned."

He could still smell it, rank and fetid, as the sweat began to run down his back. "I could hear my partner coming up the other side, and hear the woman crying. He'd sliced her up a little and she was balled up on the concrete. I couldn't be sure how bad she was hurt. I remember thinking the creep was going to be up for more than distribution. Then he jumped me. He had the knife in before I could get off a shot."

He could still feel it ripping through his flesh, still smell his own blood. "I knew I was dead, and I kept thinking that I wouldn't be able to come home. That I was going to die in that damn alley with the stink of that garbage. I killed him as I went down. That's what they told me. I don't remember. The thing I remember next was waking up in the hospital feeling like I'd been sliced in half and sewn back together. I told myself that if I made it, I was coming back here. Because I knew if I had to walk down another alley, I wouldn't come back out."

Suzanna had her arms tight around him now, her cheek pressed against his back. "Do you think because you came home instead of facing another alley, you failed?"

"I don't know."

"I did, for a long time. No one had put a knife in my back, but I came to understand that if I stayed with Bax, if I'd kept that promise, part of me would die. I chose survival, do you think I should be ashamed of that?"

"No." He turned, taking her shoulder. "No."

She lifted her hands to cup his face. In her eyes was understanding, and the sympathy he couldn't have accepted even a week before. "Neither do I. I hate what happened to you, but I'm glad it brought you here." Offering comfort, she touched her lips to his. Slowly, with a sweetness that was unbearably moving, she felt him let go.

His body relaxed against hers even as he pulled her closer. His mouth softened even as it heated. Here, at last, was the next level. There was not only passion, not only tenderness, but trust. As the wind whispered through the wild grass and the bright, brave flowers, she thought she heard something else, something so quiet and lovely that it brought tears to her eyes. When he lifted his head, when she saw his face, she knew he'd heard it, too. She smiled.

"We're not alone here," she murmured. "They must have stood in this same spot, holding each other like this. Wanting each other like this." Filled with the moment, she pressed his hand to her lips. "Holt, do you believe that fate and time can run in a circle?"

"I'm beginning to."

"They still come here, to wait. I wonder if they ever find each other. I think they will, if we can make things right." She kissed him again, then slipped an arm around his waist. "Let's go home. I have a feeling it's going to be an interesting evening."

"Suzanna," he began as they started back. "After the séance..." He trailed off, looking pained, and made her laugh.

"Don't worry, at The Towers we only have friendly ghosts."

"Right. Just don't expect me to put much stock in chanting and trances, but anyway, I was wondering if after—look, I know you don't like to leave the kids, but I thought you could come back to my place for a little while. There's some stuff I want to talk to you about."

"What stuff?"

"Just—stuff," he said lamely. If he was going to ask her to marry him, he wanted to do it right. "I'd appreciate it if you could get away for an hour or two."

"All right, if it's important. Is it about the emeralds?"

"No. It's...I'd rather wait, okay? Listen, I've got a couple of things to do before we start calling up spirits."

"Aren't you going to stay for dinner?"

"I can't. I'll be back." As they came up the slope and passed the stone wall, he pulled her against him for a brief hard kiss. "See you later."

She frowned after him and might have pursued, but her name was called from the second-level terrace. Shading her eyes, she saw her sister.

"Amanda!" With a laugh, she raced across the lawn and up the stone steps. "What are you doing back?" She gathered the new bride into her arms and squeezed. "You look wonderful—but you were supposed to be gone nearly another week. Is anything wrong?"

"No, nothing." She kissed both of Suzanna's cheeks. "Come on, I'll fill you in."

"Where are we going?"

"Bianca's tower. Family meeting."

They climbed up, then went inside to ascend the narrow circular stairs that led to the tower. C.C. and Lilah were already waiting.

"Aunt Coco?" Suzanna asked.

"We'll let her know what we discuss," Amanda answered. "But it would look too suspicious if we pulled her up here now."

With a nod, Suzanna took a seat on the floor at Lilah's feet. "So I take it this is women only?"

"No more than they deserve," C.C. said, and crossed her arms. "They've been skulking off to have their boy's club meetings for days now. It's time we set things straight."

"Max has definitely got something up his sleeve," Lilah put in. "He's acting much too innocent. And, he's been hanging around the construction crew for the last couple of days."

"I don't suppose he wants to learn how to set tile," Suzanna murmured.

"If he did, he'd have twenty books on it by now." Lilah rolled her shoulders and leaned back. "And this afternoon when I got home from work, I saw Trent and Holt powwowing in the pergola. Somebody who didn't know better might have thought they were just hanging out and having a beer, but something was going on."

"So they know something they're not telling us." Thoughtful, Suzanna drummed her fingers on her knees. She'd had a feeling something was going on, but Holt had done such a good job of distracting her, she hadn't acted on it.

"Sloan had a long, mumbling conversation with Trent on the phone two days ago. He claimed there was some problem with materials that he had to see to personally." Tossing her hair, Amanda gave a sniff. "And he thought I was stupid enough to buy it. He wanted to get back because they're on to something—and they want to keep the little women out of the way."

"Fat chance," C.C. muttered. "I'm for marching downstairs right now and demanding they tell us whatever they know. If Trent thinks I'm going to sit around twiddling my thumbs while he handles Calhoun business, he's got another think coming."

"Bamboo shoots and brass knuckles," Lilah mused, not terribly displeased with the image. "That'll just make them more stubborn. Male egos on the line, ladies. Get out your hard hats and flak jackets."

Suzanna laughed and patted her leg. "You've got a point. Let's see what we know... Sloan gets called back so they must think they're getting close. I can't see them being secretive if they thought they'd hit on the location of the emeralds."

"Neither can I." Because she thought best on her feet, Amanda paced. "Remember how stiff-necked they got when we decided to look for the yacht Max had jumped off? Sloan threatened to...what was it? Hog-tie," she said viciously. "Yes, that was it. He threatened to hog-tie me if I so much as thought about trying to find Livingston on my own."

"Trent won't even discuss Livingston with me," C.C. added, then wrinkled her nose. "It isn't good for me to be upset in my delicate condition."

From her sprawled perch on the window seat, Lilah gave a hoot. "I'd like to see any man go through childbirth then have the nerve to call a woman delicate."

"Holt says that Livingston is out of our league. *Ours,*" Suzanna explained, making a circular motion with her finger. "Not his."

"Jerk." C.C. plopped down on the window seat beside Lilah. "So are we agreed? They've got a line on Livingston and they're keeping it to themselves."

The vote was unanimous.

"Now, we need to find out what they know." Amanda stopped pacing and tapped her foot. "Suggestions?"

"Well..." Suzanna looked down at her nails and smiled. "I say divide and conquer. The four of us should be able to dig information out of them—each in our own way. Then we rendezvous here, tomorrow, same time, and put the pieces together."

"I like it." Lilah sat up to put a hand on Suzanna's shoulder. "The poor guys haven't got a chance."

Suzanna reached up to lay her hand on Lilah's as Amanda and C.C. added theirs. "And when it's over," she said, "maybe they'll realize the Calhoun women take care of their own."

Chapter 11

Holt had never felt more ridiculous in his life. He was about to take part in a séance. If that wasn't bad enough, before the night was over, he was going to ask the woman who was currently laughing at him, to be his wife.

"It isn't a firing squad." Chuckling, Suzanna patted his cheek. "Relax."

"Damn foolishness is what it is." From the foot of the table, Colleen scowled at everyone in general. "The idea of talking to spirits. Hogwash. And you—" She stabbed a finger toward Coco. "Not that you ever kept an ounce of sense in that flighty head of yours, but I'd have thought even you would know better than to raise these girls on such bilge."

"It isn't bilge." As always, the steely gaze made Coco tremble, but she felt fairly safe with the length of the table between them. "You'll see after we begin."

"What I see is a table full of dolts." Though her face remained in stern lines, Colleen's heart melted as she looked up at the portrait of her mother, which had been hung over the fireplace. "I'll give you ten thousand for it."

Holt shrugged. She'd been dogging him for days about buying the painting. "It isn't for sale."

"If you think you're going to hose me, young man, you're mistaken. I know a hustle."

He grinned at her. He would have bet his last nickel she'd hustled plenty herself. "I'm not selling it."

"It's worth more, anyway," Lilah put in, unable to resist. "Isn't that right, Professor?"

"Well, actually, yes." Max cleared his throat. "Christian Bradford's early work is increasing in value. At Sotheby's two years ago, one of his seascapes went for thirty-five thousand."

"What are you," Colleen snapped, "his agent?"

Max swallowed a grin. "No, ma'am."

"Then hush. Fifteen thousand, and not a penny more."

Holt ran his tongue around his teeth. "Not interested."

"Maybe if we got on with the matter at hand." Coco held her breath, waiting for her aunt's wrath to fall. When Colleen only muttered and scowled, she relaxed. "Amanda, dear, light the candles. Now we must all try to empty our minds of all worries, all doubts. Concentrate on Bianca." When the candles were glowing, and the chandelier extinguished, she gave a last glance around the table. "Join hands."

Holt grumbled under his breath but took Suzanna's hand in his right, Lilah's in his left.

"Focus on the picture," Coco whispered, closing her eyes to bring it into her mind since it was behind her on the wall. Tingles of anticipation raced up and down her spine. "She's close to us, very close to us. She wants to help."

Holt let his mind drift because it helped him forget what he was doing. He tried to imagine what it would be like when he and Suzanna were alone in the cottage. He'd bought candles. Not the sturdy type he kept in the kitchen drawer for power outages, but slender white tapers that smelled of jasmine.

There was champagne chilling beside the six-pack in his refrigerator, and two new clear flutes beside his coffee mugs. Even now the jeweler's box was burning a hole in his hip pocket.

Tonight, he thought, he'd take the step. The words would come exactly as he planned. The music would be playing. She would open the box, look inside. . . .

Her hands were draped with emeralds. He frowned, giving himself a little shake. That wasn't right. He hadn't bought her emeralds. But the image focused so clearly. Suzanna on her knees holding emeralds. Three glittering tiers flanked by icy diamonds and centered by a glowing teardrop stone of dreamy green.

The Calhoun necklace. He felt the chill on his neck and ignored it. He'd seen the picture Max had found in the old library book. He knew what the emeralds looked like. It was the atmosphere, the humming silence and the flickering candles that made him think of them. That made him see them.

He didn't believe in visions. But when he closed his eyes to clear it from his mind, it seemed imprinted there. Suzanna kneeling on the floor with emeralds dripping from her fingers.

He felt a hand on his shoulder and looked around. There was no one there, only shadows and light thrown by the candles. But the feeling remained, with an urgency that had his hackles rising.

It was crazy, he told himself. And it was time to put an end to the whole insane business.

"Listen," he began. And the portrait of Bianca crashed to the floor.

Coco gave a piping squeak and jolted out of the chair. "Oh, my. Oh, my goodness," she murmured, patting her speeding heart.

Amanda was already racing forward. "Oh, I hope it isn't damaged."

"I don't think it will be." Lilah released Holt's hand. "Do you?"

The clear and steady gaze made him uncomfortable. Ignoring her, he turned to Suzanna. Her hand was like ice in his. "What is it? What's wrong?"

"Nothing." But she gave a quick shudder. "I think you'd better check the portrait."

He rose to go over where the others were crouched. As he did, Suzanna looked down the length of the table at her great-aunt. Colleen's white skin had paled like glass. Her eyes were dark and damp. Without a word, Suzanna rose and poured her a brandy. "It's going to be all right," she murmured, laying a hand on the thin shoulder.

"The frame cracked." Sloan ran a finger along it before he rose. "Funny that it would fall that way. Those nails are sturdy."

Holt started to shrug it off, but when he bent closer to where the frame had separated from the backing, he went very still. "There's something between the canvas and the back." Hefting the portrait, he laid it facedown on the table. "I need a knife."

Sloan pulled out his pocketknife and offered it. Holt made a long thin slit just beneath the cracked frame and slid out several sheets of paper.

"What is it?" The question was muffled as Coco had her hands pressed to her mouth.

"It's my grandfather's writing." The emotion sprang up strong and fast. It churned in Holt's eyes as he lifted them to Suzanna's. "It looks like a kind of diary. It's dated 1965."

"Sit down, dear." Coco put a comforting hand on his shoulder. "Trent, would you pour the brandy? I'll brew some tea for C.C."

He did need to sit, and he hoped the drink would steady him. For now, he could only stare at the papers and see his grandfather. Sitting on the back porch of the cottage, watching the water. Standing in his loft, slashing paint on canvas. Walking on the cliffs, telling a young boy stories.

When Suzanna came back to lay a hand on his, he turned his palm up and gripped her fingers. "It's been there all this time, and I didn't know."

"You weren't meant to know," she said quietly. "Until tonight." When he looked at her again, she curled her fingers tight around his. "Some things we just have to take on faith."

"Something happened tonight. Something upset you."

"I'll tell you. Not yet."

Composed, Coco brought in the tea, then took her seat. "Holt, whatever your grandfather wrote belongs to you. No one here will ask you to share it. If after you read it, you feel you prefer to keep it to yourself, we'll understand."

He glanced down at the papers again, then lifted the first sheet. "We'll read it together." He took a long breath, kept Suzanna's hand tight in his. " 'The moment I saw her, my life changed.' "

No one spoke as Holt read through his grandfather's memories. But around the table, hands linked again.

There was no sound but his voice and the wind breathing through the trees outside the windows. When he was finished, the room remained silent.

Lilah spoke first, her voice thick with tears while others slid down her cheeks. "He never stopped loving her. Always, even though he made a life for himself, he loved her."

"How he must have felt, to come here that night and find out she was gone." Amanda leaned her head on Sloan's shoulder.

"But he was right." Suzanna watched one of her tears drop on the back of Holt's hand. "She didn't take her own life. She couldn't have. Not only did she love him too much, but she would have tolerated anything to protect her children."

"No, she didn't jump." Colleen whispered the words. She lifted her snifter with a trembling hand, then set it down again. "I've never spoken of that night, not to anyone. Through the years I've sometimes thought what I saw was a dream. A terrible, terrible nightmare."

Determined, she cleared her blurred vision and strengthened her voice. "He understood her, her Christian. He couldn't have written about her that way and not have known her heart. She was beautiful, but she was also kind and generous. I have never been loved as I was loved by my mother. And I have never hated as I hated my father."

She straightened her shoulders. Already the burden had lessened. "I was too young to understand her unhappiness or her desperation. In those days a man ruled his home, his family, as he chose. No one dared to question my father. But I remember the day she brought the puppy home, the little puppy my father would not have in his home. She did send us upstairs, but I hid at the top and listened. I had never heard her raise her voice to him before. Oh, she was valiant. And he was cruel. I didn't understand the names he called her. Then.''

She paused to drink again, for her throat was dry and the memory bitter. ''She defended me against him, knowing as even I knew he barely tolerated me, a female. When he left the house after the argument, I was glad. I prayed that night he would never come back. The next day, my mother told me we were going to take a trip. She hadn't told my brothers yet, but I was the eldest. She wanted me to understand that she would take care of us, that nothing bad would happen.

''Then, he came back. I knew she was upset, even frightened. I was to stay in my room until she came for me. But she didn't come. It grew late, and there was a storm. I wanted my mother.'' Colleen pressed her lips together. ''She wasn't in her room, so I went up to the tower where she often spent her time. I heard them as I crept up the stairs. The door was open and I heard them. The terrible argument. He was raging, crazed with fury. She told him that she would no longer live with him, that she wanted nothing from him but her children and her freedom.''

Because Colleen was shaking, Coco rose and walked down to take her hand.

''He struck her. I heard the slap and raced to the door. But I was afraid, too afraid to go in. She had a hand to her cheek, and her eyes were blazing. Not with fear, with fury. I will always remember that there was no fear in her at the end. He threatened her with scandal. He screamed at her that if she left his house, she would never lay eyes on any of his children again. She would never ruin his reputation. She would never throw an obstacle in the path of his ambitions.''

Though her lips trembled, Colleen lifted her chin. ''She did not beg. She did not weep. She hurled words back at him like thunderbolts." Fisting a hand, she pressed it to her mouth to smother her own tears. "She was magnificent. Her children would never be taken from her, and scandal be damned. Did he think she cared what people thought of her? Did he think she feared his power to have society shun her? She would take her children and she would make a life where both she and they could be loved. And I think it was that which drove him mad. The idea that she would choose another man over him. Over him. Fergus Calhoun. That she would toss his money and power and position back at him, rather than bow to his wishes. He grabbed her, lifting her from her feet, shaking her, screaming into her face while his own purpled with rage. I think I screamed then, and hearing me, she began to fight. When she struck him, he threw her aside. I heard the crash of the glass. He ran to it, roaring for her, but she was gone. How long he stood there while the wind and rain poured in, I don't know. When he turned his face was white, his eyes glazed. He walked past me without even seeing me. I went inside, over to the broken window and looked down until Nanny came and carried me away."

Coco pressed a kiss to the white hair, then gently stroked. "Come with me, dear. I'll take you upstairs. Lilah will bring you a nice cup of tea."

"Yes, I'll be right there." Lilah wiped her cheeks dry. "Max?"

"I'll come with you." He slipped an arm around her waist as Coco led Bianca's daughter from the room.

"Poor little girl," Suzanna murmured, and let her head rest on Holt's shoulder as he drove away from The Towers. "To have seen something so horrible, to have had to live with it all of her life. I think of Jenny—"

"Don't." He put a firm hand over hers. "You got out. Bianca didn't." He waited a moment. "You knew, didn't you? Before Colleen told us the story."

"I knew she hadn't committed suicide. I can't explain how, but tonight, I knew. It was as if she was standing right behind me."

He thought of the sensation of having a hand on his shoulder. "Maybe she was. After a night like this, it's hard for me to convince myself the picture falling off the wall was a coincidence."

Suzanna closed her eyes. "It was beautiful, what your grandfather wrote about her. If we never find the emeralds, we have that—we'll know she had that. To love that way," she said on a sigh. "It hardly seems possible. I don't want to think of the tragedy or sadness, but of the time they had together. Dancing in the wild roses."

He'd never danced with her in the sunlight, Holt thought. Or read her poetry or promised her eternal love.

When they reached the cottage, Sadie leaped out the back window of the car to race around the yard and sniff at the flower bed she'd planted for him. When Holt leaned across her, Suzanna looked down in surprise.

"What are you doing?"

"I'm opening the door for you." He shoved it open. "If I'd gotten out to do it, you wouldn't have waited."

Amused, Suzanna stepped out. "Thank you."

"You're welcome." When he reached the house, he unlocked the front door, then held that open. Keeping her face sober, Suzanna inclined her head as she slipped past him.

"Thank you."

Holt just let the screen slam shut. Brow lifted, Suzanna scanned the room.

"You've done something different."

"I cleaned it up," he muttered.

"Oh. It looks nice. You know, Holt, I've been meaning to ask you if you think Livingston is still on the island."

"Why? Did something happen?"

His response was much too abrupt, Suzanna noted and moved casually around the room. "No, I've just been wondering where he may be staying, what his next move might be." She ran a fingertip down one of the candles he'd bought. "Any ideas?"

"How should I know?"

"You're the expert on crime."

"And I told you to leave Livingston to me."

"And I told you I couldn't do that. Maybe I'll start poking around on my own."

"Try it and I'll handcuff you and lock you in a closet."

"The urban counterpart to hog-tying," she murmured. "I wouldn't have to try it if you'd tell me what you know. Or what you think."

"What brought this up now?"

She moved her shoulder. "Since we have a little time to ourselves, I thought we could talk about it."

"Look, why don't you just sit down?" He pulled out his lighter.

"What are you doing?"

"I'm lighting candles." His nerves were stretching like taffy. "What does it look like I'm doing?"

She did sit, and steepled her hands. "Since you're so cranky, I have to assume that you do know something."

"You don't have to assume anything except your ticking me off." He stalked to the stereo.

"How close are you?" she asked as a bluesy sax filled the air.

"I'm nowhere." Since that was a lie, he decided to temper it with part of the truth. "I think he's in the area because he broke in here and took a look around a couple weeks ago.''

"What?" She catapulted out of the chair. "A couple of weeks ago, and you didn't tell me?"

"What were you going to do about it?" he countered. "Pull out a magnifying glass and deer-hunter's hat?"

"I had a right to know."

"Now you know. Just sit down, will you? I'll be back in a minute."

He stalked out and she began to pace. Holt knew more than he was saying, but at least she'd annoyed a piece from him. Livingston was close, close enough that he'd known Holt might have something of interest. The fact that Holt was wound like a top at the moment made her think something more was working on him. It shouldn't be difficult, she thought, now that she already had him irritated, to push a little more out of him.

The candles were scented, she noted, and smiled to herself. She couldn't imagine that he'd bought jasmine candles on purpose. Especially a half a dozen of them. She traced a finger over the calla lilies he'd stuck—not very artistically—in a vase. Maybe working with flowers was getting to him, she thought. He wasn't pretending so hard not to like them.

When he came back in, she smiled then looked puzzled. "Is that champagne?"

"Yeah." And he was thoroughly disgusted. He'd imagined she'd be charmed. Instead she questioned everything. "Do you want some or not?"

"Sure." The curt invitation was so typical she didn't take offense. After he'd poured, she tapped her glass absently against his. "Now, if you're sure it was Livingston who broke in, I think—"

"One more word," he said with dangerous calm. "One more word about Livingston and I'll pour the rest of the bottle over your hard head."

She sipped, knowing she'd have to be careful if she didn't want to waste a bottle of champagne and end up with sticky hair. "I'm only trying to get a clear picture."

He let out what was close to a roar of frustration and spun away. Champagne sloshed over his glass as he paced. "She wants a clear picture, and she's blind as a bat. I shoveled two months' worth of dust out of this place. I bought candles and flowers. I had to listen to some jerk try to teach me about wine. That's the picture, damn it."

She'd wanted to irritate information from him, not infuriate him. "Holt—"

"Just sit down and shut up. I should have known this would get screwed up. God knows why I tried to do it this way."

A light dawned, and she smiled. He'd set the stage, but she'd been too focused on her own scheme to take note. "Holt, it's very sweet of you to do all of this. I'm sorry if I didn't seem to appreciate it. If you wanted me to come here tonight so we could make love—"

"I don't want to make love with you." He swore, viciously. "Of course I want to make love with you, but that's not it. I'm trying to ask you to marry me, damn it, so will you sit *down!*"

Since her legs had dissolved from knees to toe, she slid into a chair.

"This is perfect." He gulped down champagne and started pacing again. "Just perfect. I'm trying to tell you that I'm crazy about you, that I don't think I can live without you, and all you can do is ask me what I'm doing and nag me about some obsessed jewel thief."

Cautiously she brought the glass to her lips. "Sorry."

"You should be sorry," he said bitterly. "I was ready to make a fool of myself tonight for you, and you won't even let me do that. I've been in love with you nearly half my life. Even when I moved away, I couldn't get you out of my mind. You spoiled every other woman for me. I'd start to get close to someone, and then...they weren't you. They just weren't you, and I'd never even gotten past your back door."

In love. The two words reeled in her head. *In love.* "I thought you didn't even like me."

"I couldn't stand you." He raked his free hand through his hair. "Every time I looked at you I wanted you so much I couldn't breathe. My mouth would go dry and my stomach would knot, and you'd just smile and keep walking." His dark and turbulent eyes locked on hers. "I wanted to strangle you. You run into me and knock me off my bike and I'm lying there bleeding and—and mortified. You're leaning over me, smelling like heaven and running your hands over me to see if anything was broken. One more minute of that and I'd have dragged you onto the asphalt with me." He rubbed his hand over his face. "Lord, you were only sixteen."

"You swore at me."

His face was a picture of anger and disgust. "Damn right, I swore at you. You were better off with that than with what I wanted to do to you." He was calming, little by little. He sipped again but kept pacing. "I talked myself into believing it was just an adolescent fantasy. Even a crush, and that was tough to swallow. Then you came walking across my yard. I looked at you and my throat went dry, my stomach knotted up. We were both past being adolescents."

He set his glass down, noting that she was gripping hers with both hands. Her eyes were huge and fixed on his. Cursing both of them, he fumbled for a cigarette then tossed it aside.

"I'm not good at this, Suzanna. I thought I could pull it off. Set the mood, you know? And after you'd had enough champagne, I'd convince you I could make you happy."

She couldn't relax her grip. She tried but couldn't. "I don't need champagne and candlelight, Holt."

He smiled a little. "Babe, you were born for it. I could lie to you and tell you I'll remember to give it to you every night. But I won't."

She looked down at her glass and wondered if she was ready to take this sort of chance again. Loving him was one thing. Being loved by him was incredible. But marriage . . . "Why don't you just tell me the truth then?"

He walked over to sit on the arm of the couch and face her. "I love you. I've never felt about anyone the way I feel about you. Whatever happens, I'll never feel like this about anyone else again. There's no taking back what's happened to either of us in the last few years, but maybe we can make things better for both of us. For the kids."

Her eyes changed, darkened. "It may never be easy. Bax would always be their legal father."

"He wouldn't be the one who loved them." When her eyes filled, he shook his head. No, she hadn't needed candlelight and champagne to make her vulnerable and open to his needs. Only a mention of her children. "I won't use them to get to you. I know I could, but first it has to be between you and me. Maybe I'm stuck on them, and I want to—I think I could be pretty good at being their father, but I don't want you to marry me for them."

She took a deep breath. Odd, her fingers had relaxed on the stem of the glass without her being aware. "I never wanted to love anyone again. And I certainly never wanted to get married." Her lips curved. "Until you." Setting the glass aside, she reached for his hand. "I can't claim to have loved you as long, but you couldn't love me more than I love you."

He didn't settle for her hand, but pulled her into his arms. When he at last managed to tear his mouth from hers, he buried his face in her hair. "Don't tell me you need to think about it, Suzanna."

"I don't need to think about it." She couldn't remember the last time her heart and mind had been so at peace. "I'll marry you."

Before the words were out of her mouth, she was tumbling with him onto the couch. She was laughing as they tugged at each other's clothes, laughing still when the frantic movements sent them rolling onto the floor.

"I knew it." She nipped his bare shoulder. "You did bring me here to make love."

"Can I help it if you can't keep your hands off me?" He trailed a necklace of quick kisses around her throat.

She smiled, tilting her head to give him easy access. "Holt, did you really think about pulling me down on the street after you'd fallen off your bike."

"After you'd run into me," he corrected, nuzzling her ear. "Yeah. Let me show you what I had in mind."

Later they lay like rag dolls on the floor, a tangle of limbs. When she could manage it, she lifted her head from his chest. "It was much better that we didn't try that twelve years ago."

Lazily he opened his eyes. She was smiling down at him, her hair brushing his shoulders, the candlelight glowing in her eyes. "Much better. I wouldn't have had any skin left on my back."

She chuckled then shifted to trace the shape of his face. "You always scared me a little. Looking so dark and dangerous. And, of course, the girls used to talk about you."

"Oh, yeah? What did they say?"

"I'll tell you when you're sixty. You could probably use it then." He pinched her, but she only laughed then rested her cheek on his. "When you're sixty, we'll be an old married couple with grandchildren."

He liked the thought of it. "And you still won't be able to keep your hands off me."

"And I'll remind you of the night you asked me to marry you, when you gave me flowers and candlelight, then shouted at me and raged up and down the room, making me love you even more."

"If that's all it takes, you'll be delirious about me by the time I'm sixty."

"I already am." She lowered her mouth to his.

"Suzanna." He drew her closer, started to roll her under him, then swore. "It's your own fault," he said as he nudged her aside.

"What?"

"You were supposed to be sitting over there, dazed by my romantic abilities." He fought to untangle his jeans and pull the jeweler's box from the pocket. "Then I was going to get down on one knee."

Eyes wide, she stared at the box, then at him. "You were not."

"Yes, I was. I was going to feel like an idiot, but I was going to do it. You've got no one to blame but yourself that we're lying naked on the floor. Here."

"You bought me a ring," she whispered.

"There could be a frog in there for all you know." Impatient with her, he flipped up the top himself. "I didn't want to give you diamonds." He shrugged when she said nothing, only stared into the box. "I figured you'd already had those. I thought about emeralds, but those are something you will have. And this is more like your eyes."

When the tears blurred her vision, the light refracted. There were diamonds, tiny, lovely stones in a heart shape about the deep and brilliant sapphire. They weren't cold, as the ones she had sold, but warmed by the rich blue fire they encircled.

Holt watched the first tear fall with a great deal of discomfort. "If you don't like it, we can take it back. You can pick out what you want."

"It's beautiful." She dashed a tear away with the back of her hand. "I'm sorry. I hate to cry. It's just so beautiful, and you bought it for me because you love me. And when I put it on—" she lifted drenched eyes to his "—I'm yours."

He dropped his brow to hers. Those were the words he'd wanted. The ones he'd needed. Taking the ring from the box, he slipped it onto her finger. "You're mine." He kissed her fingers, then her lips. "I'm yours." Bringing her close again, he remembered his grandfather's words. "Eternally."

Chapter 12

Suzanna took the children to the shop with her in the morning. She couldn't tell the rest of her family the news until she'd gauged Alex's and Jenny's feelings. The day was bright and hot. Knowing it would be a busy one, she arrived a full hour before opening. Because they wanted to check the herbs they had planted, she took them into the greenhouse to look at the tender shoots.

She let them argue for a while over whose plants would be the biggest or the best, supervising as they gave the shoots their morning drink.

"Do you guys like Holt?" she asked casually, nerves drumming.

"He's neat." Alex was tempted to turn the sprayer on his sister, but he'd gotten in trouble the last time he'd indulged himself.

"He plays with us sometimes." Jenny danced from foot to foot, waiting her turn. "I like when he throws me up in the air."

"I like him, too." Suzanna relaxed a little.

"Does he throw you up in the air?" Jenny wanted to know.

"No." With a laugh, Suzanna ruffled her hair.

"He could. He's got big muscles." Reluctantly Alex passed the sprayer to his sister. "He let me feel them." Screwing up his face, Alex flexed his own. Obliging, Suzanna pinched the tiny biceps.

"Wow. You're pretty tough."

"That's what he said."

"I was wondering . . ." Suzanna wiped nervous hands on her jeans. "How would you feel if he lived with us, all the time?"

"That'd be good," Jenny decided. "He plays with us even when we don't ask."

One down, Suzanna thought and turned to her son. "Alex?"

He shuffled his feet, frowning a little. "Are you going to get married like C.C. and Amanda?"

Sharp little devil, she thought, and crouched down. "I was thinking about it. What do you think?"

"Do I have to wear a dumb tuxedo again?"

She smiled and stroked his cheek. "Probably."

"Is he going to be our uncle, like Trent and Sloan and Max?" Jenny asked.

Suzanna got up to turn off the spray before answering her daughter. "No. He'd be your stepfather."

Brother and sister exchanged looks. "Would he still like us?"

"Of course he would, Jenny."

"Would we have to go away and live someplace else?"

She sighed and combed a hand through Alex's hair. "No. He would come to live with us at The Towers, or maybe we'd go and live with him at his cottage. We'd be a family."

Alex thought it over. "Would he be Kevin's stepfather, too?"

"No." She had to kiss him. "Megan's Kevin's mom, and maybe one day she'll fall in love and get married. Then Kevin will have a father."

"Did you fall in love with Holt?" Jenny asked.

"Yes, I did." She felt Alex shift uncomfortably and smiled. "I'd like to marry him so we could all live together. But Holt and I both wanted to see how you felt about it."

"I like him," Jenny announced. "He lets me ride on his shoulders."

Alex shrugged, a bit more cautious. "Maybe it's okay."

Concerned, Suzanna rose. "We can talk about it some more. Let's go set up."

They stepped out of the greenhouse just as Holt pulled up in the graveled lot. He knew he'd told her he'd wait until lunchtime, but he hadn't been able to. He'd awakened realizing he'd rather face another alley than those two kids who could so easily reject him. He stuffed his hands into his pockets and tried to look casual.

"Hi."

"Hi." Suzanna wanted to reach out to him, but her children held her hands.

"I thought I'd drop by and . . . how's it going?"

Jenny gave him a shy smile and huddled closer to her mother. "Mom says you're going to get married and be our stepfather and live with us."

Holt had to knock back an urge to shuffle his feet. "That's the plan."

Alex tightened his fingers around Suzanna's as he stared up at Holt. "Are you going to yell at us?"

After a quick glance at Suzanna, Holt stooped down until he was eye to eye with the boy. "Maybe. If you need it."

Alex trusted that answer more than he would have an unqualified no. "Do you hit?" He remembered the swats he'd received during his vacation. They'd insulted more than hurt, but he still resented it.

Holt put a hand under the boy's chin and held it firm. "No," he said, and the look in his eyes made Alex believe. "But I might hang you up by your thumbs, or boil you in oil. If I get really mad, I'll stake you to an anthill."

Alex's lips twitched, but he wasn't finished with the interrogation. "Are you going to make Mom cry like he did?"

"Alex," Suzanna began, but Holt cut her off.

"I might sometimes, if I'm stupid. But not on purpose. I love her a lot, so I want to make her happy. Sometimes I might screw up."

Alex frowned and considered. "Are you going to do all that kissing stuff? Since Trent and Sloan and Max came, there's always kissing."

"Yeah." Holt's face relaxed into a smile. "I'm going to do all that kissing stuff."

"But you won't like it," Alex said, hopeful. "You'll just do it 'cause Mom likes it."

"Sorry, I like it, too."

"Jeez," Alex muttered, deflated.

"Do it now." Jenny danced and giggled. "Do it now so I can see."

Willing to oblige, Holt straightened and pulled Suzanna close. When he took his lips from Suzanna's, Alex was red faced and Jenny was clapping. "I hate to tell you," Holt said soberly. "but one day you'll like it, too."

"Uh-uh. I'd rather eat dirt."

With a laugh, Holt hoisted him up, relieved and delighted when Alex slung a friendly arm around his neck. "Tell me that in ten years."

"I like it," Jenny insisted, and tugged on his leg. "I like it now. Kiss me." He hauled her in his other arm and kissed her tiny, waiting lips. She smiled, big blue eyes beaming. "You kissed Mom different."

"That's 'cause she's the mom and you're the kid."

She liked the way he smelled, the way his arm supported her. When she rubbed a hand over his cheek, she was a little disappointed that it was smooth today. "Can I call you Daddy?" she asked, and Holt felt his heart lurch in his chest.

"I—ah—sure. If you want."

"Daddy's for babies," Alex said in disgust. "But you can be Dad."

"Okay." He looked over at Suzanna. "Okay."

Holt wished he could have spent the day with them, but there were things that had to be done. He had a family now—it still dazed him—and he meant to protect them. He'd already put in calls to his contacts in Portland and was awaiting the rundowns on the four names from Trent's list. While he waited, he put in calls to the Department of Motor Vehicles, the credit bureau and the Internal Revenue, stretching it a bit by giving his old badge number and rank.

Between information and instinct, he whittled the four names down to two. While he waited for another call back, he read over his grandfather's diary.

He understood the feelings beneath the words, the longing, the devotion. He understood the rage his grandfather had felt when he'd learned the woman he loved had suffered abuse by the hands of the man she'd married. Was it coincidence or fate that his relationship with Suzanna had so many similarities to that of their ancestors? At least this time, the tale would have a happy ending.

Suzanna's diamonds, he thought, drumming his fingers on the pages. Bianca's emeralds. Suzanna had hidden her jewels, the one material thing she felt belonged to her from the marriage, as security for her children. He had to believe Bianca had done the same.

So, where was the equivalent of Jenny's diaper bag? he wondered.

When the phone rang, he snatched it up on the first ring. Before he hung up again, Holt had little doubt he had his man. Going into the bedroom, he checked his weapon, balancing the familiar weight in his hand. He strapped it to his calf.

Fifteen minutes later, he was walking through the chaos of construction in the west wing. He found Sloan in what was a nearly completed two-level suite. There was a smell of new lumber and male sweat. Sloan, in a tool belt and jeans, was supervising the construction of a new staircase.

"I didn't know architects swung hammers," Holt commented.

Sloan grinned. "I got a personal interest in this job."

Nodding, Holt scanned the crew. "Which one's Marshall?"

Alerted, Sloan unbuckled the tool belt. "He's up on the next level."

"I'd like to have a little talk with him."

Sloan's eyes flashed, but he merely nodded again. "I'll go with you." He waited until they were out of range of the crew. "You think he's the one?"

"Robert Marshall didn't apply for a Maine driver's license until six weeks ago. He's never paid taxes under the name and social security number he's using. Employers don't usually check with the DMV or IRS when they hire a laborer."

Sloan swore and flexed his fingers. He could still see Amanda racing along the terrace pursued by a man holding a gun. "I get first crack at him."

"I appreciate the sentiment, but you'll have to strap it in."

The hell he would, Sloan thought, and signaled the foreman. "Marshall," he said briefly.

"Bob?" The foreman pulled out a bandanna to wipe his neck. "You just missed him. I had him drive Rick into Emergency. Rick took a pretty good slice out of his thumb, figured he needed stitches."

"How long ago?" Holt demanded.

"'Bout twenty minutes, I guess. Told them to take the rest of the day, since we're knocking off at four." He stuffed the bandanna back into his pocket. "Problem?"

"No." Sloan bit down on temper. "Let me know if Rick's okay."

"Sure thing." He shouted at one of the carpenters, then lumbered off.

"I need an address," Holt said.

"Trent's got the paperwork." They started out. "Are you going to turn it over to Lieutenant Koogar?"

"No," Holt said simply.

"Good."

They found Trent in the office he'd thrown together on the first floor, a stack of files at his fingertips, a phone at his ear. He took one look at the two men. "I'll get back to you," he said into the phone and hung up. "Who is it?"

"He's using the name Robert Marshall." Holt pulled out a cigarette. "Foreman let him go early. I want an address."

Saying nothing, Trent crossed to a file cabinet to pull out a folder. "Max is upstairs. He has a stake in this, too."

Holt skimmed the information in Marshall's file. "Then get him. We'll do this together."

The apartment Marshall had listed was on the edge of the village. The woman who opened the door after Holt's third booming knock was bent and withered and out of sorts.

"What? What?" she demanded. "I'm not buying any encyclopedias or vacuum cleaners."

"We're looking for Robert Marshall," Holt told her.

"Who? Who?" She peered through the thick lenses of her glasses.

"Robert Marshall," he repeated.

"I don't know any Marshalls," she grumbled. "There's a McNeilly next door and a Mitchell down below, but no Marshalls. I don't want to buy any insurance, either."

"We're not selling anything," Trent said in his most patient voice. "We're looking for a man named Robert Marshall who lives at this address."

"I told you there's no Marshalls here. I live here. Lived here for fifteen years, since that worthless clot I married passed on and left me with nothing but bills. I know you," she said abruptly, pointing a gnarled finger at Sloan. "Saw your picture in the paper." Reaching to the table beside the door, she hefted an iron bookend. "You robbed a bank."

"No, ma'am." Later, Sloan thought, much later, he might find the whole business amusing. "I married Amanda Calhoun."

The woman held on to the bookend while she considered. "One of the Calhoun girls. That's right. The youngest one—no, not the youngest one, the next one." Satisfied, she set the bookend down again. "Well, what do you want?"

"Robert Marshall," Holt said again. "He gave this building and this apartment as his address."

"Then he's a liar or a fool, because I've lived here for fifteen years ever since that no-account husband of mine caught pneumonia and died. Here one day, gone the next." She snapped her bent fingers. "And good riddance."

Thinking it was a dead end, Holt glanced at Sloan. "Give her a description."

"He's about thirty, six feet tall, trim, black hair, shoulder length, big droopy moustache."

"Don't know him. The boy downstairs, the Pierson boy's got hair past his shoulders. A disgrace if you ask me. Bleaches it, too, just like a girl. He's no more'n sixteen. You'd think his mother would make him cut that hair, but no. Plays the music so loud I have to bang on the floor."

"Excuse me," Max put in and described the man he had known as Ellis Caufield.

"Sounds like my nephew. Lives in Rochester with his second wife. Sells used cars."

"Thanks." Holt wasn't surprised the thief had given a phony address, but he was annoyed. As they came out of the building, he dug a quarter from his pocket.

"I guess we wait until morning," Max was saying. "He doesn't know we're onto him, so he'll show up for work."

"I'm finished waiting." Holt headed for a phone booth. After dropping in the coin, he punched in numbers. "This is Detective Sergeant Bradford, Portland P.D., badge number 7375. I need a cross-check." He reeled off the phone number from Marshall's file. Then he held on with a cop's patience while the operator set her computer to work. "Thanks." He hung up and turned to the three men. "Bar Island," he said. "We'll take my boat."

While their men prepared to sail across the bay, the Calhoun women met in Bianca's tower. "So," Amanda began, pad and pencil at the ready. "What do we know?"

"Trent's been cross-checking the personnel files," C.C. supplied. "He claimed there was some hitch in withholding taxes, but that's bull."

"Interesting," Lilah mused. "Max stopped me from going over to the west wing this morning. I'd wanted to see how things were going, and he made all kinds of lame excuses why I shouldn't distract the men while they were working."

"And Sloan shoved a couple of files into a drawer, and locked it when I came into the room last night." Amanda tapped her pencil on the pad. "Why wouldn't they want us to know if they're checking up on the crews?"

"I think I have an idea," Suzanna said slowly. She'd been chewing it over most of the day. "Last night I found out that Holt's cottage had been broken into and searched."

Her three sisters pounced on that, hammering her with questions.

"Just wait." She lifted a hand. "He was irritated with me, which is why it came out. He was even more irritated that it had. But he did tell me, because he wanted to scare me into backing off, that he was certain it was Livingston."

"Which means," Amanda concluded, "that our old friend knows Holt's connected. Who else knows besides us?" In her organized way, she began to list names.

"Oh, stop fussing," Lilah said with a negligent wave of her hand. "No one knows except the family. None of us have mentioned it outside of this house."

"Maybe he found out the same way Max did," C.C. suggested. "From the library."

"Max checked out the books." Lilah shook her head. "Maybe he found the information in the papers he stole from us."

"It's possible." Amanda noted it down. "But he's had the papers for weeks. When did he break into the cottage?"

"A couple weeks ago, but I don't think he made the connection that way. I think he got it from us."

There was an instant argument. Suzanna stood, throwing up both hands to cut it off. "Listen, we're agreed that none of us have discussed this outside of the house. And we're agreed that the men are trying to keep us from finding out they're checking out the crews. Which means—"

"Which means," Amanda interrupted and shut her eyes. "The bastard's working for us. Like a fly on the wall, so he can pick up little pieces of information, poke around the house. We're so used to seeing guys hauling lumber, we wouldn't give him a second look."

"I think Holt already came to that conclusion." Suzanna lifted her hands again. "The question is, what do we do about it?"

"We give the construction boys a thrill tomorrow, and visit the west wing." Lilah straightened from the window seat. "I don't care what he's made himself look like this time, I'll know him if I get close enough." With that settled, she sat back. "Now, Suzanna, why don't you tell us when bad boy Bradford asked you to marry him?"

Suzanna grinned. "How did you know?"

"For an ex-cop, he's got great taste in jewelry." She took Suzanna's hand to show off the ring to her other sisters.

"Last night," she said as she was hugged and kissed and wept over. "We told the kids this morning."

"Aunt Coco's going to go through the roof." C.C. gave Suzanna another squeeze. "All four of us in a matter of months. She'll be in matchmaker heaven."

"All we need now is to get that creep behind bars and find the emeralds." Amanda dashed a tear away. "Oh, no! Do you realize what this means?"

"It means you have to organize another wedding," Suzanna answered.

"Not just that. It means we're going to be stuck with Aunt Colleen at least until the last handful of rice gets tossed."

Holt returned to The Towers in a foul mood. They'd found the house. Empty. They had no doubt that Livingston was living there. Bending the law more than a little, he had broken in and given the place as meticulous a search as Livingston had given his cottage. They'd found the stolen Calhoun papers, the lists the thief had made and a copy of the original blueprints of The Towers.

They'd also found a typed copy of each woman's weekly schedule, along with handwritten comments that left no doubt as to the fact that Livingston had followed and observed each one of them. There was a well-ordered inventory of the rooms he had searched and the items he'd felt valuable enough to steal.

They had waited an hour for his return, then uneasy about leaving the women alone, had phoned in the information to Koogar. While the police staked out the rented house on Bar Island, Holt and his companions returned to The Towers.

It was only a matter of waiting now. That was something he had learned to do well in his years on the force. But now it wasn't a job, and every moment grated.

"Oh, my dear, dear boy." Coco flew at him the moment he stepped into the house. He caught her by her sturdy hips as she covered his face with kisses.

"Hey," was all he could manage as she wept against his shoulder. Her hair, he noted, was no longer gleaming black but fire-engine red. "What'd you do to your hair?"

"Oh, it was time for a change." She drew back to blow her nose into her hankie, then fell into his arms again. Helpless, he patted her back and looked at the grinning men around him for assistance.

"It looks okay," he assured her, wondering if that was what she was weeping about. "Really."

"You like it?" She pulled back again, fluffing at it. "I thought I needed a bit of dash, and red's so cheerful." She buried her face in the soggy hankie. "I'm so happy," she sobbed. "So very happy. I had hoped, you see. And the tea leaves indicated that it would all work out, but I couldn't help but worry. She's had such a dreadful time, and her sweet little babies, too. Now everything's going to be all right. I'd thought it might be Trent, but he and C.C. were so perfect. Then Sloan and Amanda. Then almost before I could blink, our dear Max and Lilah. Is it any wonder I'm overwhelmed?''

"I guess not."

"To think, all those years ago when you'd bring lobsters to the back door. And that time you changed a tire for me and were too proud to even let me thank you. And now, now, you're going to marry my baby."

"Congratulations." Trent grinned and slapped Holt on the back while Max dug out a fresh handkerchief for Coco.

"Welcome to the family." Sloan offered a hand. "I guess you know what you're getting into."

Holt studied the weeping Coco. "I'm getting the picture."

"Stop all that caterwauling." Colleen clumped down the stairs. "I could hear you wailing all the way up in my room. For heaven's sake, take that mess into the kitchen." She gestured with her cane. "Pour some tea into her until she pulls herself together. Out, all of you," she added. "I want to talk to this boy here."

Like rats deserting a sinking ship, Holt thought as they left him alone. Gesturing for him to follow, Colleen strode into the parlor.

"So, you think you're going to marry my grandniece."

"No. I am going to marry her."

She sniffed. Damned if she didn't like the boy. "I'll tell you this, if you don't do better by her than that scum she had before, you'll answer to me." She settled into a chair. "What are your prospects?"

"My what?"

"Your prospects," she said impatiently. "Don't think you're going to latch on to my money when you latch on to her."

His eyes narrowed, pleasing her. "You can take your money and—"

"Very good," she said with an approving nod. "How do you intend to keep her?"

"She doesn't need to be kept." He whirled around the room. "And she doesn't need you or anyone else poking into her business. She's managed just fine on her own, better than fine. She came out of hell and managed to put her life together, take care of the kids and start a business. The only thing that's going to change is that she's going to stop working herself into the ground, and the kids'll have someone who wants to be their father. Maybe I won't be able to give her diamonds and take her to fancy dinner parties, but I'll make her happy."

Colleen tapped her fingers on the head of her cane. "You'll do. If your grandfather was anything like you, it's no wonder my mother loved him. So..." She started to rise, then saw the portrait over the mantel. Where her father's stern face had been was her mother's lovely one. "What's that doing there?"

Holt dipped his hands into his pockets. "It seemed to me that was where it belonged. That's where my grandfather would have wanted it."

Colleen eased herself back into the chair. "Thank you." Her voice was strained, but her eyes remained fierce. "Now go away. I want to be alone."

He left her, amazed that he was growing fond of her. Though he didn't look forward to another scene, he started toward the kitchen to ask Coco where he could find Suzanna.

But he found her himself, following the music that drifted down the hall. She was sitting at a piano, playing some rich, haunting melody he didn't recognize. Though the music was sad, there was a smile on her lips and one in her eyes. When she looked up, her fingers stilled, but the smile remained.

"I didn't know you played."

"We all had lessons. I was the only one they stuck with." She reached out a hand for his. "I was hoping we'd have a minute alone, so I could tell you how wonderful you were with the kids this morning."

With his fingers meshed with hers, he studied the ring he'd given her. "I was nervous." He laughed a little. "I didn't know how they'd take it. When Jenny asked if she could call me Daddy... it's funny how fast you can fall in love. Suzanna." He kept toying with her hands, studying the ring. "I think I understand now what a parent would feel, what he'd go through to make sure his kids were safe. I'd like to have more. I know you'd need to think about it, and I don't want you to feel that I would care less about Alex and Jenny."

"I don't have to think about it." She pressed a kiss to his cheek. "I've always wanted a big family."

He drew her close so her head rested on his shoulder. "Suzanna, do you know where the nursery was when Bianca lived here?"

"On the third floor of the east wing. It's been used as a storeroom as long as I can remember." She straightened. "You think she hid the necklace there?"

"I think she hid them somewhere Fergus wouldn't look, and I can't see him spending a lot of time in the nursery."

"No, but you'd think someone would have come across them. I don't know why I say that," she corrected. "The place is filled with boxes and old furniture. The Tower's version of a garage sale."

"Show me."

It was worse than he'd imagined. Even overlooking the cobwebs and dust, it was a mess. Boxes, crates, rolled-up rugs, broken tables, shadeless lamps stood, sat or reclined over every inch of space. Speechless, he turned to Suzanna who offered a sheepish grin.

"A lot of stuff collects in eighty-odd years," she told him. "Most of what's valuable's been culled out, and a lot of that was sold when we were—well, when things were difficult. This floor's been closed off for a long time, since we couldn't afford to heat it. We had to concentrate on keeping up the living space. Once we got everything under some kind of control, we were going to kind of attack the other sections a room at a time."

"You need a bulldozer."

"No, just time and elbow grease. We had plenty of the latter, but not nearly enough of the former. Over the last couple of months, we've gone through a lot of the old rooms, inch by inch, but it's a slow process."

"Then we might as well get started."

They worked for two grueling and dirty hours. They found a tattered parasol, an amazing collection of nineteenth-century erotica, a trunk full of musty clothes from the twenties and a box of warped phonograph records. There was also a crate filled with toys, a miniature locomotive, a sad, faded rag doll, assorted yo-yos and tops. Among them were a set of lovely old fairy-tale prints that Suzanna set aside.

"For our nursery," she told him. "Look." She held up a yellow christening gown. "It might have been my grandfather's."

"You'd have thought this stuff would have been packed up with more care."

"I don't think Fergus ran a very tidy household after Bianca died. If any of this stuff belonged to his children, I'd wager the nanny bundled it away. He wouldn't have cared enough."

"No." He pulled a cobweb out of her hair. "Listen, why don't you take a break?"

"I'm fine."

It was useless to remind her that she'd been working all day, so he used another tactic. "I could use a drink. You think Coco's got anything cold in the refrigerator—maybe a sandwich to go with it?"

"Sure. I'll go check."

He knew that her aunt would insist on putting the quick meal together, and Suzanna would get that much time to sit and do nothing. "Two sandwiches," he added, and kissed her.

"Right." She rose, stretching her back. "It's sad to think about those three children, lying in here at night knowing their mother wasn't going to come and tuck them in again. Speaking of which, I'd better tuck in my own before I come back."

"Take your time." He was already headfirst in another crate.

She started out, thinking wistfully of Bianca's babies. Little Sean, who'd barely have been toddling, Ethan, who would grow up to father her father, Colleen, who was even now downstairs surely finding fault with something Coco had done. How the woman had ever been a sweet little girl...

A little girl, Suzanna thought, stopping on the second-floor landing. The oldest girl who would have been five or six when her mother died. Suzanna detoured and knocked on her great-aunt's door.

"Come in, damn it. I'm not getting up."

"Aunt Colleen." She stepped, amused to see the old woman was engrossed in a romance novel. "I'm sorry to disturb you."

"Why? No one else is."

Suzanna bit the tip of her tongue. "I was just wondering, the summer...that last summer, were you still in the nursery with your brothers?"

"I wasn't a baby, no need for a nursery."

"So you had your own room," Suzanna prompted, struggling to contain the excitement. "Near the nursery?"

"At the other end of the east wing. There was the nursery, then Nanny's room, the children's bath, and the three rooms kept for children of guests. I had the corner room at the top of the stairs." She frowned down at her book. "The next summer, I moved into one of the guest rooms. I didn't want to sleep in the room my mother had decorated for me, knowing she wouldn't come back to it."

"I'm sorry. When Bianca told you that you were going away, did she come to your room?"

"Yes. She let me pick out a few of my favorite dresses, then she packed them herself."

"Then after—I suppose they were unpacked again."

"I never wore those dresses again. I never wanted to. Shoved the trunk under my bed."

"I see." So there was hope. "Thank you."

"Moth-eaten by now," Colleen grumbled as Suzanna went out again. She thought of her favorite white muslin with its blue satin sash and with a sigh got up to walk to the terrace.

Dusk was coming early, she thought. Storm brewing. She could smell it in the wind, see it in the bad-tempered clouds already blocking the sun.

Suzanna raced up the stairs again. The sandwiches would have to wait. She pushed open the door of Colleen's old room. It too had been consigned to storage, but being smaller than the nursery wasn't as cramped. The wallpaper, perhaps the same that Bianca had picked for her daughter, was faded and spotted, but Suzanna could still see the delicate pattern of rosebuds and violets.

She didn't bother with the cases or boxes, but dragged or pushed them aside. She was looking for a traveling trunk, suitable for a young girl. What better place? she thought as she pushed aside a crate marked Winter Draperies. Fergus hadn't cared for his daughter. He would hardly have bothered to look through a trunk of dresses, particularly when that trunk had been shoved out of sight by a traumatized young girl.

It had no doubt been opened in later years. Perhaps someone—Suzanna's own mother?—had shaken out a dress or two, then finding them quaint but useless, had designated them to storage.

It could be anywhere, of course, she mused. But what better place to start than the source?

Her heart pounded dully as she stumbled across an old leather-strapped truck. Pulling it open, she found bolts of material carefully folded in tissue. But no little girl's dresses. And no emeralds.

Because the light was growing dim, she rose and started toward the door. She would get Holt, and a flashlight, before continuing. In the gloom, she rapped her shin sharply. Swearing, she looked down and saw the small trunk.

It had once been a glistening white, but now it was dull with age and dust. It had been shoved to the side, piled with other boxes and nearly hidden by them and a faded tapestry. Kneeling in the half-light, Suzanna uncovered it. She flexed her unsteady fingers then opened the lid.

There was a smell of lavender, sealed inside perhaps for decades. She lifted the first dress, a frilly white muslin, going ivory with time and banded by a faded blue satin sash. Suzanna set it carefully aside and drew out another. There were leggings and ribbons, pretty bows and a lacy nightie. And there, at the bottom, beside a small stuffed bear, a box and a book.

Suzanna put a trembling hand to her lips, then slowly reached down to lift the book.

Her journal, she thought as tears misted her eyes. Bianca's journal. Hardly daring to breathe, she turned the first page.

Bar Harbor June 12, 1912
I saw him on the cliffs, overlooking Frenchman Bay

Suzanna let out an unsteady breath and laid the book in her lap. This was not for her to read alone. It would wait for her family. Heart pounding, she reached down to take the box from the trunk. She knew before she opened it. She could feel the change in the room, the trembling of the air. As the first tear slid down her cheek, she opened the lid and uncovered Bianca's emeralds.

They pulsed like green suns, throbbing with life and passion. She lifted the necklace, the glorious three tiers, and felt the heat on her hands. Hidden eighty years before, in hope and desperation, they were now free. The gloom that filled the room was no match for them.

As she knelt, the necklace dripping from her fingers, she reached into the box and took out the matching earrings. Strange, she thought. She'd all but forgotten them. They were lovely, exquisite, but the necklace dominated. It was made to dominate.

Stunned, she stared down at the power in her hands. They weren't just gems, she realized. They were far from being simply beautiful stones. They were Bianca's passions and hopes and dreams. From the time she had placed them in the box until now, when they had been lifted out by her descendant, they had waited to see the light again.

"Oh, Bianca."

"A charming sight."

Her head jerked up at the voice. He stood in the doorway, hardly more than a shadow. When he stepped into the room, she saw the glint of the gun in his hand.

"Patience pays off," Livingston said. "I watched you and the cop go into the room down the hall. I've been losing quite a bit of sleep wandering these rooms at night."

As he came closer, she stared at him. He didn't look like the man she remembered. His coloring was wrong, even the shape of his face. She rose very slowly, clutching the book and earrings in one hand, the necklace in the other.

"You don't recognize me. But I know you. I know all of you. You're Suzanna, just one of the Calhouns who owes me quite a bit."

"I don't know what you're talking about."

"Three months of my time, and not a little trouble. Then there was the loss of Hawkins, of course. He wasn't much of a partner, but he was mine. Just as those are mine." He looked down at the necklace and his mouth watered. They dazzled him. More than he had dreamed, more than he had imagined. Everything he wanted. His fingers trembled lightly on the gun as he reached out. Suzanna jerked away. He lifted a brow. "Do you really think you can keep them from me? They're meant to be mine. And when they are, everything they are will be mine."

He stepped closer, and as she looked around for the best route of escape, his hand closed over her hair. "Some stones have power," he told her softly. "Tragedy seeps into them, making them stronger. Death and grief. It hones them. Hawkins didn't understand that, but he was a simple man."

And the one she was facing was a mad one. "The necklace belongs to the Calhouns. It always has. It always will."

He jerked her hair hard and fast. She would have yelped, but the gun was now pressed against the racing pulse in her throat. "It belongs to me. Because I've been clever enough, I've been determined enough to wait for it. The moment I read about it, I knew. Now tonight, it's done."

She wasn't certain what she would have done—given it to him, tried to reason. But at the moment, her little girl moved into the doorway. "Mom." Her voice trembled as she rubbed her eyes. "It's thundering. You're supposed to come get me when it thunders."

It happened fast. He turned, swinging the gun. With all her strength, Suzanna hurled herself at him, blocking his aim. "Run!" she screamed to Jenny. "Run down the hall to Holt." She shoved, and raced after her daughter. The decision had to be made the minute she hit the doorway. As she watched Jenny streak toward the right and—she hoped—safety, Suzanna plunged in the opposite direction.

He would follow her, not the child, she told herself. Because she still had the necklace. The next decision had to be made at the steps. To go down to her family and risk them. Or to go up, alone.

She was halfway up the stairs when she heard him pounding behind her. She jerked in shock as a bullet plowed into the plaster an inch from her shoulder.

Breathless, she streaked up, only now hearing the boom of thunder that had frightened Jenny and made her look for her mother. Her single thought was to put as much distance between the madman behind her and her child. Her feet clattered on the winding metal staircase that led to Bianca's tower.

His fingers darted through the open treads and snatched at her ankle. With a sound of terror and fury, she kicked out, dislodging them, then stumbled up the rest of the way. The door was shut. She nearly wept as she threw her weight against the thick wood. It gave, with painful slowness, then allowed her to fall inside. But before she could slam it closed, he was hurtling in.

She braced, certain it would be only seconds before she felt the bullet. He was panting, sweating, his eyes glazed. At the corner of his mouth, a muscle ticked and jerked. "Give it to me." The gun shook as he advanced on her. A flash of lightning had him looking wildly around the shadowy room. "Give it to me now."

He's afraid, she realized. Of this room. "You've been in here before."

He had, only once, and had run out again, terrified. There was something here, something that hated him. It crawled cold as ice along his skin. "Give me the necklace, or I'll just kill you and take it."

"This was her room," Suzanna murmured, keeping her eyes on his. "Bianca's room. She died when her husband threw her from that window."

Unable to resist, he looked at the glass, dark with gloom, then away again.

"She still comes here, to wait, and to watch the cliffs." She heard, as she had known she would, the sound of Holt racing up the steps. "She's here now. Take them." She held the emeralds out. "But she won't let you leave with them."

His face was bone white and sheened with sweat as he reached for the necklace. He gripped it, but rather than the heat Suzanna had felt, he felt only cold. And a terror.

"They're mine now." He shivered and stumbled.

"Suzanna," Holt said quietly from the doorway. "Move away from him." His weapon was drawn, gripped in both hands. "Move away," he repeated. "Slow."

She took one step back, then two, but Livingston paid no attention to her. He was wiping his gun hand over his dry lips.

"It's over," Holt told him. "Drop the gun, kick it aside." But Livingston continued to stare at the necklace, breathing raggedly. "Drop it." Braced, Holt moved closer. "Get out, Suzanna."

"No, I'm not leaving you."

He didn't have time to swear at her. Though he was prepared to kill, he could see that the man was no longer concerned with his weapon, or with escape. Instead, Livingston merely stared down at the emeralds and trembled.

With his eyes trained on Livingston, Holt reached up to grasp the wrist of his gun hand. "It's over," he said again.

"It's mine." Wild with rage and fear, Livingston lunged. He fired once into the ceiling before Holt disarmed him. Even then he struggled, but the struggle was brief. With the next crash of thunder, he howled, striking out wildly even as the others raced into the room. Disoriented or terrified, stunned by Holt's blow to his jaw or no longer sane, he whirled.

There was the crash of breaking glass. Then a sound Suzanna would never forget. A man's horrified scream. Even as Holt leaped forward to try to save him, Livingston pinwheeled through the broken window and tumbled to the rain swept rock below.

"My God." Suzanna pressed back against the wall, her hands over her mouth to stop her own screams. There were arms around her, a babble of voices.

Her family poured into the tower room. She bent to her children, pressing kisses on their cheeks. "It's all right," she soothed. "It's all right now. There's nothing to be afraid of." She looked up at Holt. He stood facing her, the black space at his back, the glitter of emeralds at his feet. "Everything's all right now. I'm going to take you downstairs."

Holt pushed the gun back in its holster. "We'll take them down."

An hour later, when the children were soothed and sleeping, he took her by the arm and pulled her out on the terrace. All the fear and rage he'd felt since Jenny had run crying down the hallway came pouring out.

"What the hell do you think you were doing?"

"I had to keep him away from Jenny." She thought she was calm, but her hands began to shake. "I suddenly had an idea about the emeralds. It was so simple, really. And I found them. Then he was there—and Jenny. He had a gun, and God, oh God, I thought he would kill her."

"All right, all right," Holt said. Suzanna didn't choke back the tears this time, but clung to him as they shuddered out of her. "The kids are fine, Suzanna. Nobody's going to hurt them. Or you."

"I didn't know what else to do. I wasn't trying to be brave or stupid."

"You were both. I love you." He framed her face in his hands and kissed her. "Did he hurt you?"

"No." She sniffled a little and wiped her eyes. "He chased me up there, and then...he snapped. You saw how he was when you came in."

"Yeah." Two feet away from her, with a gun in his hand. Holt's fingers tightened on her shoulders. "Don't you ever scare me like that again."

"It's a deal." She rubbed her cheek against his, for comfort and for love. "It's really over now, isn't it?"

He kissed the top of her head. "It's just beginning."

Epilogue

It was late when the family gathered together in the parlor. The police had finally finished and left them alone. They were drawn together, a solid, united front beneath the portrait of Bianca.

Colleen sat, a dog at her feet, the emeralds in her lap. She had shed no tears when Suzanna had explained how and where she had found them, but took comfort in having that small, precious memory of her mother.

There was no talk of death.

Holt keep Suzanna close, his arm firm around her. The storm had passed, and the moon had risen. The parlor was washed with light. The only sound was Suzanna's soft, clear voice as she read from Bianca's journal.

She turned the last page and spoke of Bianca's thoughts as she'd prepared to hide the emeralds.

"'I didn't think of their monetary value as I took them out, held them in my hands and watched them gleam in the light of the lamp. They would be a legacy for my children, and their children, a symbol of freedom, and of hope. And with Christian, of love.

"'As dawn broke, I decided to put them, together with this journal, in a safe place until I joined Christian again.'"

Slowly, quietly Suzanna closed the book. "I think she's with him now. That they're with each other."

She smiled when Holt's fingers gripped hers. Looking around the room, she saw her sisters, the men they loved, her aunt smiling through tears, and Bianca's daughter, gazing up at the portrait that had been painted with unconquerable love.

"It was Bianca, more than the emeralds, who brought us all together. I like to think that by finding them, by bringing them back, we've helped them find each other."

Beyond the house, the moon glimmered on the cliffs far above where the sea churned and fought with the rocks. The wind whispered through the wild roses and warmed the lovers who walked there.

SILHOUETTE·INTIMATE·MOMENTS®

COMING NEXT MONTH

#401 DESERT SHADOWS—Emilie Richards

Private investigator Felice Christy's latest assignment was driving her crazy! Stuck in a convent pretending to be a nun in order to protect a *real* sister, she had to deal with new handyman Josiah Gallagher, too. His drifter act didn't fool her for a moment. But did he spell trouble for her mission . . . or her heart?

#402 STEVIE'S CHASE—Justine Davis

Chase Sullivan's shadowed past made him a loner by necessity, *not* by choice. Then sweet Stevie Holt stepped into his life, and he dared to dream that things could be different. Suddenly he realized that he'd placed Stevie's life in danger, and unless he did something—quickly—they would *both* be dead.

#403 FORBIDDEN—Catherine Palmer

Federal narcotics agent Ridge Gordon's cover as a college football player didn't stop him from making a pass at sexy English professor Adair Reade. But when new evidence pointed to her involvement in the very drug ring he'd been sent to bust, he fumbled. Was he falling in love with a drug runner?

#404 SIR FLYNN AND LADY CONSTANCE—Maura Seger

When Constance Lehane's brush with date rape ended in tragedy, she hired criminal lawyer Flynn Corbett to defend her against a possible murder charge. Instinctively she knew that his passion for the law would save her, yet the flames that burned between them hinted at a different sort of passion altogether. . . .

AVAILABLE THIS MONTH:

Take 4 bestselling love stories FREE

Plus get a FREE surprise gift!

SILHOUETTE®
OFFICIAL SWEEPSTAKES RULES

NO PURCHASE NECESSARY

1. To enter, complete an Official Entry Form or 3"× 5" index card by hand-printing, in plain block letters, your complete name, address, phone number and age, and mailing it to: Silhouette Fashion A Whole New You Sweepstakes, P.O. Box 621, Fort Erie, Ontario L2A 5X3.

   No responsibility is assumed for lost, late or misdirected mail. Entries must be sent separately with first class postage affixed, and be received no later than December 31, 1991 for eligibility.

2. Winners will be selected by D.L. Blair, Inc., an independent judging organization whose decisions are final, in random drawings to be held on January 30, 1992 in Blair, NE at 10:00 a.m. from among all eligible entries received.

3. The prizes to be awarded and their approximate retail values are as follows: Grand Prize — A brand-new Ford Explorer 4×4 plus a trip for two (2) to Hawaii, including round-trip air transportation, six (6) nights hotel accommodation, a $1,400 meal/spending money stipend and $2,000 cash toward a new fashion wardrobe (approximate value: $28,000) or $15,000 cash; two (2) Second Prizes — A trip to Hawaii, including round-trip air transportation, six (6) nights hotel accommodation, a $1,400 meal/spending money stipend and $2,000 cash toward a new fashion wardrobe (approximate value: $11,000) or $5,000 cash; three (3) Third Prizes — $2,000 cash toward a new fashion wardrobe. All prizes are valued in U.S. currency. Travel award air transportation is from the commercial airport nearest winner's home. Travel is subject to space and accommodation availability, and must be completed by June 30, 1993. Sweepstakes offer is open to residents of the U.S. and Canada who are 21 years of age or older as of December 31, 1991, except residents of Puerto Rico, employees and immediate family members of Torstar Corp., its affiliates, subsidiaries, and all agencies, entities and persons connected with the use, marketing, or conduct of this sweepstakes. All federal, state, provincial, municipal and local laws apply. Offer void wherever prohibited by law. Taxes and/or duties, applicable registration and licensing fees, are the sole responsibility of the winners. Any litigation within the province of Quebec respecting the conduct and awarding of a prize may be submitted to the Régie des loteries et courses du Québec. All prizes will be awarded; winners will be notified by mail. No substitution of prizes is permitted.

4. Potential winners must sign and return any required Affidavit of Eligibility/Release of Liability within 30 days of notification. In the event of noncompliance within this time period, the prize may be awarded to an alternate winner. Any prize or prize notification returned as undeliverable may result in the awarding of that prize to an alternate winner. By acceptance of their prize, winners consent to use of their names, photographs or their likenesses for purposes of advertising, trade and promotion on behalf of Torstar Corp. without further compensation. Canadian winners must correctly answer a time-limited arithmetical question in order to be awarded a prize.

5. For a list of winners (available after 3/31/92), send a separate stamped, self-addressed envelope to: Silhouette Fashion A Whole New You Sweepstakes, P.O. Box 4665, Blair, NE 68009.

PREMIUM OFFER TERMS

To receive your gift, complete the Offer Certificate according to directions. Be certain to enclose the required number of "Fashion A Whole New You" proofs of product purchase (which are found on the last page of every specially marked "Fashion A Whole New You" Silhouette or Harlequin romance novel). Requests must be received no later than December 31, 1991. Limit: four (4) gifts per name, family, group, organization or address. Items depicted are for illustrative purposes only and may not be exactly as shown. Please allow 6 to 8 weeks for receipt of order. Offer good while quantities of gifts last. In the event an ordered gift is no longer available, you will receive a free, previously unpublished Silhouette or Harlequin book for every proof of purchase you have submitted with your request, plus a refund of the postage and handling charge you have included. Offer good in the U.S. and Canada only.

SLFC - SWPR

SILHOUETTE® OFFICIAL SWEEPSTAKES ENTRY FORM

4-FCSIS-2

Complete and return this Entry Form immediately – the more entries you submit, the better your chances of winning!

- Entries must be received by **December 31, 1991.**
- A Random draw will take place on **January 30, 1992.**
- No purchase necessary.

Yes, I want to win a FASHION A WHOLE NEW YOU Sensuous and Adventurous prize from Silhouette:

Name _____ Telephone _____ Age ____

Address _____

City _____ Province _____ Postal Code _____

Return Entries to: **Silhouette FASHION A WHOLE NEW YOU,**
P.O. Box 621, Fort Erie, Ontario L2A 5X3   © 1991 Harlequin Enterprises Limited

PREMIUM OFFER

To receive your free gift, send us the required number of proofs-of-purchase from any specially marked FASHION A WHOLE NEW YOU Silhouette or Harlequin Book with the Offer Certificate properly completed, plus a check or money order (do not send cash) to cover postage and handling payable to Silhouette FASHION A WHOLE NEW YOU Offer. We will send you the specified gift.

OFFER CERTIFICATE

Item	A. SENSUAL DESIGNER VANITY BOX COLLECTION (set of 4) (Suggested Retail Price $60.00)	B. ADVENTUROUS TRAVEL COSMETIC CASE SET (set of 3) (Suggested Retail Price $25.00)
# of proofs-of-purchase	18	12
Postage and Handling	$4.00	$3.45
Check one	☐	☐

Name _____

Address _____

City _____ Province _____ Postal Code _____

Mail this certificate, designated number of proofs-of-purchase and check or money order for postage and handling to: **Silhouette FASHION A WHOLE NEW YOU Gift Offer,** P.O. Box 622, Fort Erie, Ontario L2A 5X3. Requests must be received by December 31, 1991.

ONE PROOF-OF-PURCHASE

4-FWCSI-2

To collect your fabulous free gift you must include the necessary number of proofs-of-purchase with a properly completed Offer Certificate.

© 1991 Harlequin Enterprises Limited

See previous page for details.

THE
CALHOUN WOMEN

BY NORA ROBERTS

If you've enjoyed SUZANNA'S SURRENDER in the Silhouette Intimate Moments line, be sure to order any of THE CALHOUN WOMEN titles you missed:

COURTING CATHERINE
Silhouette Romance #801 ($2.50)

A MAN FOR AMANDA
Silhouette Desire #649 ($2.75)

FOR THE LOVE OF LILAH
Silhouette Special Edition #685 ($3.25)

To try other Silhouette Intimate Moments books, see special savings offer on the back.

Silhouette Books®

SILHOUETTE·INTIMATE·MOMENTS®

Enter a world of excitement, of romance heightened by suspense, adventure and the passions every woman dreams of. Let us sweep you away.